KERI ARTHUR

Shadow's End

A LIZZIE GRACE NOVEL

Published by KA Publishing PTY LTD

Cover Art by Lori Grundy from Cover Reveal Designs

All characters and events in this book are fictitious. Any resemblance to real people, alive or dead, is entirely coincidental.

ISBN: 978-1-923169-06-7

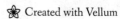 Created with Vellum

With thanks to:

The Lulus
Skyla / Indigo Chick Designs
Hot Tree Editing
Debbie from DP Plus
Robyn E.
The lovely ladies from Indie Gals
Lori Grundy / Cover Reveal Designs for the amazing cover

CHAPTER ONE

The thing about my dreams was, they almost always came true. The five or so percent that didn't were generally *real* dreams—ones based on wants, desires, or even fears—rather than being prophetic.

This one had me walking barefoot through a forest—I mean, why? It was summer, for God's sake, and snakes abounded, even at night. The air was warm and alive with golden threads that danced around me, a firestorm of power that was mine to use even if it would never belong to me. A figure padded lightly beside me, two more behind, and another two whose weight I could feel through the earth but could not see were moving toward us from the other side of this woodland.

Light of a different kind filtered through the trees ahead. It wasn't moonlight or even firelight, but something far darker.

Mage fire.

A deeply dangerous purple fire that could kill with just a touch.

And I knew, without knowing how, that its source was a vampire almost as old as time itself.

Fear slithered through me, and there was a part of my brain screaming that I needed to wake, that I didn't want to see what lay ahead. But these dreams were always relentless.

I walked on, feet barely touching the ground, the soil under my toes warm and filled with an energy as sharp as the air. The closer I moved to the deadly light, the more dread grew, until my heart raced fiercely and every breath was a short, sharp explosion of fear.

I moved through trees wilting under the glow of the mage fire into a clearing that held neither life nor death, and yet wasn't empty.

A man—a *naked* man—lay in the middle of a dark pentagram. Black candles burned at each of the cardinal points, but they weren't the source of the deadly mage fire, nor was the large protection circle surrounding the pentagram. In the three-foot scrap of ground between the two, creatures roamed. Creatures that were wispy and insubstantial, yet all teeth and talons.

The man in the middle of the pentagram was pale of skin and thin to the point of emaciation. His legs and arms were spread-eagled, each limb pinned to the ground by wooden stakes driven through his flesh. Thick, red veins of poison extended away from each entry point, suggesting those stakes were white ash—a wood historically deadly to vampires.

This man wasn't a vampire, but he was the next best thing—a thrall, beings who'd dined on the flesh of their mistress or master, thereby receiving eternal life in exchange for eternal service.

He also *wasn't* a stranger. This was Roger, who was

not only Maelle's thrall, but also, in many respects, her sanity. Our resident vampire was already walking a tightrope of control after Roger had barely survived two previous attempts on his life. Of course, she was also the *cause* of one of those near-death experiences. She'd physically drained his energy to the point of death after my mad —and now very dead—ex had bombed her nightclub and almost killed her. A third, this time successful, attempt on Roger's life would definitely end whatever grip on sanity she had.

I stopped well beyond the protection circle and the creatures that roamed within it and waited to see if Roger lived or not.

After several long seconds, his chest rose a fraction. It was enough to indicate life; thralls already walked the twilight world, and there was plenty of debate as to whether they actually *needed* to breathe.

The dream forced me closer. The insubstantial creatures bared teeth and prowled back and forth, red eyes gleaming with hunger. Spirit eaters, instinct whispered, not flesh.

I shivered and rubbed nonexistent arms.

Shadows moved on the other side of the clearing, and a figure stepped into view. She was small and dainty, with golden hair curled on the top of her head to resemble a crown. She looked no more than sixteen or seventeen years old, but she was far older. Centuries older.

This was Marie Nicolete Bouchier, who was not only Maelle's former lover *and* her maker, but a dark mage even more powerful than Maelle.

I knew then this wasn't just a prophetic dream. She'd called me here. Or, more precisely, called my spirit here. How or why, I had no idea, but it scared the hell out of me.

Because I couldn't wake. As much as I wanted to, I just couldn't. The dream's grip remained far too tight.

And would, I knew, until she'd said whatever she'd called me here for.

I flexed my fingers and tried to remain calm. I was still wearing the protection charms around my neck, even in this dream, and the multiple spells and wild magic layered within them burned against nonexistent skin. It *was* acting against whatever magic was at work here, even if it wasn't strong enough to prevent it. And Marie, for all her power, was not a spirit eater.

Of course, the things that roamed that three-foot strip of barren ground *were*. But if she'd intended them to consume my soul, surely she would have simply sent them directly into my dreams rather than keeping them leashed like this.

They were a warning, nothing more.

I stopped just short of the protection circle. Its energy burned over me, a dark and dangerous blanket that could smother in an instant. Goose bumps prickled, and my heartbeat leapt, becoming a fierce drumbeat that echoed across the clearing's silence.

From the other side of the flames came Marie's soft laugh.

"Ah," she said, her voice soft, melodious, and very heavily French accented. "Human fear. It is such a delicious sound."

I flexed my fingers again. Heat pressed against their tips but didn't spark around them as it would have in the real world—perhaps because she didn't know about it. I doubted the wild magic that had initially accompanied me in this dream—or nightmare, or whatever the hell it actually was—could be used because it, like the shadows who'd padded beside and behind me, hadn't entered this clearing. But my inner wild magic—which had fused to my DNA after Mom had been sent to contain and protect a newly emerging wellspring when she'd been unknowingly pregnant with me—could not be curtailed so easily, even by someone as powerful as her.

And that press of heat said it was here with me now.

Of course, it did mean that, unless she'd lured me here to kill me, I also couldn't use it. It would reveal too much about me, and she already knew far too much, thanks to her recent mind invasion of the man who lay in her circle.

But again, I doubted her intent was to kill. Not tonight, at any rate.

"Why have you called me here, Marie?"

She raised a pale eyebrow. "She speaks."

"You'd prefer I didn't?"

"That is always my preference, yes. Listening to victims whine is not only tedious but can ultimately spoil the pleasure of a meal."

"Then I will definitely speak a whole lot more."

She laughed and waved a pale hand, the movement eloquent. Regal. Long before she'd come into this reservation seeking bloody revenge on Maelle, I'd had a vision of her sitting on a throne of dark red velvet. At the time, I thought it meant she was royalty, and in some respects I hadn't been wrong. She was the queen—the maker—of her coven.

Until Maelle had all but erased it in a fit of bloody fury, of course.

"False courage is always preferable to whining, so please do."

"Are you going to tell me what you want? Or are we just going to throw threats at each other for a few minutes and then go our separate ways?"

Her responding smile was warm and friendly, and it chilled me to the core. "I gave you a warning not to interfere—"

"Technically," I cut in, probably unwisely, "that warning came from Jaqueline rather than your good self."

"She and I speak as one."

"Do you, though? She's Maelle's child by birth, even if yours by rebirth. Bloodlines always matter."

It hadn't for me when it came to one of my parents, of course, but she wasn't to know that. Unless, of course, that was one of the things she'd pulled from Roger's mind. Maelle seemed to know entirely too much about me and my family.

"If you are trying to rile me, you will not succeed. It is also not very wise, especially when I hold you in this walking dream."

"Do you, though?" I repeated, and called to the power within. With a flick of my fingers, I willed myself onto the other side of the fire, standing six feet away from her.

If only it was that easy to break out of this goddamn dream.

Surprise flitted briefly through her expression before her scary-as-fuck smile fell back into place. "Interesting. I had not thought you capable of such a feat, especially when your connection to the wild magic has been curtailed. I shall have to ramp up my defenses."

Not what I'd intended, but still ... "Underestimating those within this reservation would be a big mistake, Marie."

Her gaze swept me, cool and amused. "Oh, I am well aware of what this reservation is and isn't capable of. Dear Roger gave me a great deal of useful information in that regard."

"Dear Roger" hadn't done so willingly. She'd used a telepath to trample through his memories, not only ripping everything vital from his brain but setting him up to attack us. Belle—who was not only my best friend and familiar, but also one of the strongest telepaths around—had prevented the latter but neither she nor even Maelle had been able to fully restore all of his memories. Though, to be honest, I think Maelle only cared about the ones involving her.

I crossed my arms, aware it could be seen as a defensive gesture—and perhaps it was. The cold amusement rolling from her certainly had more goose bumps crawling across nonexistent skin. But it was also very necessary. The heat pressing at my fingers was growing, as was the need to unleash.

Restraint, restraint, I intoned to myself.

I'd already shown her I was not as enthralled by this dreaming spell as she'd hoped. That was more than enough.

"To yet again repeat my earlier question," I said, somehow managing to keep my voice flat and without emotion. "What do want with me, Marie? Or did you just call me here to impress me with your power? Because, granted, I am impressed, but it won't stop me from coming after you."

"Courage. I do like it." She waved eloquently toward Roger. "We both know that he is her sanity. Tell her that she has twenty-four hours to present herself to our court of justice or I will kill him and then destroy her."

"And this court of justice? Are you going to give me an address or are we just leaving it to chance and guesswork?"

"She will know where to meet. She has always known."

With that, I was sent tumbling out of her dream and back into reality.

And woke, gasping and shaking, wrapped in arms that were warm and familiar. *Aiden*. He didn't say anything. He knew well enough there was no waking me while the dreams held me in their grip, and little point in offering meaningless words of comfort after.

I drew in a shuddering breath, then turned and pressed my cheek against his bare chest, listening to the rapid beat of his heart and drawing in the warm, musky scent of him, which was tinged with just the faintest hint of fresh paint—the latter coming more from the bedroom's air than his skin. This house—which he'd inherited from his grandfather—was in the midst of a complete internal renovation. In fact, this bedroom and its en suite were the only really useable rooms in the house, and even in here the walls still needed their final coat of paint and there was no furniture aside from this boat-sized bed. Aiden had been doing the renovations in his spare time over the last few months—without telling me, of course, because hey, why would he? It wasn't like he'd intended this place to be our home once we'd married or anything ...

The thought had me smiling. Alpha werewolves weren't big on sharing emotions or intentions until absolutely necessary, and it had taken me splitting up with him and then heading to Canberra for a couple of weeks before he finally admitted to himself and to me just how deeply he loved me.

Of course, having made the decision to fully include me in his entire life, not just on the periphery, he basically went in all guns blazing. He'd not only asked me to marry him, but had confronted his alpha bitch of a mother and then his whole damn pack, demanding I be allowed to live within the reservation.

The resulting vote had fallen in our favor, and said bitch was no longer the other pack alpha. While it was a position that normally went to the alpha's mate, I was a witch rather than a wolf and couldn't realistically speak on their behalf or vote at the reservation's council meetings. I had, however, been allowed to pick a suitable proxy.

I'd chosen his sister, Ciara.

His mom had hated that. And me even more.

It would certainly make living within the pack's compound very interesting over the next couple of months, especially when there were factions within the five different bloodlines making up the O'Connor pack who'd sided with Karleen when it came to my presence amongst them.

As my breathing evened out, Aiden kissed the top of my head and then said, in a voice that was rumbly and warm, "Would you like a coffee? Or maybe a hot chocolate?"

"The latter is always appreciated." I brushed the sweaty strands of hair from my face and scanned his sharp but lovely features. Faint shadows lined his blue eyes, but that was due more to the long hours we'd been spending working on this place than my dreams keeping him awake. Still ... I grimaced and added, "Sorry for waking you so damn early."

"I accepted long ago that my life with you was never going to be boring." A smile tugged at his luscious lips. "As for sleep, well, you're pregnant with our daughter, so I'd best get used to having none of it."

I laughed. "I'd rather spend the next seven and a half months stocking up on sleep, thank you very much."

"The dreams obviously didn't get *that* memo."

No, they fucking didn't.

He swung his legs off the bed and padded naked toward the main room, where we'd set up a camp kitchen. I took a moment to admire the sheer perfection of the man—like all wolves, he was built lean but powerful, with a V-shaped torso that drew the eye down to a butt made for jeans, and lovely long legs that could run all day through a forest or fully support a woman when her back was pressed against the wall, her legs were wrapped around his waist, and she was riding him hard and fast ...

Desire stirred anew, and there was a part of me—a big, will-never-get-enough-of-the-man part—that wanted to drag him back into bed and make love until the last wisps of the dream were erased from my mind.

But the clock was counting down, and we couldn't afford to waste a minute of it, let alone several hours. I sighed, reached for my phone, and called Maelle. The call rang for several seconds, then flipped over to her message service.

"Maelle, this is Lizzie Grace. I need to talk to you urgently. Please ring me back ASAP." I paused. "If I don't hear from you in half an hour, I'm driving over to see you."

I waited a few more heartbeats to see if she picked up. Her nightclub had yet to reopen, but I had no doubt she'd be there, either marshalling the workers or feeding from her menagerie of "kept" men and women. Unless she was in the middle of one such session, she should have answered. That she hadn't worried the hell out of me.

I dropped my phone onto the bed, then pushed the sheet off my legs and padded out to the longhouse's large main living room. An oversized stone chimney dominated the center of the room, separating what would eventually be our kitchen-diner from the living area. There were four rooms on the other side of the building—three bedrooms and what would be a bathroom. The bedrooms had all been plastered but needed new flooring and painting, while the bathroom, like the kitchen, was little more than a shell.

Aiden had lit the two-burner camp stove we were using until our kitchen was installed and was pouring milk into a pot. The glow coming from the embers in the nearby fire-place warmed his skin and highlighted the silver in his dark golden hair. The O'Connors were silver wolves, though their coloring could range from complete silver to a muddy blond. These days I actually looked more like a wolf than a witch—hair wise anyway, because I was not, and never would be, built lean—after full immersion in the wellspring had turned my once crimson-colored hair to full silver. Aside from one lone stubborn streak in my fringe, anyway.

I trailed my fingers across his butt cheeks, and the scent of desire instantly stung the air.

"Tease," he said.

"Says the master of that art."

I opened the bread and popped a couple of slices into the toaster. It might be three in the morning, but I was hungry—a seemingly constant state for me these days. Being pregnant had certainly increased my appetite, though thankfully it hadn't yet affected my waistline. But it was early days yet.

Amusement danced through his eyes. "I didn't hear any complaints earlier this evening."

"And likely will never. That doesn't alter the fact."

He laughed and picked up a spoon to stir the milk and prevent a skin forming while it heated up, though his amusement quickly faded. "What was the dream about? It looked pretty nasty from my side of things."

"It was." I grimaced and gave him a bare-bones rundown. "We've twenty-four hours before Marie unleashes the hell that will be Maelle without Roger."

"I heard you leave her a message—are we going down there if she doesn't reply?"

"What's this 'we' business? You have work in the morning."

"You seriously think I'm not going to accompany my wife-to-be—"

"Said wife-to-be is well able to protect herself."

"I'm aware of that—"

"*This* is one of those moments we discussed, you know."

Confusion flickered briefly across his expression. "What moments?"

"A 'going all alpha wolf, must protect mate,' moment."

He rolled his eyes, poured the frothing milk into the cups, then dumped a couple of spoons of chocolate into each. "I'm being sensible. Marie targeted you with that dream. It may well be a trap—a means of drawing you out of the compound so she can grab you."

"It wasn't. If she can draw me to her in a dream despite the spells I've set up around this longhouse, she could have undoubtedly just walked in here and grabbed me. It was a show of strength, nothing more."

"For now."

"Yes. Hopefully we can find and stop her before that becomes a problem."

"Things have never been that easy before, and I suspect it won't be so in this case." He stirred the chocolate in and slid a mug over to me. "It might be better if we stay full-time at the café—at least until this idiotic vampire war is over."

I picked up the drink and took a sip. "That will mean you putting up with my shower."

He smiled. "I can put up with almost anything when you're by my side."

"You say this now, but you'll be complaining when you bang your elbow on the shower glass for the umpteenth time."

"If I'm banging you when it happens, I assure you I won't."

I snorted and threw the tea towel at him. He caught it with a laugh and then added, more seriously, "Is she powerful enough to break the café's protections?"

"Possibly. But the wild magic is thickly woven through the spells there, and there are few witches or mages who'd risk tackling its unpredictability." I took another drink. "Seriously, though, I don't believe she has any intention of coming after me just yet. I think I'm dessert—a tempting little treat after the main course that is Maelle."

"Well, that's comforting."

It was dryly said, and I smiled. "You can escort me down to my car to make sure I get there safely, if you want."

"I want."

The toast popped, so I slathered walnut toffee butter all over both pieces, then offered him a slice.

He shook his head. "Do you think Maelle will acquiesce to her demand?"

"Not a chance in hell." I munched on the toast for a bit. "She *will* expect me to find and save Roger, of course."

"And if you don't?"

"She's long wanted to taste the power in my blood. Which, before you say anything, she will never be able to do. My inner wild magic is an instinctive beast, and her teeth won't get within an inch of my neck or thigh or whatever other bit of flesh she likes to dine on."

I crossed mental fingers as I said all that because, hey, fate did like being tempted, and I'd just sent a doozy out into the ether.

"*That* I do find comforting." He picked up his chocolate and took a sip. "So, describe this clearing. Maybe I know it."

I did so, and he wrinkled his nose. "It sounds like a pretty generic forest clearing of which we have hundreds, and that isn't going to make finding him any easier."

"I know." I finished my piece of toast and then took a drink. "And Maelle is of the opinion my psychometry will never find him because he will read too much like her."

"Which may not matter if she's beside you and you're able to feel a secondary if fainter pulse."

"True, but—" I stopped as my phone rang, then put down my cup and ran for the bedroom. The screen said it was Maelle, so I hit the answer button. "Maelle, thank you—"

"I haven't the time to linger on the phone," she cut in, her normally melodious tone brusque. "Be at my nightclub in half an hour if you wish to speak."

And with that, she hung up. I blinked and stared at the phone's screen for a second. Maelle was very many things but rarely brusque to the point of rudeness. Something must have happened. Something *other* than Roger.

I swore, threw the phone down onto the bed, and started pulling on clothes. The night remained hot, so I dressed in little more than shorts and a tank top, but I did add socks and thick boots, just to prepare for any snakes that might be slithering about.

Aiden came in and quickly pulled on jeans and boots, but didn't bother with a shirt. He grabbed my backpack—which was filled with all sorts of witch paraphernalia, including my silver blade—from the doorless walk-in wardrobe and slung it over his shoulder.

"I poured your hot chocolate into a travel mug so you can take it with you."

"You're a good man, Aiden O'Connor."

He smiled. "I've heard horror stories of husbands not catering to their pregnant partner's cravings, so I'm getting ahead of the curve."

I laughed, pulled him close, and kissed him. "As long as

you keep a steady cache of chocolate on hand, I think you'll be fine."

"I will remind you of this statement when you're craving pickles at three in the morning."

I snorted but didn't deny the possibility. While I hated pickles, he didn't, so maybe our daughter would follow in his footsteps and start demanding the horrid things even before she popped into the world.

I headed out of the bedroom, detouring to grab the travel mug and my remaining bit of toast, then followed him out into the night. The stars were bright in the sky thanks to the moon being little more than a sliver, the air rich with the scent of eucalyptus. The latter was a bit of a worry—while we were very early into summer and the hottest months remained ahead of us, the bush was already starting to dry off, and both the trees and their oils were highly flammable.

It wouldn't take much to cause a disaster.

And yet, disaster is coming ... I frowned at the insight, but as per usual with these things, nothing in the way of explanatory information followed it.

I walked through the pretty garden and its white picket fence—something Aiden had built because I once said I'd wanted the whole white picket fence and family ideal—and followed him into the silent heart of the reservation. It was here—in the remains of an old volcanic crater—where you could find all the main residences of the various family alphas within the pack. The grand hall, which was where the pack met, debated, and made decisions over all things affecting their compound, was also here. It was lovely old building that was, in a complete juxtaposition with the long-houses surrounding it, circular in design with an angular earthen roof that pitched up to the stone chimney domi-nating the center of the structure.

A flicker of movement through the trees had my heart leaping, but it was only one of the wolf guards Aiden had placed around this central area slipping through the trees to check on us.

Aiden gave him a nod, then caught my hand and led me quickly into the canyon. While it narrowed the farther down the mountain you moved, this initial section was filled with more, albeit smaller, longhouses that even on an almost moonless night glimmered like jewels thanks to the quartz stone used in their construction. Few lights were on in any of the places either here or farther down, though I had no doubt many were aware of our passing. Wolves tended to sleep lightly.

Once we were out of the canyon, we followed the winding track through to the lower forest area. Another guard stepped out from one of the well-hidden tree platforms, gave Aiden a nod, and then moved back into the thick greenery.

I clicked open my SUV—which still bore a multitude of bullet holes thanks to the fact we simply hadn't had the time to get it repaired after the granny killer had shot the hell out of it and tried to do the same to us. Aiden opened the door, threw my pack onto the passenger side of the car, then helped me climb in.

"Ring me once you've finished with Maelle. Don't go chasing after Roger without any of us there."

"Stupid, I am not."

Careless of your own safety, you can be, came Belle's sleepy comment, her words almost perfectly echoing Aiden's.

What the fuck are you doing awake at this hour of the morning? I asked, then said aloud, "I promise I'll not go anywhere from Maelle's without calling in the troops—which, my dear ranger, might not include you."

"As long as it at least includes Monty and Belle, I'm satisfied."

"She's already online bitching about me waking her so early."

I did not bitch. She paused. *Well, not yet anyway.*

Aiden slammed the door shut and stepped back. I started the SUV and then wound down the window.

"Call me," he reiterated. "Or at the very least, send a text."

I raised an eyebrow. "This overprotective thing might get annoying going forward."

"Probably, but if the situation were switched, you'd be asking the same damn thing."

I laughed. *"That* is a certainty."

I reversed the SUV and headed down the narrow, uneven track that was the compound's main entry point. There were others, but they generally weren't vehicle accessible.

So, what disaster has gotten you out of bed on this too-warm night? came Belle's comment,

I could ask you the same thing.

In my case, it was the urgent need to pee. I'm figuring that's not your excuse.

I turned onto the main road and headed for Castle Rock. *I dreamed. Well, kind of.*

You need to be more specific. The heat has sapped my brainpower of late.

I couldn't help grinning. *You sure it's not all the good loving you're getting?*

Positive. Her mental tone was dry. *Even Monty has*

decided it's too freaking hot. He's currently researching weather spells.

Seriously?

Yes. Now stop hedging and give with the information.

Marie reached out to me in a prophetic dream.

Well, fuck.

Yeah. She has Roger staked in a pentagram and has given Maelle twenty-four hours to hand herself over to them or he dies.

She's going to kill him whether Maelle goes or not.

Yes, but I think she'll wait until she has Maelle in custody. Even Marie doesn't want a crazy-as-fuck, all-bets-are-off vampire coming after her.

The headlights picked out a shape on the side of the road—a kangaroo, and a big one at that—so I hit the brake and cruised past slowly. Thankfully, he remained where he was rather than play dare with my SUV.

So why call you into the situation? Wasn't it only days ago she warned us to stay out of it?

I didn't take notice of her warning, so now she's bringing me into play.

How did she call you though? You've run protections around the longhouse—

They obviously weren't enough. We're going to return to the café until this mess is sorted.

So where are you now?

Heading for Maelle's.

Why not just ring her?

I tried. When she finally answered, she sounded ... brusque. She didn't give me the chance to tell her what I saw, just told me to be at the nightclub in half an hour. I paused and glanced at the time. Still fifteen to go, and I was on the outskirts of Castle Rock now. *I think something has happened.*

Of course it has, because problems rarely hit one at a time. I'll get dressed and meet you there. And don't say "don't", because you are not going in there without backup.

I half smiled. *Wouldn't think about it.*

Liar. She paused. *Monty's coming, too.*

She probably won't let him in. She hadn't the last time he'd accompanied me.

Exactly what he said, but he's insisting he be the backup plan. He'll wait outside and come a-running if we need it.

Fair enough. I'm about ten minutes away.

We'll meet you there.

The mental line went dead. I flicked on the radio and wound my way through the silent streets of Castle Rock, eventually arriving at Maelle's nightclub eight minutes later. Monty and Belle hadn't arrived yet, so I stopped on the opposite side of the street to the club and studied it.

The last time I'd been here the walls had been repaired but missing the biomechanical alien forms that had made it something of a tourist attraction. They remained absent, but the roof had now been restored, and the walls were in the process of being painted—though not right at this particular moment. Painting at night was never ideal, because the lights needed to see what you were doing generally attracted far too many bugs—and real-life rotting bug carcasses probably wouldn't be the attraction the alien forms had been.

Two other things had changed.

One, there were now multiple layers of protection spells surrounding the building.

And two, the hulking, not-quite-human men who generally guarded the doors were absent.

Something *definitely* had happened.

Twin lights speared through the SUV's rear window as a car pulled up behind me, and the accompanying rattle of the engine told me who it was. Monty's old Ford had a very distinctive sound.

I grabbed a couple of bottles of holy water from my backpack, then climbed out and walked down to them.

Monty wound down the window. "Hey, cuz. Nice night for a bit of magic."

I smiled. Though my relationship with my mom was now on the improve, during the bad old days of growing up in Canberra, Monty had been one of the few relatives I'd not only gotten along with but had actually liked. My grandfather was the other, but he'd died long before the forced marriage mess that had sent Belle and me on the run for nearly thirteen years.

Like most royal witches, Monty had deep crimson hair and silver eyes, but his pleasant features held a lot more warmth and humor than was usual amongst the royal lines. He'd been in love with Belle for as long as I could remember, and I couldn't have been happier that the two of them were finally engaged.

"I'm thinking you might *not* be referring to the witch kind there," I replied, voice dry.

"Then you'd be thinking wrong. As Belle said, it's entirely too hot, even for me."

"Are you ill?" I pressed the back of my hand against his forehead. "A little hot but wouldn't call it a fever—"

He laughed and knocked my hand away. "I see the repairs on Maelle's place continue to rocket along. No guards though—do you think she's replaced them with all those protection spells?"

"Honestly?" I replied, "No, because she uses them as a

visible deterrent to the human population. It's possible they're helping with whatever situation caused Maelle to sound so harassed."

"Possible, but unlikely." Belle climbed out of the passenger side of the car and walked around the front of the car. "We're all aware how Maelle deals with 'problems,' and I'm thinking she wouldn't want witnesses."

"Except her guards aren't exactly human." They weren't thralls either, but appeared to stand somewhere between the two. "They're her creatures, and it's doubtful they would—or even could—report her to the rangers for any sort of misdemeanor."

"If she's grumpy, then whatever has happened in there will be more than a misdemeanor." She stopped beside me and studied the club through slightly narrowed eyes. Like me, she was wearing a tank top and shorts, but, unlike me, she was built like an Amazon and looked absolutely stunning. She was a Sarr witch, so had their coloring—black skin, silver eyes, and straight black hair that was currently pulled back into a ponytail. I was paler, rounder, and four inches shorter, with freckles across my nose that tended to become more noticeable in summer months.

"I'm only sensing two people inside—Maelle and one other," she added. "Can't tell you who that second person is, because I don't want to risk Maelle's wrath by doing anything deeper than a mind brush."

"Always a sensible goal when it comes to magically powerful old vampires," Monty said. "Could you tell if the person with her is male or female?"

"Female, so not one of the guards."

"Could be one of her feeders," I said.

"Possible, but I did catch a hint of distress."

"Unsurprising, because having a vampire attached to

your neck, sucking on your blood, would undoubtedly be a rather distressing experience," Monty replied in a sage sort of tone.

"She actually prefers the inner thigh, rather than the neck," I said. "Apparently, the closer the blood is to the sexual organs, the sweeter it tastes."

His gaze jumped to mine, expression a mix of surprise and disbelief. "Seriously? You know this how?"

"She told me. Or at least, she told me the first bit, and I was left in no doubt about the second."

"And why were you discussing such a matter?"

"Maelle volunteered the information. Maybe she thought I'd be curious enough to be tempted."

"And maybe," Belle drawled, "she simply figured that if you allowed a werewolf to go down—"

"Belle!" I cut in, and pushed her arm. "Monty does not need that sort of image in his mind."

"Monty does not," he agreed. "So why don't you two head on into that club before this conversation disintegrates any further. Just be careful."

"Aside from the fact Maelle's expecting me, she wants me to rescue Roger. She won't hurt either of us just yet."

"If she damn well even tries," Monty growled, "Roger won't be the only one fucking staked."

He found a source for white ash stakes, Belle explained. *They arrived a few days ago.*

You didn't mention it.

Thought I'd let you enjoy a few days of engagement bliss before the shit hit the fan again.

Thanks. I paused. *Has he checked his stock to make sure none are missing?*

The minute you mentioned Roger being staked. All are accounted for.

Ah, good. I switched my attention back to Monty and patted the arm he was resting on the windowsill. "Just remember that she likes a bit of violence with her meals."

He rolled his eyes and pointed at the club. I grinned and obeyed, although my smile quickly faded as I stepped onto the pavement and a curtain of dark and dangerous energy descended.

It wasn't aimed at us, and it wasn't a spell of any kind. It was emotions. Raw, deep, and darkly furious emotions.

"Oh," Belle muttered, "that does not feel good."

"No."

I studied the airlock-like front door but couldn't see anything to indicate violence or forced entry. Yet that veil very much confirmed that something bad had happened—if not here, then somewhere else.

I took a deep breath that did little to ease the gathering tension, then slowly reached out and gripped the door handle. The metal was oddly cold to the touch, and though my skin crawled, I had no sense of evil or danger.

I opened the door and stepped inside, Belle a couple of steps behind me. The foyer area was in the same state of disrepair as before, although the booth where you checked your coats and paid the entry fees now had a new glass and metal window installed. The doorway into the main club area remained covered by heavy plastic, but this time, doors were here, ready to be installed. I pushed the plastic aside, stepped through, and held it up for Belle.

But as I dropped the plastic back into place, a cloud of raw emotion hit, its force so strong it felt like a punch to the gut. I gasped and leant over, sucking in air as I frantically raised additional mental barriers to quell the emotional tide. Belle's presence sharpened in my mind, and a heartbeat later, the tide dissipated. Not fully, but enough that I could breathe and think again.

"Thanks," I said, pushing upright again. "I should have thought to strengthen my shields, given what we sensed outside."

"I don't think either of us expected—" She stopped, her gaze widening in shock.

My head snapped around.

Maelle walked toward us, her normally meticulously bound chestnut hair falling like string all around her face, and her eyes ... Fear stepped into my heart.

Her eyes were usually a gray so pale there was only the slightest variation between her irises and the white. But here—now—they were black. All black. Ghoulish black.

I'd seen that happen once before, and it had ended with my ex being torn apart before she'd bathed naked in his bloody remains.

She wasn't naked now, but her normally pale and perfect skin was splattered with blood, and her clothes—a deep green riding habit with a high-collar, white lace under-shirt—dripped with fluids, some of which was obviously blood, while the rest ...

The rest were human remains.

CHAPTER TWO

My stomach heaved, but I gulped in air and somehow avoided being sick. Which was a damn good thing given every instinct I had was screaming, "don't move, don't show any sign of repulsion, and for God's sake, don't show any fear lest it unleash the demon so evident in her eyes."

Because there was absolutely nothing human in her gaze right now.

There were many people—even to this day—who believed vampires weren't created via magic and the sharing of a vampire's blood, but were indeed true demons who'd simply taken over the flesh of the living—or even the newly dead—to prey on others.

Maelle was living evidence as to why those superstitions had formed.

I flexed my fingers and resisted the press of wild magic. It might ache to be released, but aside from the pall of inhumanity that currently surrounded her, there was also the magic. It clung to her like a cloak, a cloud of viscous dark purple threads that threatened violence.

If either of us tried to spell right now—if we even reached for something as simple as a protection spell—that violence would hit us.

I guess we were about to discover whether the recently boosted charms we both wore would protect us against a vampire walking the thin edge of sanity.

I fucking *hope they do,* Belle said, *because holy cow, if she unleashed that power—fully unleashed—it could take out everything and everyone in the near vicinity.*

And the scary thing is, Marie is at least her equal magic wise. If they got into a one-on-one battle, the whole damn reservation could be destroyed. *Have you any sense of the other woman?*

Yes, she's upstairs, in Maelle's aerie.

Alive?

Yes.

Which at least meant the ... bits ... all over Maelle's body weren't that other woman's. Which of course only led to the next obvious question—whose was it? The blood was too fresh, too red, for it to have happened any earlier than a few minutes ago, and yet Belle hadn't sensed anyone else in the club.

It's possible that whatever happened for her to be covered in ... Belle's mental tones faded briefly as she gulped ... *all this stuff happened in the private rooms. They weren't destroyed in the explosion, remember.*

Because they weren't located within the club itself, but rather underground some undefined distance away. The main entrance had been here, though, and it had used some sort of transport spell to take her customers into that area.

Perhaps that's where the door bouncers are, too.

Unless, of course, the bits are the bouncers. There's a lot

26

of black threaded in amongst the other ... things ... and that seemed to be their color of choice.

I can't see her attacking her own people.

And yet she all but destroyed the vampire coven because Marie broke her promise not to turn anyone else from Maelle's bloodline—no children, grandchildren, or great-grandchildren—and you can bet your ass plenty of those she murdered that day were her people.

Maelle stopped at the base of the stairs that divided the upper platform—where the bar and the seating booths were —from the main dance floor. The chunks of flesh and the strings of muscle and veins decorating her clothing were more evident this close, and the scent of it all ... Dear God, she smelled like blood and raw meat, and it was all I could do not to turn and run.

For several seconds she said nothing and did nothing, but her fingers were clenched and those darkly violent threads surrounding her pulsed erratically.

That pulse, I realized in horror, matched the frantic beat of my heart.

And mine.

Maelle's fists clenched a fraction more, her knuckles glowing in her blood-splattered hands. She *wanted* to attack. She was desperate to attack.

But somewhere deep under all that fury and violence a spark of sanity remained—and it was all that kept her from following baser need.

The silence stretched on endlessly. She didn't move, and I didn't dare lest it break the tenuous hold she had on control. As time ticked past, my erratic heartbeat began to slow, and the dark threads echoed the descent. The black leached from her eyes, though it left the faintest stain

27

around her irises, a reminder that the violence might be checked but it had not disappeared.

She flexed her fingers, and I briefly echoed the movement. Her gaze flicked to my hands, but thankfully, the sparks that sometimes played around their tips in dangerous situations were absent. Perhaps my inner wild magic was as frightened by the woman in front of us as I was.

Justifiably so, Belle said. *Though if I had to guess at a reason for the lack of a light show, I'd say it's more to do with you gaining control over it now that you've done the well thing and come to an agreement with its tenants.*

"Its tenants" being the souls of the Fenna—witch-werewolf crosses who'd been specifically bred in the fires of newly emerging wellsprings to become guardians of the wild magic. It was a practice that hadn't survived into present day—hell, there'd only been one book in the main witch archives up in Canberra that even mentioned the Fenna—but that had all changed the day I'd gotten pregnant. The daughter I was carrying would be the first true Fenna born in who knew how many generations, and to save the O'Connor compound, I'd forever bound her to the older wellspring.

That I'd had no real choice didn't ease the guilt of choosing a life and a path for her that she might never have wanted.

"If you came to warn me of an attack on my people, you came far too late." Maelle's French accent was almost lost to the fury that burned through her voice. "They are gone. They are all gone. All bar Lucille."

My gaze flicked to Maelle's lair—a dark glass and metal room built into the point where the building's ceiling arches met, giving her a three-sixty-degree view of her venue while concealing her from casual sight. The vague outline visible through one of those dark panes suggested Lucille was watching us.

My gaze returned to Maelle. "Did their attackers escape?"

Her smile was short, sharp, and dangerous, even without her canines fully extended. "No, they did not. But then, I doubt Marie ever intended them to."

My gaze flicked briefly to her splattered, stained clothes. If she'd done the whole "swimming in their remains" thing, then it was unlikely there'd even be enough left to identify them ...

I gulped and brutally pushed down the images that rose. Maelle emoted so strongly that, despite all the barriers now ringing my psi senses, my psychometry and clairvoyance skills were working in tandem to pick up bits and pieces of her memories.

"Is that where your guards are? They're cleaning up the attackers' remains?"

She smiled her violent smile. "Oh, there is very little remaining, but yes."

"Did this happen here? Or were each of your people tracked down and killed individually?"

"It happened in the club's privacy rooms. I thought it safer if I kept my people close. I was wrong."

"But how did they get in?" Belle asked. "I saw how secure those rooms were. Even if she'd magically smashed her way through, you would have had warning."

"Indeed, and if they had done that, there'd be more than one feeder alive right now. But there was no need to break the barriers, because they have Roger, and he has access to all areas."

I frowned. I'd already seen what was happening to Roger, so that didn't really make much sense. He simply couldn't have been here if he'd already been staked out in that forest. Unless, of course, what I'd seen was some sort of insight into what would be rather than what was. Given it wasn't really a precognitive dream, but rather a meeting of minds or even spirits that had been orchestrated by Marie, anything was possible.

"Why didn't you change his access when he disappeared?" I asked.

"It would have been pointless. He is my creature and would read as me to any barrier raised."

"Surely you can refine the spells," Belle said. "He has very different physical attributes than you."

"Indeed, but he shares my energy, and that is what underpins all the spells. It cannot be altered."

"But if Roger had been forced here to open the gateways and allow Marie's people entry, wouldn't you have sensed him?"

"Under normal circumstances, yes."

"And under *these* circumstances?" I asked.

She smiled her scary smile. "He did not come through here."

Instinct prickled. "Not here, but he *was* in the private rooms, I take it?"

"Yes. It is what drew me away from my lair and Lucille."

Lucky Lucille. Because if the two of them had been in the middle of a feeding sex session when the murders happened, she might have taken her fury out on the other woman—even if not intentionally. "I take it that means there's a second entry?"

"More an escape route. By the time I arrived, he was gone, but the barriers had been breached and the slaughter almost complete." She paused, and the black in her eyes briefly increased. "I finished what they started. Such blood-shed ... it is irresistible."

Dear God ... she killed her own people. Belle's mental tones were filled with horror. *No wonder Lucille is quaking in her boots.*

While there was a part of me sympathetic to Lucille's terror, she'd willingly become a bloodsucker's blood bank and had to be aware of the damn dangers that came with that.

"The attack on your feeders isn't what I came here to warn you about," I said.

She raised an eyebrow, the movement almost languid. Overfeeding did have that effect ... I shoved the thought away. I did *not* need it or the resulting images that teased mind and imagination. My stomach remained really unstable, and it wouldn't take much for me to start puking.

"Then what did you come here for?"

"Marie stepped into a dream. She gave me a message to give to you."

She straightened as the shadows rolled through her eyes again. "What message?"

"That you have twenty-four hours to meet her at the court of justice, or she will kill Roger and come after you."

"There is no justice in her court. There never has been. She is also well aware I am her equal in magic, and all of this is nothing more than a means of ensuring she has the upper hand."

"Is that why—at least in the dream—I saw him staked with white ash?"

The black flooded her eyes again. "She has him staked? That would certainly explain my recent ... hungers. He is drawing more from me to fight the deadly infection that comes with such piercing."

"Is it survivable?" I couldn't help but ask.

"Of course." The reply was curt. "He is not a vampire, just the creature of one. Staking him will never kill him, even if his heart is pierced, but he will continue to draw more from me as the infection grows. You must find him before I am forced to completely cut him off."

I frowned. "It's going to take more than twenty-four hours to search every glade in this reservation, Maelle."

"Then use the other gifts you have in your possession."

"You told me they would be useless—that he would read as an extension of you."

"That is neither here nor there. I wish you to at least try."

By wish, she means demand, Belle said dryly.

No doubt about that. To Maelle, I added, "Then I will need something of his to use. Something closely connected to him."

She immediately pulled a gold ring off the small finger on her left hand and held it out to me. I didn't take it. "It needs to be his, not yours."

"He is me. You can use this to find an echo of my presence."

Which was exactly what Aiden had said earlier. The man understood more about my gifts and how they worked than I'd given him credit for.

That's to be expected, given just how often said gifts have been employed under his very watchful eye over the last year, Belle said, mental tones dry. *I'm just hoping that Monty's declaration that these two will be the last of the big bads to come into the reservation comes to pass. All of us deserve a goddamn break.*

And how often have you warned me about tempting fate with comments like that?

Difference is, I didn't say it out loud. Thoughts are perfectly safe.

Maelle waved the ring at me, the movement impatient. I held my breath and stepped forward, not wanting to inhale the scent of blood and meat that hung like a pall around her. It was bad enough from a distance, but the closer you got ...

I pulled an old tissue from my pocket, folded it several times, then gingerly plucked the ring from her grip, being extra careful not to touch her hand. My shields were holding against the raw emotion she was still broadcasting, but a direct touch might well blow them apart.

Even through the layers of tissues, I felt the life within the ring. Her presence dominated, but there very definitely was a distant echo. Whether I'd be able to trace it was another matter entirely—and a question I couldn't answer until I opened the gates holding my psychometry in check.

I moved back to stand beside Belle and released the breath I'd been holding. Though to be honest, the air quality was only fractionally better here.

"Are you sensing anything?" Maelle asked, voice sharp.

"I haven't even tried—"

"Then do so."

I frowned at her. "It's never wise to chase a rabbit down a hole without full protections when said rabbit is caught—"

Maelle was suddenly several steps closer, even though I hadn't even seen her move. "What is *unwise* is not doing what I ask, when I ask it."

My insides clenched, but I continued to meet her dark gaze evenly. "You can't afford to kill me, Maelle. You're outnumbered, and you need all the fucking help you—"

"Oh, I won't kill you, Elizabeth," she cut in smoothly. "But this reservation? The people you care about? Different matter entirely."

In that moment, I saw Marie in her. Saw just how similar the two were, despite Maelle's thicker coat of civility. But what did I expect? She was, in the end, Marie's creation—a product of her blood and her magic.

I clenched my fists and stepped so close to her that we were almost nose to nose. The stench rolling off her was horrendous, and the darkness in her eyes a smothering blanket that was all-consuming ... then my inner wild magic flared, the blanket fell away, and her eyes became nothing more than inky spots of fury.

"I hope your threat is nothing more than the lingering madness of bloodthirst you mentioned earlier." My voice was flat, utterly devoid of the fury and the fear that roiled through me. "But if it is not, be warned. Harm any of my friends, or anyone I love, and I will erase your stain from existence."

She stared at me for the longest moment, then threw her head back and laughed.

"Ah, Lizzie Grace, I do wish there were more around like you. You are balm for the soul."

Thank the fuck that gamble paid off, Belle said, *because I was getting ready to fry the bitch's mind.*

Maelle respects strength and courage, even if she doesn't believe I could ever best her in a one-on-one fight.

She doesn't, but if you ever do get into a one-on-one, you know I'll be along for that ride. She paused. *Monty suggests not taking the ring back to the café, because it's possible it could provide her with a magical access point.*

I frowned. *But I revoked her access—*

Via the usual means of entry. But mages are fully capable of transport spells, and the ring could provide a navigational lock point on the café that will allow her to bypass all protections and restrictions and port directly in.

Is it possible to guard against that sort of thing?

There was a brief pause, then she said, *If we place a repelling spell around it and then encase it in silver, he thinks that should do the trick.*

"Please," Maelle continued, in that same amused manner, "proceed as you wish, where you wish."

I hesitated. "It's probably best if we do the search here, but we'll need to create a protective circle to ensure whatever traps Marie might have laid don't snare—"

"If this is a trap, Elizabeth, a mere protection circle will not actually protect you."

"If it was only one circle, that might be true. But three working in tandem have defeated the most determined demon in the past. At the very least, it will hold off *your* demon long enough to retreat." I paused. "I take it you have no objections to us bringing Monty in to help?"

Monty was in fact the reservation witch—a position assigned by the High Witch Council and one that usually meant doing nothing more than passing on the occasional high council decree and providing the rangers with magical assistance when needed. I'd officially become his assistant a few months ago, but that didn't moot the point that Maelle should have been dealing with him rather than me. But as Belle had noted previously, she wanted to get her teeth into my flesh, not his, and had basically started—very politely—blocking his attempts to talk to her.

And one did not push the buttons of a crazy powerful vampire unless it was absolutely necessary.

Thinks the woman who constantly pushes said buttons, Belle noted dryly.

I didn't bother refuting the statement. Couldn't, in fact, when it was nothing but the truth.

"Marie would be incensed to hear you call her a mere

demon." Amusement played around Maelle's lips again but the violence surrounding her had retreated further. Though none of us dared relax just yet, it was at least a sign that the immediate threat of becoming a vampire's lunch had greatly lessened. "But yes, you can bring Monty in. The poor fellow might well have a heart attack if it keeps beating at such a rapid rate."

Holy fuck, she can hear it from here? Belle said.

The senses of all predators are attuned to their prey.

Yeah, but I had no idea it was that sensitive.

Wolves can hear sounds from six to ten miles away, depending on the terrain and wind. While I doubt her hearing is that keen, I can't imagine up to a mile would be much of a stretch. To Maelle, I added, "Where would you prefer us to set up?"

She waved a hand casually. "Wherever. I have ... things I have to take care of, but I will remain nearby if you need me."

I nodded. She turned and walked away, disappearing into the deeper shadows that haunted the dance floor. The air suddenly became easier to breathe.

I glanced at Belle. "Monty's on the way?"

She nodded. "He's just grabbing your spell stones from your pack."

"Just as well I didn't lock the SUV then."

"You could leave the keys in the ignition and put a 'feel free to steal' sign on that thing, and absolutely no one would take you up on the invitation."

I grinned but turned around as Monty came through the plastic.

"Where's our resident vamp?" he asked.

"Dealing with 'stuff' but close enough to hear and see what is going on," Belle said.

"Ah." He handed me and Belle the small silk bags containing our spell stones. "I suggest you two interweave your stones while I provide an outer layer. Belle can remain in the inner circle with you, just to be doubly safe."

Belle raised an eyebrow. "I think it would be best if the three of us are in the center. Safer all round if this is a setup."

"I disagree, and I am the boss in the field."

She grinned and patted his arm. "You keep on believing that, if it makes you happy."

He rolled his eyes. "Just get to it, both of you."

We did. After Belle and I had placed our spell stones, we raised the protective magic, weaving the separate threads through each other's to create a stronger whole.

Once we were done and the circle was raised, Monty placed his own spell stones, then stepped inside his barrier and raised it.

"Right," he said, turning to face us. "You're good to go."

I nodded and sat cross-legged on the ground. Belle followed, then inched closer so that our knees were touching.

We'd done this hundreds of times before, but my stomach nevertheless clenched. Probably because this time, unlike the other times, I knew exactly what might be waiting.

"You'll be fine," Belle said softly. "I'll pull you out the minute I sense anything untoward."

"I know."

But knowing didn't ease the fear and uncertainty, however. In cases like this, it probably never would.

I took one of those deep breaths that did absolutely nothing, then carefully wiped away any smears of blood from the ring before releasing it from its tissue prison.

The minute the gold hit my skin, my psi talents exploded to life, drawing me hard and fast down a rabbit hole of images and information. In quick succession I saw two golden wattles, red boulders, a cavern shaped like a mouth, and a deep body of water. Then feet, and legs, and then arms, but no torsos. No heads.

None of the parts belonged to Roger. But he was here, somewhere.

His intermittent pulse ran across the darkness, a spark of life in a cavern that held nothing but death.

Realization hit. This was a pen.

A stockyard.

A place Marie and her people took their human "cattle" before they dined on them.

CHAPTER THREE

I shuddered and released the ring, which shattered the connection and let the horrific images dissipate. The gut-churning horror remained, however.

The ring chimed lightly as it hit the floor and bounced away. Monty caught it before it could roll down the steps, but in the shadowed darkness that surrounded us, it glimmered with bloody fire. My psychometry surged to life one more time, giving me a final image—that of a lake rich and red in hue, and in which faces floated. Faces that were forever frozen in fear and horror.

My stomach roiled threateningly. I gulped down air as I battled the urge to be sick. Belle caught my hands, and her mind flowed into mine, pushing the images back from the forefront of my memories and giving me room to breathe, to think.

"Thanks," I said eventually. My gaze rose to hers. "Did you see ...?"

"Some of the stronger images certainly came through, but you're doing a damn good job of shutting me out these days." She squeezed my hands then released them. "What you saw is not unexpected, given who and what we're dealing with."

I guess it wasn't, given there were at least a dozen vampires remaining with Marie—including, of course, Maelle's daughter Jaqueline—and they did all need to be fed.

I just hadn't expected it to be so ... centralized.

Monty disengaged his circle and collected his spell stones. "I take it you located Roger?"

"I saw the cavern where I think he's imprisoned, but he's not alone there."

Belle and I released our entwined protection circle, then rose and picked up the spell stones.

Monty's eyebrows rose. "They have other prisoners?"

"More like other victims." Belle's reply was grim. "Think charnel house, but in a cave."

"Ah, fuck." Monty scraped a hand across his bristly chin. "Though *that* does make me wonder why there hasn't been an avalanche of missing persons reports."

"The reservation is filled with small farms and out-of-the-way shacks," I replied. "The werewolves might notice one of their own going missing, but they're unlikely to notice anyone else doing so unless its reported or they deal with them on a daily basis."

"True." He hesitated. "Did you see anything that will give us an idea of general location? Or are we just going to tootle around with the ring until we find a pulse—"

"I would hope your use of 'tootling' does not imply a lack of urgency" came Maelle's comment from somewhere deep in the shadows behind Monty. "Roger needs to be found within that twenty-four-hour deadline we were given."

Her use of 'we' definitely suggested there'd be personal

ramifications for us if we didn't, and that they wouldn't be coming from Marie.

But then, if we failed to save Roger, be it within that deadline or not, there'd be ramifications for the whole damn reservation, not just us.

"Just where is this court she mentioned?" I couldn't help asking. "She said you'd know, but how is that even possible if you two haven't communicated yet?"

Maelle remained in the shadows, but I nevertheless felt the cold flash of her smile. "The court is not a physical entity, but rather one that lies in the realm between life and death. It is a plane on which evil plays, and one that we who live on the lives of others, who conjure from the blood of others, or who barter with the darker forces of this world can traverse at will."

I stared at the darkness in which she stood for several seconds. "That's how Jaqueline escaped the explosion at the shearers' shed, isn't it?"

She hadn't, as we'd presumed at the time, scrambled down into the old mine shaft that ran underneath the shed, but rather had simply stepped into this shadow realm.

"Indeed," Maelle said, amusement evident. "And if not for the fact that the spells around your café have the wild magic woven through them, you would have already fallen victim to Marie's wiles."

"And there you go, underestimating me again."

"I underestimate nothing, my dear Elizabeth. Now, you had best go and find Roger, otherwise annoyance might get the better of me."

It was so calmly, so politely said, but there was no doubting the threat within. A chill ran down my spine and, as one, the three of us turned and got the hell out of there.

"Talk about being caught between a rock and a hard

place," Monty grumbled once we were clear of the building. "We've one vampire who'll kill us if we don't find her man, and a fucking dozen who will kill us if we do."

"At least we have the sunlight on our side right now," I said. "No matter what else they might be capable of, they simply can't roam about in it."

"Which may not matter if they're able to use this shadow plane as some sort of supernatural highway to get about."

"I can't imagine it would be easy to enter or use," Belle said. "All magic has its costs, but the darker the spell, the greater the price paid."

"Except the dark plane isn't reached via a spell," Monty replied.

I glanced at him, eyebrows rising. "You've heard about it before?"

"It was mentioned in one of the classes about dark mages and darker magics at uni, though they called it a path rather than a plane." He grimaced. "Like most classes related to anything involving either subject, it was high on theory and low on fact."

"Maybe because those teaching the class don't know all that much on the subject," Belle said.

"The Heretic Investigations Center exists, remember, and they have a pretty extensive library about dark magic and its uses, given their specialty is hunting down dark witches and mages."

"Did these classes ever mention how the plane is reached, if not by a spell?" I asked.

He grimaced. "As I said, it was theory more than fact. They believe there're numerous entry points into the plane that only those who deal with darkness and death can see. Regular witches can't see them, apparently, and most of those who can are rarely given the chance to answer questions about them."

"Because the HIC's 'most wanted' list is also a kill list," I commented.

He nodded. "Did you get anything specific that might pin down the search area?"

I wrinkled my nose. "Maybe—I'll need to talk to Aiden first."

"I think it might also be worth giving Ashworth and Eli a heads-up," Monty said. "If that cave is charnel in nature, it's likely to be well protected. It wouldn't hurt to have additional magical help."

Ira Ashworth worked for the Regional Witch Association—the government body charged with dealing with any situation witch-related within regional communities. Eli, his husband, had also worked for them, but was now retired. Both men had basically become substitute grandfathers to me over the course of the last year. I'd even asked Ashworth if he would walk me down the aisle.

"You ring them; I'll ring Aiden." I'd promised to update him anyway, though this wasn't the sort of update I wanted to be doing.

As Monty nodded and pulled out his phone, I leaned against the SUV's bullet hole-ridden rear door and made my call.

The phone barely had time to ring before Aiden answered. "You obviously survived the wrath of our resident vampire."

I smiled. "I will admit it was touch-and-go for a little while there. She's one scary mother, I can tell you that."

"All mothers are scary when their young are threatened. Roger may not be her bloodline, but he is of her flesh."

Which was very true, but her fierceness was more a

result of the damage his death could do to her than any sort of maternal instinct. Hell, I wasn't even sure her demand we leave Jaqueline alive was maternal in nature, despite her protestations and the fact that her daughter was one of the few who'd survived her destroying their coven.

"Did you manage to persuade her to let you use psychometry to find him?"

"I did, and I did."

"And you're ringing to get my help with the location?"

I smiled. "That, and because I was missing your dulcet tones."

He snorted. "Yeah. Likely."

I laughed. "In the vision, I saw two golden wattles, red boulders, and a cavern shaped like a mouth. Does that ring any location bells?"

"Wrong time of year for the wattles to be out—"

"They weren't in flower, but I recognized the leaves."

"Ah. Well, the red boulders suggest it could be situated around the Eureka Reef area."

"I take it there are plenty of old caves there?"

"Plenty of mines. There's a self-guided two-kilometer walking track situated there, but we generally encourage tourists to keep out of the deeper forests surrounding the reef because of the mine shaft dangers. I take it he's not located anywhere easy to get to?"

"Are they ever?" I responded. "It still might be worth driving around the area first to see if I can pick up a signal from the ring Maelle gave me. It could save us some time."

Could waste it, too, but given my tendency to find mine shafts the hard way, I'd really prefer not to be walking around an area full of them.

"We can certainly do that."

I smiled. "There's no need for you to accompany us. I'll

call if we find something. Besides, you surely have more important things to do than drive around the reservation with the three of us."

"There *is* nothing more important than sorting out this whole vampire mess right now, because you and I need to marry, and the sooner the better."

I laughed again. "I'm not going to run away on you, Aiden. And it's not like a marriage certificate will stop that if I do decide to run."

"I know. I just ..."

Want to make you mine. Officially. He didn't say that, but it nevertheless seemed to sing down the line between us.

"I was, and always will be, yours," I said softly. "Nothing will ever change that."

"Wish I could echo the first part of that statement, but it took me too damnably long to realize you'd stolen my heart."

"I forgive you," I said lightly. "You are a werewolf, after all, and sometimes the alpha trait gets in the way of common sense."

He laughed. "Says the witch who constantly ignores common sense."

I smiled, but it quickly faded. "Aiden, has there been an uptick in missing person reports of late?"

"Not that I'm aware of. Why?"

"Because I saw what looked to be the vamps' feeding ground, and there were a lot of bodies in there."

"Ah, fuck," he muttered. "I'll contact the alphas and get them to check the isolated farms near their compounds. If too many people had gone missing from towns, we would have received reports by now. Where are you now?"

"Outside Maelle's."

"Then head back to the café and I'll meet you all there.

My truck can cope with the rougher tracks up near the Eureka Reef better than either yours or Monty's."

"Monty's can barely cope with a dirt road."

Aiden laughed. "Don't let him hear you say that. He's inordinately fond of that rust bucket of his."

So fond he'd given her a name—Beast. Which, in many ways, was appropriate, because it certainly was a beast of a thing to drive—in a bad way, not good.

"I'll see you soon, then."

I hung up and glanced at Monty. "Aiden's going to meet us at the café."

"Ashworth asked if we could pick him up on the way through," Monty said. "Eli's going to contact a cousin in Canberra and see what he knows about the dark path."

My eyebrows rose. "Did his cousin work for the HIC?"

"Quite some years ago, apparently, but he still has access to their resources and can do a search for us. Whether it'll result in a means of tracing or even blocking these entry points is anyone's guess."

"Maelle can obviously see them," Belle commented. "It would be handy if she started coming to the party with some information."

"I wouldn't hold your breath waiting for that to happen," Monty muttered. "Shall we go?"

I nodded, and jumped into the SUV, doing a U-turn, and led the way back to the café. I parked around the back, then, after dropping the ring into the center console, out of immediate sight, I grabbed my pack and walked up the steps, avoiding the stained patch of concrete—all that was left of the vampire who'd been incinerated there not long ago. Not by me, but by the sun.

The air sparkled briefly as I entered the reading room, a clear indication the thickly layered spells encircling and protecting the room remained active. The warm scent of cinnamon, clove, lemon, and sandalwood—all of which provided either protection or enhanced focus and concentration—filled the air, and it was a scent that would only get stronger in the run-up to Christmas. Belle was one of the strongest spirit talkers around, and it was an ability that was now bringing in customers from far and wide. With Christmas only a few weeks away, it seemed everyone wanted to speak to lost loved ones. It was a good revenue stream, but doing so many each and every day did take a toll on Belle strength wise. I'd suggested she take an additional day off, but so far she was resisting.

"And you know why," she commented from behind me. "The readings don't cover the cost of hiring an additional staff member."

"The café is now running at a profit, Belle."

"Only just. And please don't give me that whole 'we're both millionaires now' line, because that money hasn't yet come through."

"But it will." Anthony, the Black Lantern attorney who'd represented me at the mediation meeting with my ex's other heirs, would ensure it.

I pressed my hand against a panel in the bookcase that covered the entire rear wall—one of thirty-six we'd had installed. Magic crawled across my fingers, then the lock released, revealing an eight-inch hidden compartment. This one held multiple bottles of holy water and a couple of packets of blessed salt. Salt worked as a deterrent for most supernatural beasties, because as a general rule they couldn't cross an unbroken line of it. Blessed salt was new and totally untested, but the priest we now purchased our holy water from—for a sizeable donation to his church—had said it might strengthen the salt's deterrent factor and could even work as a cleanser. We had nothing to lose by trying it—nothing other than another large donation to his church, of course.

I tossed the salt across to Belle and then grabbed a nearby box and stacked six bottles of holy water into it. After closing that panel, I moved across to the next and pulled out a bag of sage smudge sticks. We generally dispensed a mix of dried sage and lavender to clients wanting to banish negative energy, but the smudge sticks were useful to cleanse and purify spaces.

This cave, however big it was, would need both if the number of faces I'd seen floating in that bloody pond was anything to go by. That many deaths in one confined area could lead to the formation of a tenebrum cloud—a swirling cloud of darkness imbued with all the fear, the horror, and the pain of those who'd died. It could drown those who entered it unprotected with all its emotional weight, and often resulted in madness.

Of course, sage was also useful for banishing evil spirits, but I very much doubted it would work against the evil currently using the Faelan Reservation as a hunting ground, if only because they weren't spirits but rather flesh and blood.

I tucked the bag and a box of matches into my pack and then handed Belle a silk bag to place the ring in once we were back in the car. I really didn't want to touch it with bare fingers, given the images that might lie in wait. The silk wouldn't kill my ability to track the pulse of Roger's presence, but it would at least mute those images.

I scooped up the box of holy water and followed Belle out into the main café area. Monty was behind the counter, helping himself to cake.

"You were a hobbit in a previous life, weren't you?" I said, amused.

"Hey, I haven't had first breakfast yet, let alone second." He waved the serving knife toward the carrot cake he'd taken out of the cake fridge. "You want some? I can highly recommend it. The cream-cheese icing really sets it off perfectly."

"Says the biased man who sleeps with the woman who made said carrot cake and cream-cheese icing," I said dryly. "And it's probably better if I don't, given the unsteady nature of my stomach of late and what we're about to head into."

"Ah, yeah, sorry." Monty bagged three more pieces, then scooped them up and followed me out the back door. After collecting and bagging the ring, we walked around to the front to wait for Aiden.

Gentle hues of pink and gold began to stain the horizon even though shadows still hugged the ground. The dawning day remained hot and still, and there was very little in the way of birdsong to be heard. Even the magpies had apparently decided it took too much energy to warble in this heat.

Aiden's truck came around the corner a few seconds later. He pulled up in front of us, then leaned across to open the passenger door for me. Monty ushered Belle into the rear seat, then scooted in beside her and offered Aiden one of the bags.

"Nothing nicer than a crumbly cake when you're driving," he said wryly. "But thanks for the thought."

"Quite happy to eat it if you don't," Monty replied.

"Which was no doubt your plan all along."

"Oh, no doubt about it," Belle said.

Aiden laughed, then checked his mirrors and pulled

out. "I take it we're picking up Ashworth on the way through?"

I nodded and tried to ignore the delicious scent of cake invading the cabin. As much as my stomach was rumbling, it would appreciate my forbearance later.

It didn't take us long to get across to Ashworth's. He and Eli lived in a pretty miners' cottage with a white picket fence and a path lined with flowers and roses. The backyard was even prettier, which was why I'd asked if we could use it to get married in.

Ashworth was waiting at the front for us. He was a short, squat, and powerfully built bald man with a heavily lined face and muddy silver eyes. Today he was wearing oil-stained jeans and his favorite Black Sabbath T-shirt, which Eli had long ago declared should have been binned. He was at least wearing decent leather boots, rather than his usual threadbare sneakers. Anyone who didn't know him would probably write him off as some kind of hobo, but any witch would know better—the power that rolled off him when he wasn't tamping it down was breathtaking.

Monty moved across to make room for him. Ashworth threw his pack into the back of Aiden's truck, then climbed in beside Monty and did up the belt.

"Morning all," he said, sounding altogether too cheerful for such an early hour. "I brought along some white ash shavings. Thought they might come in handy."

"White ash shavings?" I looked around. "That wouldn't kill them, would it?"

"No, but it does prevent vampire entry if appropriately placed. They can't cross it. They can't even touch it."

"Couldn't they just jump over it?" Belle asked. "Or just blow it away?"

"No, because we'll link a shield to the shavings. That'll

result in the white ash's properties infusing the spell and means they won't easily be able to dismantle said spell without endangering their own lives."

"I'm betting Marie will just get one of her subordinate vamps to take the risk."

"Most likely, but he or she will pay the price, and that'll mean one less vamp for us to deal with."

"They never mentioned shavings when we did the unit on vampires," Monty said.

"Because those who teach rarely have field experience." Ashworth's voice held a hint of contempt. "Need and experimentation is sometimes the best teacher."

"I'm not going to argue with that," Monty said.

"That would be a change," Ashworth said. "Are you feeling all right?"

"He's only had the one piece of cake," Belle explained. "His sugar levels are suffering."

"Ah well, I'll go easy on the lad then."

"Thank you," the lad said dryly.

Silence fell, though it was far from an easy silence, given we were all too aware that what we were racing toward might well be a trap.

Once we were well on our way to the Eureka Reef, Belle handed me the silk bag containing the ring. The minute it hit my palm, the distant pulse of life jumped into focus. A heartbeat later, a thin, shadowy line began to reel out in front of the truck. It was a physical emanation of the link between the ring and Roger—a tracking guide rope, if you will. It was a very recent development, one born of the changes the inner wild magic was making to my psi talents.

"Got him," I said. "He's still alive."

Aiden glanced at me. "Is the connection a strong one?"

"Yes, so we're close. I'd slow down because who knows when it's going to rip us off the main road."

"Knowing your psi senses," Monty commented, "they'll do so at the most inappropriate time."

He'd barely finished saying that when the translucent rope jagged sideways into the trees.

"Like left right now," I said, even though there really didn't appear to be a road or track to drive onto.

Aiden swore and yanked the wheel sideways. Tires squealed and the truck rocked violently onto two wheels, forcing me to grip the panic bar to stop being thrown into Aiden's side. He gunned the engine, the truck thumped back down onto four wheels, and we plunged into trees, branches scraping across the windows and the roof of the truck. We bumped along for several minutes, then the heavier forest gave way to what might mockingly be called a road, though it was little wider than a goat track.

"Remind me never to put something like that into the ether again," Monty said. "Are we on a track, or just plunging willy-nilly through the forest?"

"It's hardly willy-nilly, given I am being guided," I replied.

"That was a serious question aimed at our driver—no answers from the peanut gallery, please."

I laughed and did a quick handball motion to Aiden.

"It's one of the old four-wheel driving tracks," he replied, amused. "The practice was banned quite a few years ago, after several fires were started by hot exhaust pipes."

"And are there any mines about these parts?"

"Not big enough to lose a truck in."

"Well, that's at least something."

"Given Liz's tendency to fall down the things, it's more than merely something," Aiden said, voice dry.

"That's a truth no one will argue with." Belle paused. "Is it my imagination, or is this forest getting darker rather than lighter?"

"Darker," Ashworth replied. "We broke through a veil several minutes ago."

"What sort of veil?" Monty asked, a frown I couldn't see evident in his voice. "I felt a slight ... pressure along the magical lines, but it didn't feel like any sort of spell that I'm aware of."

"It's not a spell in the true sense of the word," Ashworth said. "More of a charm-based deterrent that works in the same manner as a protection circle. It's designed to discourage anyone walking into a set area. It didn't apply to us because we're in the truck."

"How big an area can these deterrents cover?" Belle asked. "Because it looks to me like the truck's headlights are on but struggling to make a dent in the gloom."

"They are, which is why we're now crawling." Aiden glanced at me. "Any idea how much farther we have to go?"

I tightened my grip on the silk-bagged ring for a second. Images of death and darkness pressed at the back of my mind, but they had a weirdly distant feel to them this time. Instinct was suggesting there was a good reason for that, but I ignored it and concentrated instead on the irregular pulse. Right now, our priority had to be rescuing Roger. I could work on the deeper puzzle inherent in this connection later.

"Hard to say," I said eventually. "I guess we just stop and walk once the truck can't go any further."

He nodded and kept following my directions. But the deeper we drove into the forest, the harder it became to see the ground ahead and the trees around us. Eventually, we had no choice but to stop.

I grabbed my backpack and climbed out. A hint of woodsmoke ran underneath the scent of eucalyptus in the air, which suggested there might be a fire nearby. I hoped it was someone who'd just lit a campfire, rather than the beginnings of a bushfire. *That* was the very last thing we needed right now.

Aiden got a couple of flashlights from the back of his truck, but they did little more than flare weakly across the gloom surrounding us. The light orb Monty cast into the air had a little more luck in folding back the veil, but even then visibility remained down to only a few yards.

It was going to make spotting the cave or even mine shafts difficult. Which, I guess, might have been the whole point of the veil in the first place.

I swung my backpack on, and with Aiden by my side, headed left into the trees, following the rising ridge of red rock up the mound-strewn hillside. It was surprisingly hard to walk—the veil wasn't only keeping it artificially dark, but it also seemed to be thickening the air, making every step more of an effort. Sweat trickled down my spine, and I tugged a hairband from the backpack's side pocket and pulled my hair into a ponytail to get it off my neck.

The ridge continued to grow in height. Dotted along its length were various shafts, their entrances barely visible in the golden glow of Monty's light orb, their caverns hiding a darkness even deeper than the veil. None of them were guarded by trees, let alone wattles.

The scent of smoke continued to strengthen, and I glanced worriedly at Aiden. "Is that anything to be concerned about?"

"Don't know." He eyed the bush ahead for a second.

"But there're no burn-offs planned in the area that I'm aware."

"So, it's not just a campfire?"

"Afraid not."

"Isn't it a bit early for bushfires?" Monty asked.

"Sadly, no. Especially not with the heat we've been getting lately." Aiden half shrugged. "I haven't received an alert on my phone, and I would have if there was a fire in the area."

Because the rangers were always called in on fires, if only to keep onlookers at bay so the brigade could do their jobs.

The shadowed string guiding me did another sharp turn, this time to the right. I swung the flashlight that way. Directly ahead was a towering rock face, in the middle of which was a blot of blackness. Either side of this stood the two wattles I'd seen in the vision.

The string went straight into the mouth of that blackness and disappeared.

We'd found the cavern.

And every inch of my being screamed we couldn't—shouldn't—go inside.

That if we did, we would die.

The scents drifting from the cavern's mouth backed up that insight, because that air wasn't only filled with death, but also the thick, acidic scent of demon.

That cave might be a charnel hellhole, but it was also a trap.

CHAPTER FOUR

"Roger's in that cave," I said quietly.

"And that cave is filled with something *other* than bodies and magic." Ashworth's voice was grave. Despite the early hour of the day and the fact he was probably fitter than anyone here aside from Aiden, he was sweating profusely. The veil wasn't taking it easy on anyone, it seemed. "Whatever it is, it doesn't feel right."

"I think that would have to be the understatement of the year," Monty said.

I glanced at them both. "It's a demon."

"And one that's fucking hungry," Belle added, with a shiver.

"Then obviously, it's either a trap or a means of diverting us to wherever the hell they actually want us to go," Aiden said.

"Possibly, but surely Marie can't have known we'd try ..." I let the rest trail off. Marie had been correctly guessing our every move up to this point, so why wouldn't she have known this would be our next one?

"Given what obviously awaits inside *this* tunnel,"

Monty said, "it's worthwhile to at least check out other options, even if that's what they want us to do."

"I think there's an open seam around behind the ridge that dives into a smaller connecting cavern," Aiden said. "I'll run over and—"

"Not alone," I snapped.

"I can move faster in wolf form—"

"Your wolf can't outrun magic," I growled. "It can't even see it. And I'm the only one here who has any chance of keeping up with said wolf."

I would never be able to shift into wolf form, but the DNA changes being made to my body had at least given me wolf-like speed. Whether I could keep up with him in this soup was another matter entirely.

He hesitated then nodded. "Fine."

Both his expression and his voice were mild, but I knew him well enough by now to know he was anything but. I grinned and, as he turned and walked toward the left edge of the towering seam of red rock, glanced back at Ashworth. "Might be worth creating a barrier around that entrance to prevent any future bushwalkers from heading inside."

"I was thinking the very same thing, lass," he said. "The three of us will attend to that while you check out this other entrance."

I nodded, shoved the silk bag containing the ring into my pocket, and ran after Aiden. A few yards beyond the cavern's entrance, the shadows began to ease, and moving seemed less of an effort. Which was odd, in many respects. Why have a wide protection arc on one side of the mine's entrance but not the other? Or was it a deliberate ploy to funnel the unwary into an easier to defend entrance?

Doubtful came Belle's comment. *This looks like a main*

entrance and would be pretty easy to defend. The demon inside is overkill.

Marie seems to have a penchant for that. Stones slid from under my foot, and Aiden caught my hand, stopping me from slipping back down. He didn't release me, but kept a firm hold as we continued on.

Marie has a penchant for games, just like Maelle. Maybe it comes with the territory.

The territory being a very old vampire. *Or maybe it's a trait of their bloodline—something Marie passes on to all those she turns.*

Possible. It's not like any of us know all that much about vampires.

I'm tempted to say, "and thank the fuck for that," but our lack of knowledge isn't helping us right now.

Which is why I've all things crossed that, at the very least, the things that worked on the vamp who turned Karen will work on this lot.

It should.

"Should" doesn't mean will.

My, you're suddenly very pessimistic. My mental tones were dry. *Any reason?*

She hesitated. *Not really. I'm just getting bad vibes about this whole situation.*

It's usually me getting the bad vibes.

Aiden and I finally reached the top of the scree slope; he released my hand and led the way across the ridge's gentle rise, slowly at first but with increasing speed as I managed to keep him in sight.

And maybe this is just a rare bleed over from you, Belle said, *but I've got this weird feeling something is about to happen. Something other than the likelihood we're walking into a trap.*

Something like a fire, perhaps? The scent of smoke was certainly stronger up on this ridge. *It might be worth checking the Emergency Services app for fire warnings. I wouldn't put it past Marie to set off a fire and force us into the arms of her demon.*

I will ... just be careful.

Always am, I repeated with a mental grin.

She snorted. *Seriously, that reply is getting old.*

And yet, I will continue to use it.

She mentally rolled her eyes, and the connection between us faded back. I switched my full attention to following Aiden through the thick scrub, leaping over rocks and fallen tree trunks with an ease and sureness that wouldn't have been possible six months ago.

As we crested the ridge, Aiden swung right, onto another long scree slope. I cautiously followed him down. Loose bits of stone and earth slid away from every step, creating a mini avalanche that chased Aiden's heels. He made it safely to solid ground, then turned and waited for me.

"You okay?" He caught my hand and helped me down the few final feet.

I nodded, squeezed his fingers, then released them. "How far away is the other entrance?"

"Just down there." He pointed to the right, where two sections of rough red stone rose sharply, forming a narrow crevice between them. "Are you sensing anything?"

I shook my head. "Doesn't mean there isn't anything there, though. I'll lead." I paused. "Any known vertical shafts I need to worry about?"

He half smiled. "No, though given your tendency to find them, it might be wise for us to tie on, just in case."

I arched my eyebrows, amusement teasing my lips. "For

safety reasons? Or because you're desperate to tie me down?"

He grinned. "I refuse to answer that question on the grounds I might incriminate myself."

I snorted softly and moved on cautiously. As we neared the crevice, several tiny but luminous threads of wild magic drifted toward me. I raised a hand, and they looped around my wrist. Energy surged around me, through me, and suddenly I was *mentally* falling toward a pool of light—a bright, fierce light that was not only filled with power but also voices. Speaking to me. Warning me.

Surprise had me stumbling, and I probably would have hit the ground if Aiden hadn't lunged forward and caught me. "I'm fine," I said, even though he hadn't said anything, my mind still on the whispers rather than my surroundings.

"You're not," he retorted. "What just happened?"

"It's the wild magic. It's speaking to me."

"Hasn't it always spoken to you?"

"Katie speaks to me through it, yes, but this isn't her."

Katie O'Connor had been Aiden's youngest sister, and her soul—along with the ghost of her witch husband, Gabe—now protected the second, much newer wellspring within the reservation.

"Then who is it?"

"The Fenna."

There was an edge of surprise—and perhaps even wonder—running through my reply. I'd thought they'd rejected me outright, but these whispers suggested that was not the case. I'd been judged, true, and the wolf in Mom's bloodline considered insufficient to fully contain and control the sheer depth of power that lay within the wellspring, but Belle had been right. They had not vetoed my use of its power and there was no curtailment in the power I could draw. They were simply limiting it to what my body could safely contain without harming myself or the child I carried. In those brief, confused, mind-blowing, awe-inspiring moments when I'd stepped into the wellspring and found myself in the presence of hundreds of powerful souls, I'd misunderstood the stream of information flowing through and around me.

No surprise there. I did tend to do that.

"What are they saying?" Aiden asked.

"They're warning me about what lies in wait up ahead."

And it was a threat that would take every ounce of my power to contain.

Because what waited was not a demon, but a vampire.

Not Marie. Jaqueline.

I stopped and spun. "You can't go any further, Aiden."

He looked at me like I'd suddenly gone mad. And maybe I had, because with the threads wrapped around my wrists and the Fenna's whispers ringing in my ears, I felt nothing. No uncertainty. No fear. And I should. I knew I should.

And then, with a sickening lurch, I realized what else I wasn't feeling.

Belle? You out there?

No reply. I couldn't feel her, couldn't hear her. The mental line between us was deathly silent. The Fenna had cut me off from her. That *did* scare me, because up until now we'd always believed there was absolutely nothing that could ever break our bond.

If the wild magic could do this, then maybe Marie could, too.

Or Maelle.

Now fear surged. Fear, and an odd sense of foreboding.

"Liz?" Aiden placed a hand on my cheek, but the

warmth of his skin against mine did little to chase away the ice creeping through my veins.

I swallowed heavily, doing my best to ignore the fear, trying to concentrate. The whispers were growing louder. They wanted me in that cavern, wanted me to confront the darkness within. Not just the vampire but also the weight of blood and death that stained the rocks and sullied the water.

They wanted—*needed*—the area to be cleansed before the foulness reached too deeply into the earth and forever altered its energy.

I pressed a hand against Aiden's chest, felt the rapid pounding of his heart. "I'm fine, and I need you to ring Belle and tell her that—the wild magic has blocked our connection, and I can't seem to restore it. I need you—and everyone else—to remain out here, in the sunshine, until I say otherwise."

"But what—"

"Jaqueline's inside. If you—or any of the others—take one step into that cavern, she'll attack you to get at me."

"You can't go up against Jaqueline alone—"

"I'm not alone—the wild magic is with me." I curled my fingers into a fist and lightly punched his chest. "Please, listen to me. Don't come in. Things will go badly if you do."

He hesitated and then nodded. "Don't get dead."

The words "I won't" once again teased my tongue, but I wasn't about to tempt fate by putting that out there. I kissed him, then quickly turned and walked toward the crevice. Power hummed around and through me, but the voices had fallen silent, at least for the moment. They'd gotten what they'd wanted. I couldn't help but wonder if that was the end of it, or whether they'd lend guidance or help with Jaqueline.

I guess I'd find out soon enough.

The crevice was narrow, the sides jagged and sharp. I squeezed through as best I could, somehow managing to avoid slicing my arms open in the process. The last thing I wanted to be doing was confronting a vampire while bleeding like a stuck pig. She'd undoubtedly take it as some sort of invitation.

Her mother certainly would have.

Another rush of trepidation swept through me. The confrontation I'd always feared was coming. Maelle was coming. Maybe not right at this moment, but soon. Far too soon.

I flexed my fingers and did my best to push away the fear. I was safe for the moment. Or, rather, I was safe for as long as Roger lived. If he died ...

I shivered and stopped at the entrance to the cavern. Unlike the main one, this was little more than a jagged split in the rock face. The scent of death was absent, as was the hungry fury of whatever demon guarded the larger cavern. I had no sense of Jaqueline—if not for the wild magic, Aiden and I might have walked into this place, straight into whatever trap awaited.

I swung my pack around and pulled out two bottles of holy water, tucking one into the back pocket of my jeans and keeping the other in my hand. The wild magic—both mine and the wild threads clinging to my wrist—would protect me, but I couldn't risk using it against her. She was a dark mage and wouldn't take to being caught and caged very easily. The last thing I needed was to stain the wellspring's wild magic with her blood or her magic.

I took several wary steps into the cavern, then paused again, waiting for my eyes to adjust to the deeper darkness. My sight, like my hearing, was now wolf-sharp, and I was soon able to see the sloping, rock-strewn path leading deeper into the cavern. I walked on warily, keeping close to one wall, all senses on alert and my heart galloping uncomfortably in my chest.

Which, considering who I was about to confront, was not ideal. But maybe the enticing pulse of life would distract her. Or, better yet, make her act rashly.

In reality, it was doubtful either would happen. She was her mother's daughter, after all.

I edged on, drawing in deeper breaths, trying to get some sense of the threat that waited. The air smelled slightly musty, and I could hear the distant bubble of water, suggesting there was a good-sized stream running through this cavern somewhere. What remained absent was the heavy weight of death, as well as the demon. Perhaps the caverns weren't as closely linked as Aiden had thought and I was simply too far away to gain any "feel" of the demon.

And perhaps its presence was, as Aiden had guessed, nothing more than a means of diverting at least some of us to this entrance. Why else would Jaqueline be here?

I crept on, wild magic pressing against my fingertips and pulsing on my wrists. The voices were still, but the need for caution nevertheless emanated through the silent connection.

It was a warning I didn't really need. Not when every instinct was screaming the very same thing.

After another dozen steps, the tunnel or shaft or whatever the hell this was began to widen out into a larger cavern. I paused, scanning the visible area, seeing ragged rock walls and various metallic bits and pieces suggesting that even if this cavern was a natural occurrence, it had been mined at some point.

What I couldn't see was a large area to my right.

Or Jaqueline.

But she was here.

My senses, and the voices, told me that.

I took a deep breath that as usual did little to calm my nerves and popped the cork off the bottle of holy water. I could cast it faster than I could cast a spell. A cage spell nevertheless burned across my free hand—which, along with a repelling spell, had recently become my body's automatic magical response to any sort of threat—but I was reluctant to use it until I knew exactly what sort of game or trap Jaqueline and Marie had planned. It might well be nothing more than another means of testing just how strong my magic was, and how well it meshed with the wild magic.

And it *was* meshed, even in something as simple as a repelling spell and this more complicated cage spell. It might be my inner magic rather than the wellspring's, but it was doubtful Jaqueline or Marie would feel the difference.

"I know you're in there, Jaqueline." Thankfully, my voice showed little of the tension roiling through me. "What do you want?"

Her laughter ran across the shadows, the warm mocking sound so reminiscent of her mother that a chill ran through me. "I didn't think you would be fooled for long."

The shadows parted, and she stepped through. She was tall and supple, with copper hair and pale, flawless skin. Aside from the color of her hair and eyes—which were blue —and her more modern clothing, she was the image of Maelle.

I clenched my free hand against the deepening burn of magic pressing against my fingertips, fighting for dominance against the cage spell. I might be wary of unleashing my inner wild magic, but my inner energy seemed to have other ideas. No sparks danced across my fist just yet, but they couldn't be that far off.

"What game do you and your mistress play now, Jaqueline?"

"Oh, I assure you, this is no game." Her voice held echoes of Maelle's accent, but it was nowhere near as cultured.

"Then what is it? Why do you haunt the shadows of this cavern when your dining room lies no more than a hundred or so yards away?"

"It is not our dining room. Hasn't been for a week now, but I believe you are already aware of this." Her voice was gently mocking. "I also believe you are here not to save the souls of the dead, but rather the life of one who has never deserved it."

Which only made me wonder what Roger had done to her, given he apparently hadn't existed until well after Maelle had destroyed the coven.

Or was that not the case?

If it wasn't, then it meant I truly couldn't believe anything any of them were telling me.

"That would be my ultimate goal, yes," I said. "Maelle without the man who is basically her sanity is not someone any clear-thinking person would want to deal with."

She chuckled again. "If you believe the face she presents to the world is her true one, then you have been sadly misled."

"Oh, I'm well aware of who and what she is—"

"No," Jaqueline cut in. "I do not think you are."

"Then why don't you tell me?"

She took a step closer. I didn't back away, but my grip instinctively tightened on the bottle of holy water. Her gaze briefly flickered down, and she smiled.

It was not a pleasant smile.

"If you think such a small vial will do me serious damage, you are deluded, young witch."

"Oh, I am under no delusions as to what holy water can and can't do. Take one step closer, and perhaps we will see which of us is right."

She studied me for several wildly erratic heartbeats—mine, not hers—and then laughed. It was the first time I'd ever heard anything approaching *real* warmth from her, and my psi senses stirred.

Nothing in this situation was what it seemed, and to believe one person's truth over the other's might be the biggest mistake I'd ever make.

"I am not at liberty to speak of that which passed between my maker and my mother—"

"How convenient," I drawled.

"But if it is truth you seek," she continued, ignoring my comment, "then at least some of it can be found in the next cavern, with that which waits."

"Meaning the souls of those you and your fellow vamps murdered? Or your leashed demon?"

"I have never been overly concerned with souls—they are troublesome creatures at best, and for the most part deserving of what came to them."

Anger surged. "None of those people in there—"

"A few did." She shrugged, an eloquent gesture that again reminded me of Maelle. "But as wolves hunt for food, so must we."

A chill ran through me. Though her words contained no actual threat, it was nevertheless a gentle reminder that the chaos they'd already inflicted on the O'Connor pack could very easily be repeated—this time with vampires rather than a basilisk.

The wild magic pulsed through me, and I ached, truly

ached, to unleash it. To capture this bitch and drag her back to her mother to deal with. But my psi senses continued to urge caution.

I shifted uneasily from one foot to another, and that's when I caught it—the faint flicker of a spell. I narrowed my gaze and studied it. It was intricately woven, with multiple layers of protection spells threaded through it, and what looked to be some sort of capture spell. Beyond them, sitting much deeper in the heart of the multi-layered spell, were thick and ominous-looking threads that had a chill tripping across my skin even if I was too far away to see what they were—and I had no desire to get any closer and find out the hard way.

I swallowed heavily against increasing trepidation, although, rather weirdly, my fear seemed to be easing. Whatever was happening here, it presented no immediate threat to me. "Why are you waiting here, Jaqueline? You can't have known we would find this place."

She raised an eyebrow, a cool, almost contemptuous smile playing around her lush red lips. She'd fed recently. Very recently. Which didn't mean she wouldn't be tempted to take a sip from me if the opportunity presented itself, but it did at least lessen the chance of her hunger getting the better of her.

"You forget we have a greater understanding of my mother's ways than you ever could or would."

"That doesn't answer the question."

Her playful contempt increased, and once again I saw Maelle. "Did you not find Roger via some possession my mother gave you?"

I frowned. "Yes, but my psychometry—"

"Was guided. Maelle has always known where to find

Roger. He is a part of her—a product of her own flesh in a way more basic than even me."

"You can't get much more basic than giving birth to a child, and you are that, not him."

She raised a mocking eyebrow. "He dined on her flesh and bound himself to her for eternity. I did not. It made him hers in a manner I never will be."

At least that meant what we'd been told about thralls was true. "That doesn't explain your statement that my psi seeking was guided."

"The item you were given was not his but rather hers. When you opened your mind to her possession, she simply used it to show you where he was."

If Jaqueline was right—if Maelle *had* guided my seeking, despite the presence of our entwined protection circles and without me ever suspecting something was off—that was fucking scary.

"Maelle couldn't have known what else lies in that cavern."

"In that, you are very wrong, as you will no doubt soon discover. But you also forget that she sees through his eyes and knows full well her demon is leashed to her thrall. I would wager she did not mention that fact, and you had no idea it existed until you reached the cavern's entrance."

"*Her* demon? You didn't conjure it?"

"No. We are not the reason it has come to this reservation, though we are the reason it is tethered here. You need to understand exactly what you're dealing with. It is not us you need to fear."

"Say the women who have repeatedly threatened to kill us all if we got in the way of their vengeance."

"That warning still holds. Step back, and you will be safe.

We are not after you." She paused. "Although it is undoubtedly true that you have an intriguing way with the wild magic that should not exist, and which would be interesting to ... sample."

Over my dead body. But I well and truly kept that thought to myself. No need to tempt evil more than she already was. "If what you are saying is correct—"

"And it is, I assure you."

"Why would Maelle simply not tell us? Why wouldn't she mention the demon?"

"Because she hopes you will kill it. You must not."

I blinked. "Why not? It's a fucking demon."

"It's not any old demon—it is *her* demon. That is a vastly different thing."

"I don't understand—"

"No matter what Maelle might have made you believe, she is not more powerful than Marie. They are equals. They always have been. To destroy the coven, my mother made a deal with her devil. Roger is a part of that deal, the leash that keeps her safe from the demon that continues to feed."

Was that confirmation Roger *hadn't* been created after the destruction, as we'd been led to believe, but was instead an intrinsic part of it? Or had my earlier guess been right, and the truth lay somewhere between their two stories?

"So Roger's soul was gifted in exchange for Maelle's power boost?"

"No. As I said, he is the leash and the control."

My confusion deepened. "Meaning he controls the demon? Or that he *is* the demon?"

I'd never gotten any sense of that from him but then, it wasn't like I'd ever—*ever*—come across a thrall or a situation like this before. Hell, I didn't think there'd be many in Canberra who could make such a claim, not even amongst those who hunted dark mages for a living.

"He is more the"—she paused, as if considering her words—"gateway. The means through which this demon enters her world to feed as their agreement requires. To kill the demon while it is leashed in *this* world rather than the one it was called from would leave the gateway open and allow others—others who would be unrestrained—to enter. It would basically mean the end of this reservation."

"Ah, fuck."

"A crude but appropriate sentiment," Jaqueline said, tone dryly amused.

I drew in a breath and released it slowly. "But by pinning her demon to this world, aren't you basically doing the same thing?"

"Not for as long as Roger remains alive. Besides, you will banish it, will you not? It then will not be a problem going forward."

When she or Marie finally got around to killing Roger, she meant. "Why would Maelle send me here, knowing I'd discover her demon and more likely kill rather than banish it? That makes no sense if it is indeed her 'battery.'"

"Its death would allow her to call forth another— possibly stronger—demon."

I studied her for a second, uncertain just how much I should believe her. "Why are you telling me all this? Why do you even care?"

Her smile was cool—almost mocking. "I *don't* care—not about you, or indeed this place. I certainly do not wish to be here any longer than necessary. But Mother must be dealt with, once and for all."

Then why didn't you fucking do so eons ago? Why bring your war here?

But I already knew the answer—or, at least, a part of it. An unprotected wellspring always drew evil to its shores. Maelle

71

might deny it was the reason for her presence here, but Castle Rock wasn't the sort of place any serious businesswoman would set up a nightclub like hers. It might have been a success, but the area simply didn't have the population to sustain it long term.

And now, the wellspring's echoes and her presence had drawn her hunters here.

Monty had theorized not so long ago that the call of the wellspring's unprotected power was beginning to fade, and that these dark intrusions would soon end. If that were true, Fate had obviously decided we needed to go out with one hell of a bang, and called the biggest bads of them all into the reservation.

I reached out for Belle again, needing nothing more than the comforting buzz of her presence in the background of my mind, but the deadness remained.

"You do not believe us, but there are always two sides to every story," Jaqueline continued. "The truth lies in the past —look to places such as Holtham, Elvedon, and Greysdown —and at the nature of the Stragulum demon. Then step aside and let us do what must be done, the way we wish to do it."

"Only if you stop kidnapping, draining, and then tearing apart your victims."

Her smile flashed. "In that, I am a product of my maker, as much as my mother is. Her demon only amplified what already existed."

"Then you and I remain on opposite sides of this war."

"That would be a great shame." She paused. "One more thing—when you learn the truth, you must not kill her. She is ours, and only ours."

And with that, she stepped back into the shadows and was gone. As was the barrier that had stood between us.

Had she been nothing more than a projection? It wouldn't be the first time, but there hadn't been such a heavily layered spell between us previously. There hadn't been any spell evident at *all*. Did that mean the unknown threads layered into the spell separating us had been some sort of transport spell?

Possibly.

I studied the rest of the cavern for a moment longer, not seeing or sensing anything untoward, then swung around and made my way back to Aiden. His relief when I emerged out of the crevice was so strong it briefly overwhelmed my senses.

"What happened? Did you find Jaqueline?"

"Yes. She came with another warning."

"They seem very big on warnings, which is rather odd, considering."

"They're aware of the wild magic. I think they want to avoid unleashing its wrath via pissing me off."

"Which is very sensible, given it's never a good idea to piss you off. I know this from experience."

I laughed and let him catch my hand and pull me into his embrace. For several seconds, I did nothing more than rest the side of my head against his chest, drawing in his strength and warmth and love, replenishing the well that fear and trepidation had drained.

Continued to drain.

"Belle, Monty, and Ashworth are on their way here," he said, his voice a deep rumble that vibrated through me. "They've protected the main entrance as best they can."

"Good, although according to Jaqueline the demon is leashed."

Pissed off, but leashed.

"I wouldn't think it a good idea to trust the vampire who not so long ago threatened to kill you."

"Actually, she threatened to 'have' me, which isn't quite the same thing." I glanced around as Belle came into view.

"What the fuck has happened to our link?" she immediately asked.

"The wild magic has somehow cut us off."

"*Your* wild magic?"

I shook my head and lifted my wrist, revealing the luminous threads that remained attached. She frowned. "I thought the wellspring—and the Fenna who command it—had abandoned you, except in times of need?"

"Apparently I was wrong."

"Huh." She frowned. "Any idea why it has cut us off, then? That never happened when you've used it before."

"I don't think it's a result of the wild magic per se, but rather the Fenna. The minute their whispers started, we were cut off."

"What are they whispering?" Monty said, as he stopped beside Belle.

"They warned me about Jaqueline, and they want that cavern cleansed ASAP." I switched my gaze to Ashworth as he appeared "What do you know about Stragulum demons?"

"Stragulum? Now there's a breed of beastie I've not heard mentioned in a very long time."

"Then you do know about them?"

He nodded. "I take it that's what awaits us?"

"If Jaqueline is to be believed, yes." I quickly updated them, then added, "She told me not to kill it because doing so would leave a gateway open and risk us being overrun by evil. Is that true?"

"It's not so much evil as darker emotions," Ashworth

said gravely. "They're demons that feed off the worst excesses of the living. Unlike most of their kind, they do not barter for the soul of the summoner but rather an alliance— a boost in magical energy for negative energy feasts."

"That's why she bathes in the broken bodies of those she kills," Belle said suddenly. "She might enjoy it, but she also has to feed her demon."

Ashworth nodded again. "If a Stragulum is killed, all the negative energy it has collected is released. If it is a very old Stragulum, as this one probably is, then think of that release as an emotional tsunami."

"How the hell do we deal with it then?" Aiden asked.

"We banish it."

"Which is what Jaqueline said we should do," I said. "Apparently, they only called it forth so that we knew exactly what Maelle truly is."

"Like we didn't already know," Belle muttered.

"I don't think any of us understood the true depths of her depravity, even if we knew she was far darker than her polished veneer would have us believe." I returned my attention to Ashworth. "How will banishing it help? Won't she just call it back to her side?"

"Banishment breaks their agreement. If she calls it back, she would need to renegotiate the deal, and the demon is now well aware of what she faces and will drive a harder bargain."

"I wouldn't think there would be much more it could do than force her to tear her living victims apart and swim in their remains," Monty said.

"Oh, you would be wrong there, laddie, and there're a few places that can attest to that."

"Like Holtham, Elvedon, and Greysdown?" I said.

Ashworth glanced at me. "I don't know Elvedon or

Greysdown, but Holtham is certainly a good example of what happens when you kill a Stragulum. Those few who survived there were never the same."

Which meant that perhaps the cleansing the Fenna wanted wasn't only the weight of blood and death, but the presence of this demon. If its store of negative energy *was* unleashed, it could fatally stain *both* wellsprings. Katie wasn't yet strong enough to protect hers from such a wave, and even if I worked in tandem with Belle, it was doubtful either of us could hold it back for long.

"One thing does strike me as odd," Belle said. "If Jaqueline and Marie knew this demon is the source of her power, why summon it to show us? Why not just banish it themselves?"

"Maelle said she can't retaliate against them unless they make a direct attack on her," I said. "Perhaps attacking her demon could be considered a direct attack."

"And Roger isn't?" She raised her eyebrows. "How does that work? In many respects, he's linked to her more intimately than this demon."

"Given none of them appear to be telling the whole truth, who fucking knows." Frustration and more than a bit of anger crept into my tone. I did my best to squash it down and glanced at Ashworth. "If we're using the banishment spell that we used on the basilisk, will we need to call in Eli or can Belle slip into his spot?"

"This demon is no basilisk, and Belle is perfectly capable of stepping in." He half shrugged. "Truth is, the demon may well welcome being banished, as it will allow renegotiations. The contract would have been blooded a long time ago."

"Happy to step in, but I wasn't there when you

banished the rusalka or the basilisk," Belle said. "You'll need to walk me through it.

"Liz can guide you." Ashworth returned his gaze to mine. "Is Jaqueline still in there?"

"No. I was either speaking to a projection again, or she used some sort of spell to transport away." Maybe even that "other" plane Maelle had mentioned earlier.

"Well then, let's get this show on the road." Monty waved me forward. "After you, dear cousin."

"Thanks."

It was wryly said, and his smile flashed. "You've only yourself to blame. If you don't want to lead, stop collecting all these new and wonderful abilities that allow you to do things like see in the dark."

I laughed and lightly pushed him. "Yeah, because I have a choice in any of it."

Just as my daughter didn't have a choice.

It was a sobering thought, and I couldn't help but wonder again what sort of life I'd committed her to. I hoped her link to the Fenna would be along the same lines as Belle's link to her spirit guides, but so little was known about the Fenna and the wild magic that I couldn't be sure. And until she was old enough to understand what I'd done, I wouldn't know.

Would she hate me, as Jaqueline hated her mother?

The circumstances were different—presuming Maelle told the truth about Jaqueline being a willing participant in the ceremony, and there was no guarantee now that she was —and the reason very different indeed, but that didn't alter the fact that I'd done to her what my father had done to me.

And it was something that would haunt me through the long years ahead.

Not wanting to dwell on *that*, I spun and walked back

into the canyon. Aiden stepped in behind me, then the others followed in single file. I stopped when we reached the smaller cavern's entrance, once again checking for any sign of magic. The place remained silent and empty.

I wished I could say the same for the larger cavern.

The ghosts were moaning. Loudly. It was as if they sensed salvation was at hand.

I glanced around at Belle. "They've practically got a choir happening in that other cavern—are you going to be okay?"

She nodded, though sorrow haunted her silver eyes. "Their emotional weight rests heavily on the air, which will affect you more than me. I'll be fine as long as I don't connect."

"You'll have to connect to help them move on, though, won't you?" Monty asked, with a frown.

She hesitated, tilting her head slightly sideways as she listened to her spirit guides. "It's apparently possible to do a bulk 'move on' spell without connecting, as long as the souls are confined to the one area."

"And the souls that refuse the call?"

"Will remain in that cavern. I cannot alter that. I've never been able to."

It was rare for souls to refuse moving on, but there were always some outliers who couldn't accept their death, or who wanted to remain close to those they'd loved, even if only in spirit form. We'd certainly come across a couple over the years.

"Why would any soul want to remain in such an awful place?" Monty asked, then touched Belle's arm lightly. "If you need to stop at any point, just shout."

She nodded and dropped a quick kiss on his cheek. "I'll be fine."

I wasn't so certain, and the quick look she cast me suggested she was worried about us both. I frowned down at the threads on my wrist; the whispers had fallen silent, but the buzz of their power skated across the back of my thoughts. I reached out, trying to connect with them mentally, and felt a slight pop in the power stream. An acknowledgement of my attempt, perhaps? I had no real idea, but it didn't hurt to try. *I need Belle's help to cleanse. You have to stop blocking her.*

The request seemed to echo across that band of static but there was no immediate lifting of the barrier that had cut us off.

I cursed silently and stalked toward the tunnel. It turned out to be man-made, and the heavy wooden beams supporting the ceiling and walls in this section looked in surprisingly good condition. I doubted it would stay that way, given the steady trickle of water I could hear running deeper within the tunnel.

Monty's light sphere bobbed above our heads, its pale light washing across rough red walls that still bore the pick marks of those who'd carved it into existence. It was easier to move through than the crevice had been, but I nevertheless walked on cautiously. Just because all I'd sensed were the ghosts and Maelle's demon didn't mean Marie or Jaqueline hadn't left another surprise for us.

The deeper we moved into the tunnel, the louder the moaning became. Thick waves of agony and fear washed across my senses, making it increasingly harder to force my feet on. My shields were on high, but without Belle running interference—

The connection between us flared to life with a suddenness that had me blinking back tears of relief. The Fenna had finally acknowledged my need and lifted the blocking shield. Their static still ran through the far reaches of my mind, though their voices were now a distant murmur I couldn't really understand.

Maybe the fact that I wasn't naturally telepathic meant that I could only mentally deal with one connection at a time.

Possible came Belle's thought. *Have they gone completely?*

No, and I suspect they'll break our connection again if they have something to tell me. I paused. *You can't hear their static?*

No, but I haven't got the right blood in me. Whatever the reason for our reconnection, I'm glad it happened. Aside from the fact your absence felt plain wrong, we'll need to pull on each other's strength to get through what awaits.

That was a certainty. And probably why the Fenna had, in fact, relented.

We were deeper into the tunnel now and it was becoming increasingly degraded. Water dripped from the ceiling, and the rock underfoot was slippery with slime. Rubble scattered the floor and, up ahead, barely visible in the sphere's pale light, a ceiling support had partially collapsed, spilling rocks across the ground, and narrowing the tunnel considerably. Moss hung over the uprights and the cracked half of the ceiling support that remained lodged in the wall, suggesting it wasn't a recent fall. But the smell of rot now vied with blood in the air. One wrong move, and this whole tunnel could come down on top of us.

"I'm thinking this *isn't* the tunnel they used to bring their prisoners in," Monty said. "There's no way they could herd frightened people through here without causing an accident."

"That's presuming their captives weren't spelled into

submission," Ashworth replied. "Or that vampires capable of transport spells would be bothered walking their dinner into whatever dining room they might be using."

"According to Jaqueline, they stopped using this one," I said. "I also asked her to stop killing. She refused."

"She's Maelle's daughter, so that's also unsurprising," Monty said.

"Maelle doesn't kill her feeders," I replied.

"As far as we're aware," Monty said. "But given what we now know of her, I doubt that was always the case."

Especially given the three names Jaqueline had dropped. Which meant, of course, the bloody destruction could just as easily be Maelle's and her demon's as Marie's and Jaqueline's.

I guess we'd find out soon enough.

I wouldn't be asking Maelle if she and her demon engage in regular blood baths, Belle said. *Even if Roger was at full strength and her state of mind on an even keel, that would be a dangerous question to ask.*

Never fear, I have no intention of poking the demon's mistress any more than necessary, especially with questions that don't in the end matter.

We reach the partially collapsed bracing. I sucked in a breath, not daring to breathe as I turned side-on and carefully eased through it. A fine rain of dirt sprinkled down, and I quickly glanced up. There was a decidedly worrying large crack running from the beam's broken back to the supporting wall prop. It wouldn't take much of a bump to bring it all down ...

I didn't bump it. Neither did anyone else.

Once Monty, the last in line, had cleared the collapse, we continued on. This section of tunnel bore further evidence of its fragile nature. Rubble lay everywhere, and the dripping water became an almost steady stream running down the slope toward the main cavern. Moss rippled in the clear current and spread across the stone, making each step that much more treacherous.

The closer we got to the cavern, the more intense the wailing of the ghosts became. The waves of emotion that accompanied their song was so strong my skin vibrated with its force. I flexed my fingers, tension rippling through me. If my shields cracked, I was going to be in a whole world of trouble.

They won't, Belle said, with a certainty I didn't feel. *But if they do, I'll shore them up.*

You need to worry about yourself.

I've heard such choruses before, even if the freshness of these deaths intensifies their song. Besides, connecting with a soul or souls is a conscious decision for me, whereas your empathetic ability can be set off by a simple, unguarded touch.

Not so much these days, but that had certainly been a problem in the past. I continued in, picking my way through the water, rocks, and ... were those bone fragments? My stomach stirred, even as instinct whispered an affirmative.

And it wasn't just bone fragments. There were also bits of cloth, knots of hair in hues of browns and blonde, and long strings of what looked like flesh or intestines.

Some of their victims had tried to escape.

Some had made it as far as this partial collapse.

None of them had gotten any farther.

Oh God ... I swallowed heavily against the bitter rise of bile, but forced my feet on and kept my gaze ahead rather than looking down at what was crunching under each step. The wailing intensified abruptly, as did the empathic wave, and, up ahead, air shimmered. It was the ghosts who'd died in this tunnel, huddled together in confusion and despair. We'd have to walk through them to get into the cavern.

I stopped. I just couldn't do it.

"Belle?" I said softly. "I don't suppose you …?"

My voice faded as she moved past Aiden and stopped beside me. "It's a small group—six in all. I'll move them on."

She swung her pack around, pulled out a bottle of holy water, and then handed me the pack. After a deep breath to center her energy, she began to spell, though it was in a language I'd never heard used before.

"That's Latin," Ashworth said, surprised. "There are few enough spells around these days that use it. I'm surprised she even knows it."

"She doesn't," I replied. "Her spirit guides are guiding her."

"I thought there was a rule in the spirit world against direct intervention?" Monty said. "This would surely fall under that category, wouldn't it?"

"Generally, yes, but it does depend on the situation and the guide." I shot him an amused glance. "Your spirit guide may have the temperament of a gutter cat who wouldn't go out of his way to help you unless it was absolutely necessary, but not all of them are so mean."

"Eamon is *not* mean." Amusement glimmered in his eyes. "He merely senses your fear and, like all real felines, likes to tease."

"He has a very liberal definition of tease," I said dryly. And I had the scars to prove it. The ginger terror had very sharp claws.

"Love taps, nothing more," he said. "Trust me, you'd know if he was serious about harming you."

I rolled my eyes and returned my attention to Belle. She was circling the glimmering veil of souls, the force of her magic increasing in tempo with the spell as she sprinkled the holy water onto the ground. While her spirits guides—unlike most witches she was gifted—plagued?—by a number of them—would never harm her, we had no idea what else waited in that tunnel ahead. Just because I was sensing nothing didn't mean something in there wouldn't take advantage of her concentration being on the spell rather than her surroundings.

Belle reached the point where she'd begun and raised a hand, making a sweeping motion as she tied off and then initiated the spell. Power hovered in the air, and ghosts thrummed in tune with it. Then gradually, a bright light formed in the center of the ring she'd created, and one by one, the ghosts entered and disappeared. The light died, the spell died, and the ghosts—or at least these ones—were gone. They'd moved on to whatever fate their next life would bring.

I hoped it was a far kinder one than this.

Belle took a deep breath, then turned to face us. "They all chose to move on."

"Let's hope the rest do," I murmured and touched her arm lightly. *You okay?*

We seem to be asking each other that a lot recently.

You've spent a lifetime worrying about me, so it's about time I returned the favor, I replied dryly. *And don't say it comes with being a familiar, because there's no way in hell Eamon worries about Monty the way you do me.*

Her amusement ran down the line between us. *Eamon is a law unto himself. But his witch also doesn't have the habit of throwing himself into situations and thinking about it later.*

Are we talking about the same Monty?

"Will you two stop having private conversations?" the

man in question said wryly. "We have a demon to banish and a thrall to rescue. Let's not piss off the unstable vampire any more than necessary by wasting time."

I saluted lightly. "Moving on as ordered, boss."

He snorted. "I may technically be head reservation witch, but we all know who that mantle really belongs to."

I grinned and moved on, still trying to avoid the bones even if their ghosts were no longer present to moan in distress over us stepping on them. But I'd only gone a few more yards when the tunnel began to widen out into the larger cavern. I slowed, scanning the darkness, all senses alert for any sign of magic or a trap.

Nothing.

The demon scratched and growled to the right of the cavern, hidden by the deeper darkness, its anger so palpable the air practically burned with its force. I had no sense of Roger, though, so I reluctantly retrieved the ring from my pocket and wrapped my fingers around its silk casing.

The pulse of life was distant.

Maelle distant.

Meaning this is something else Jaqueline was truthful about, Belle said. *Not that I think we can believe everything else is the truth.*

Agree. But right now, her ratio of truth to lie was sitting pretty high. I shoved the ring back into my pack and glanced at Aiden as he stopped beside me.

"I'm not smelling Roger or anyone else in there," he said. "The scent of blood and flesh lingers, and there's an odd sulfuric scent I presume is the demon, but Roger is absent."

"What does Roger smell like to you?" I asked curiously.

He glanced at me, his eyebrows raised. "Like Maelle, just not as ... dead."

"Ha." I returned my gaze to the cavern. "Jaqueline said she'd pinned the demon to Roger, so he has to be here somewhere."

"I think we need a little more light on the subject," Monty said, and cast his sphere out into the cavern.

Its pale light washed across stained stone and the remains that floated in the nearest lake—there were two, one far smaller than the other—but didn't really touch the deeper shadows. Monty's magic briefly surged, and the sphere brightened.

Revealing the demon. Its skin was as black as sin and covered with fine hair that seemed to move with a life of its own and reminded me somewhat of a sea anemone. Its features were narrow, almost animal like, with cat-like eyes that glared at us, a long narrow nose, and no mouth. But this thing fed on emotions rather than flesh, so I guess that wasn't surprising.

My gaze dropped to the ground, looking for Roger, and my stomach twisted.

Jaqueline had lied. The demon wasn't leashed to Roger.

It was leashed to his severed *leg*.

CHAPTER FIVE

"A h fuck," Ashworth said. "Our resident vamp is not going to take this well."

"No," Monty said, "but if there's something to salvage out of this, it's the fact we won't have to tell her it's happened. She'll already know."

"And didn't bother warning us," Belle said. "I wonder why?"

"Given everything else she didn't warn us about, it's pretty obvious she's treating us all as nothing more than pawns in her game" came Aiden's grim comment. "It's definitely past time we had a serious chat to the council about revoking her trading license."

By "we'" he meant he, because it was doubtful the council would take too much notice of anything us witches said.

"I suspect our resident vampire will not only use anyone and everyone in an effort to survive, but also unleash every nasty trick in her repertoire to remain here if she does," Monty said. "If it wasn't for the fact both sides are taking out innocent bystanders, I'd be voting for the 'stand back and let the bitches erase each other' option."

"You wouldn't be the only one," I muttered.

I walked on cautiously, studiously keeping my gaze away from the larger body of water and the death that lay within it. I couldn't so easily erase the scent, however, and my stomach was twisting with ever increasing intensity.

Aiden reached into his pocket and held out a small blue tub. "Use this."

I accepted it gratefully. It was basically an extra strong mentholated ointment that was dabbed under the nose to counter the worst odors. I'd used it before, and it was pretty damn good for cutting the foulness down to an acceptable level. I dabbed some on, then offered it to the others before giving it back to Aiden.

He applied some then tucked it back into his pocket. "I'll start recording the scene while you deal with that demon."

I nodded and motioned Ashworth and Monty to precede me. The demon snarled and growled, but its leash —magical, not physical—was relatively short, and its agitated movements were restricted to little more than a six-foot circle around Roger's leg. *It* remained pinned by white ash, the stake not only driving through Roger's flesh but also deep into the stone. Either the ash had been magically strengthened or they'd used a spell to anchor it. I couldn't tell because I simply wasn't seeing any spell threads.

And that was scary, if only because if they could so easily hide this spell, what other types of spells could they hide? I really, really, didn't want to think about that, though I also suspected we might find out sooner rather than later.

"Will we need to use multiple protection circles?" I

asked. "Or do you think a weave of mine and Belle's will suffice?"

"I honestly don't think it will be necessary, given the nature of this demon and the fact banishment works in its favor," Ashworth said, "but I would also never advise doing any sort of banishment spell without a protective circle, especially when we're dealing with a beastie connected to a dark mage."

I nodded and tugged my spell stones free from my pack. After ensuring I was well out of the demon's reach, I began to spell, placing each stone on the ground and attaching the threads before moving on. Belle interwove her spell through mine and, once we'd both finished, we simultaneously activated them. A wall of power rose, shimmering softly and running with glittering luminous threads.

"Well, *that's* a new development," Monty said, surprise evident. "Has it anything to do with the wild magic you've leashed around your wrist?"

The threads around my wrist pulsed, and the voices briefly rose. It wasn't a confirmation, but it wasn't a denial, either. I wrinkled my nose. "Possibly? They want this place cleansed, and that would definitely include sending this demon back to whatever hell it came from."

"Which suggests the Fenna might be far more than mere advisory spectators," Ashworth said. "It makes me wonder what the future holds for your little one. It'll be interesting watching her grow and develop."

Worry briefly flitted through me again. "I wish we knew more. I wish so much hadn't been forgotten."

Wished I could jump into the future, if only in my dreams, and see what might lie ahead for her. But my dreams, while precognitive in nature, just weren't playing ball.

"Indeed, lassie, indeed." Ashworth grimaced and moved to the far side of the circle. Monty went right, Belle left, and I remained where I was, opposite Ashworth. The demon paced and growled, its anger stinging the air and its short tentacles darting in and out of its flesh, an agitated movement that made me wonder if it was trying to taste our intent.

I took a deep breath to steady nerves that never were by such an action and began to spell. A few lines into it, the demon stilled, and an almost anticipatory gleam shone in its golden eyes. It knew what we were doing. Wanted it, if the wave of satisfaction that swiftly replaced the anger rolling from it was anything to go by.

Once I'd finished, I guided Belle through her section, then Ashworth did his, and Monty finished off.

A deep void swirled into existence behind the demon, and its body began to vibrate, its tentacles becoming translucent smoke that was swiftly sucked into the void. As its body began to disintegrate, its gaze came to mine, and it bowed, either in acknowledgement or gratitude. Then it was swept away, and the void closed with an audible snap.

The ring in my pocket pulsed, and from deep in the distance came an infuriated scream. Maelle. She knew she'd just lost her demon.

Trepidation shivered through me, but I did my best to ignore it. Right now, we had bigger problems, like moving the ghosts on and cleansing this place.

"Well," Monty said, once we'd dismantled the spell. "That was a whole lot easier than I thought it would be."

"Aye," Ashworth agreed. "But I dare say it was only because it recognized what we were doing. That beastie was a very old and powerful one."

"Maelle likely made her deal with it just before she

destroyed her coven, which means it has had centuries of feasting to grow in strength and power." I collected my spell stones and tucked them away. "She felt it go. I heard her scream via the ring."

"Well, she's only herself to blame," Belle said. "If she'd been semi-honest about what awaited, we might have killed rather than banished it."

"I don't understand the bitch's motivations at *all*," Monty growled. "How does she benefit from us erasing what is basically her backup battery?"

"Said bitch is in an unstable state of mind," I said mildly. "I'd avoid calling her that anywhere near her, otherwise she might just unleash."

"And we have a future wedding to plan," Belle added dryly. "I'd really appreciate you not getting unleashed upon."

He laughed and blew her a kiss. "That doesn't answer my question."

"It's possible she hoped that the release of centuries of angst and darkness her demon had collected would erase Marie as well as the reservation," Ashworth said. "Or perhaps she simply hoped it would affect Marie enough to ensure an easier kill."

"An emotional tsunami would also take out Jaqueline, though," I replied, "And she's stated numerous times she doesn't want her daughter harmed."

"As you noted, she unstable and obviously *not* thinking clearly." Belle motioned toward Roger's leg. "Do we remove the stake and give her back his leg or what?"

Given how ungenerous I was feeling toward Maelle right now, I was tempted to vote for "or what" and just leave the fucking thing exactly where it was and let her suffer.

That, of course, wasn't a practical or even safe thing to do, given her tenuous hold on sanity.

"If we remove the stake, it will at least ease some of the pain Roger is backwashing to Maelle," Monty said.

"Not when there are three other stakes in him," I muttered. And it wouldn't be the last limb he'd lose, either, if Jaqueline's comment was anything to go by.

"Three is better than four, lass. As for the leg—" Ashworth shrugged. "If we can remove the white ash and preserve what is left of his leg, it's possible we can use it to find him."

I blinked. "There's a spell that allows you to track someone through severed bits of flesh?"

He nodded. "It's not one I know personally, but I know Heretic Investigations have used it. I've already contacted someone I know and requested access to the relevant information as a matter of urgency."

"*That* suggests you believed we'd be finding bits of Roger strewn about long before we actually did." Belle rubbed her arms, her skin littered with goose bumps, though I suspected its source was the increasing intensity of the ghosts' grief rather than anything else.

"This is not my first vampire rodeo, and they do have a tendency to inflict bodily harm on each other's servants." He motioned to the limb. "Monty and I will deal with this. You two best tend to the ghosts and the cleansing."

I nodded and glanced at Belle. "Is there anything I can do to help you with the ceremony?"

She shook her head. "Thankfully, the bulk of them are clustered in the alcove area between the two lakes."

"And the ones that aren't?" There were at least three that I was aware of roaming through the far shadows, and there was likely more I wasn't sensing.

She thrust a hand through her sweaty hair, pulling several strands from its ponytail. "There're only five. From the wisps I'm getting, I think they feel safer apart from the main group. If I haven't got the strength to deal with them after the main, I'll come back tomorrow. Their presence won't be adding much weight to the darkness of this place."

Given her weariness was already humming down the line between us, there was no doubt we'd be coming back here tomorrow.

"Yell if you do need anything."

She nodded, though I knew she would never yell or draw on my strength unless she absolutely had to.

Yeah, and I wonder where I got that bad habit from?

Her mental tone was wry. I smiled, touched her arm, then headed over to Aiden, who was recording the area behind the larger lake. I stopped a few yards away from the shoreline opposite him, still making every effort to avoid looking at the water and its gruesome contents.

"Aiden, is it okay if I begin the cleansing ritual?"

He glanced up, his expression neutral but his blue eyes furious. At Marie and her crew for committing such atrocities, at Maelle for doing nothing to stop them or help us. "What will it involve?"

"A mix of burning sage, sprinkling holy water, and spells to erase the weight of evil that might linger."

I'd never actually performed the spell before and only knew of its existence thanks to the library Belle had inherited from her gran. And given I'd read said spell several years ago now, I could only hope I remembered it correctly.

"Try not to contaminate any hard evidence, and just be careful where you're placing your feet, as there're bits of bone and flesh scattered about everywhere," he said. "I'm going to be here awhile yet, so avoid that section over near the ledge to your right, because I haven't recorded the bones and body fragments over there yet."

I motioned to the bodies in the water without actually looking at them. "If they haven't been reduced to bone, why would those in the tunnel or over near that ledge have been? Water doesn't preserve; it bloats and increases the decomposition rate, doesn't it?"

"In warmer, shallower waters, yes. But in this particular case, I would think the bones and skin scraps in both the tunnel and near the ridge have been here much longer."

"But it can take years—decades, even—for a body to break down that thoroughly, can't it?"

"Normally, yes" came Ashworth's comment from the other side of the cavern. "But it's possible to enhance the rate of putrefaction and decay through a variety of different means, including magic."

"By how much, though?"

He half shrugged, his concentration more on the magical shovel he was helping Monty create than me. "It could reduce it from years to months, at best."

I stared at him for a second and swallowed heavily. "Then that has to mean this is *Maelle's* charnel cave. Marie and her crew simply made use of what already existed."

"Even if that is true, I doubt we'll ever find evidence to confirm it." Aiden's voice was grim. "Not that we actually need evidence to revoke Maelle's trading license and escort her out of the reservation."

"The chances of her allowing *anyone* to escort her anywhere she didn't want to go are exactly zero," I said. "But surely so many people could not have gone missing—"

I cut the rest off. It was highly unlikely that *any* of these bodies had originated from within the reservation. In fact, perhaps part of her fury over Roger's absence was the fact that he could no longer gather suitable dining options from beyond the reservation and bring them back for her and her demon to enjoy.

Bile rose up my throat, and I swallowed heavily, managing to control the surge. But if I got through the rest of this day without losing the contents of my stomach, it would be an utter miracle.

I think what made this whole situation far worse was the fact she'd fooled me. Totally and utterly pulled the wool over my eyes. I'd always known she was dangerous, always known she could not be entirely trusted, but even after what she'd done to Clayton, even after knowing she'd bathed in human remains up in her aerie, I still hadn't grasped the true depths of her depravity. Her evil.

I wasn't alone in that, of course, but that didn't ease the guilt and the "should have known" refrain already running through my brain. I was the psychic. I was the one with the nose for evil. I should have picked up the depths of hers.

Of course, she'd had centuries to build her façade and hone her lies, but that didn't help ease the guilt.

I guess the deeper question was, how could I maintain any sort of calm in her presence now, knowing what I knew? I couldn't kill her—aside from the fact it would probably take the wellspring's magic to counter hers, and that was something I really couldn't risk, there was Jaqueline's warning to consider.

I closed my eyes and scrubbed them wearily. Maybe I simply needed to avoid her—though that would, undoubtedly, bring its own set of problems, given she still needed us to find Roger.

Or, at least, whatever remained of him.

Light footsteps echoed, but before I had a chance to look up, Aiden wrapped his arms around me and pulled me close. I pressed the side of my face against the muscular planes of his chest and breathed in the warm, musky smoke scent of him. And felt safer than I ever had in my entire life, even if it was nothing more than an illusion that could so easily be shattered if we didn't find a way to stop Marie and Maelle from unleashing hell on the reservation.

"Perhaps you should leave," he said softly. "These deaths have stained the earth for some time now—one more day will not make a difference."

"The Fenna beg to differ." I pulled back and kissed him tenderly. "I'll be fine."

He smiled and gently skimmed my cheek with a knuckle. "No, you won't, but you also won't admit it."

"That's a truth I cannot deny."

"Will you at least go home once the cleansing ceremony is done?"

I hesitated and then nodded. "Belle won't be in any state to hang around. I'll have to take her home and ply her with energy potions."

Though she was deep in the midst of her spell, I heard a faint, *Oh no, you fucking won't.*

As a smile teased my lips, Aiden tugged the truck's keys from his pocket and gave them to me. "The team should be here in fifteen minutes, so I can catch a lift back to the café with one of them."

"How long do you think it'll take?"

"Honestly, I have no idea. Why?"

"Just wondering if I need to plan something for dinner or not."

"I'm hoping we'll be finished well before then, but if we're not, I'll be ordering everyone out at five. There's no way I'll be leaving anyone in a place like this when there're vampires roaming about using the reservation as a diner."

"Can a curfew be placed?"

"I'll issue an order for restricted movement, but with summer on us and a multitude of tourists in the area, it's going to be next to impossible to enforce. Especially when we can't explain why without causing widespread panic."

"Perhaps you could use that smoke we smelled to your advantage and—"

"And the first thing anyone with a bit of nous will be doing is checking the emergency services app for warnings."

I grimaced. "Then at the very least, we'll have to supply all your rangers with stronger charms."

"Deal with the vampires, and we won't have to worry about the charms."

"Yeah," I said with a smile. "But creating the charms will probably be far easier than dealing with the vampires."

"Another truth that cannot be denied." He kissed me, his lips lingering on mine, as if reluctant to give them up. Eventually, he murmured, "I can taste your tiredness. And yes, I know, you're fine."

I laughed, pulled out of his arms, and moved across to the other side of the cavern. I pulled out everything I needed from the pack and then shoved the ring into it—the last thing I wanted to be doing was carrying an item that reeked of foulness when I was attempting to cleanse the area—then lit the first smudge stick. After encouraging it to smoke with a gentle spell, I walked around in a large square, being careful to avoid the darker stains and slivers of bone as I gently wafted the smoke through the area and murmured the cleansing spell. Once I'd scattered the ashes across the inner part of my imaginary square, I repeated the process with the holy water. Even though I was wearing boots, I could feel the warm thrumming that ran through the sanctified ground; a heartbeat later, the air shimmered and a dark veil lifted from the stone then faded away.

The cleansing had worked. The heavy weight of death and darkness no longer sat on this section of stone.

But this was just one small area. There was a ton more to do.

I drew in a deeper breath, then began the next section. As Belle continued to work with the ghosts, gently ushering them toward the softly glowing light, I continued to perform the ritual. Once Monty and Ashworth had removed Roger's leg and bagged both it and the stake, they retrieved the sage sticks from Belle's pack and helped me. Aiden's team finally arrived, their shock echoing through the vastness of this place in a way their voices didn't. I suspected the horror of what had happened here would linger here for a very long time, despite the ghosts being moved on and the cavern cleansed. Sometimes, there was simply nothing that could be done about the residue weight of emotion that remained after such a tragedy. Time might eventually strip its potency, but I suspected this place, like many others, would become an area anyone with any degree of psi sensitivity would avoid for some time to come.

With three of us performing the cleansing ritual, it took just under an hour to cover the rest of the cavern. Aiden and his team were now working on retrieving the bodies from the water, so it was impossible to do anything about the two lakes, but the Fenna were apparently satisfied with our efforts, as the wild magic unleashed itself from my wrist and floated away.

It left me feeling bone-tired, though it was nothing compared to Belle's. Her exhaustion was a pulse that beat inside me as loudly as a heartbeat, though she was still refusing to draw on my strength.

I sat down on a rock and rested my arms on my knees. The veil of ghosts being moved on was down to just a couple of wisps now, and I could only see one lingering beyond the area she was working. Perhaps Belle—or rather, her spirit guides—had altered the spell to draw them in and give them the choice.

Monty sat next to me and slung an arm around my shoulders. "You should go home once Belle has finished up. You look like shit."

A wry smile touched my lips. "I can always count on you to boost my ego."

He laughed. "Would it help if I said my one true love looks even worse than you do?"

"No, it would not." I sniffed. "Will you and Ashworth stay here? I doubt Marie or Jaqueline will attack now they've gotten what they wanted, but—"

I stopped and shrugged.

"I'm not leaving until Aiden and his people do." He stared at the dark water for a second, his expression contemplative. "If Maelle has always known Roger's location, why didn't she simply tell us? Why make us faff around like that? It makes no sense whatsoever, given the more he's tortured, the more it drains her."

"Because she's well aware Roger is bait."

"Yes, obviously, but it's not like she cares about us. Hell, she sent us here to confront her demon without any sort of warning. If it had killed us, where would she be?"

"Probably receiving a power boost right now as her demon swims in our flesh and our agony."

"Well, that image will haunt me for the rest of my life." He half waved a hand. "I just get this bad feeling we're missing something."

"Yeah, the truth." Because right now, I didn't think either side was being completely honest.

He nudged me lightly with his shoulder, his gaze on Belle. There were only two more souls to go, and one of them was little more than a wisp of fractured air, which to me suggested he or she was far older than most of those here. Perhaps it wasn't a vampire victim at all, but rather a soul who'd lost his life in some mining disaster ...

My mind froze on that last word, and instincts leapt.

Disaster.

It was coming to the reservation. To the O'Connors. To all of us.

I sucked in air and tried to chase the insight down, desperate to get more information. But it was moonlight quick and just as impossible to catch.

"Monty," I said abruptly, "you and Belle need to come stay at the café until all of this is over. You can even bring that wretched cat of yours with you."

His gaze swung to mine. "I can protect—"

"I know, but thanks to Roger, Marie knows how vital Belle is to me. She will go through you to get to Belle if things go bad."

Or if we didn't back off.

A shiver stole through my soul. I'd come close to losing Belle once before. I did not want to go through that ever again.

Monty studied me for a second. "A premonition? Or just being extra cautious?"

I hesitated. "Both? I mean, I've seen nothing definite, but destruction is coming, and I can't risk losing either of you."

A smile tugged at his lips. "I'm glad to be included in that."

I nudged him far harder than he had me, sending him sideways with enough force that he had to throw a hand down onto the rock to steady himself. "Idiot. You know that you're the one family member aside from Mom that I can stand."

"Speaking of your mother, it might be worth talking to her about what is happening here. Not with the vampires. With you and the wellspring."

I frowned. "We can't risk the high council—"

"She already knows about the wild magic, Liz, and she has contacts that we don't. There must be information about the Fenna somewhere in this damn world. She wants to help you. Wants to help her granddaughter. I think you should let her."

"I don't know, Monty—"

"It takes a village to raise a child," he cut in softly. "And you have that village here, with all of us. But your child will never be ordinary, and we all need to know what we might be facing—what *she* might be facing—in the future."

I drew in a deeper breath and released it slowly. He was right. I knew he was right. But I'd spent well over ten years running from my family and relying on no one else except Belle. The habit was so ingrained it remained hard to break.

But I also wanted—maybe even needed—to mend more bridges with Mom. This might be a good way of doing that.

"When did you get so damn smart?"

He laughed. "I'll grab some clothes once we finish here and then drive over to the café." He paused, and though his voice retained its seriousness, there was a twinkle in his eyes. "Just as well Red is safely tucked away in off-site storage. I'd hate for something to happen to her if they hit our place."

I rolled my eyes. Red was his classic Mustang and,

according to Belle, he was so in love with the damn thing he crooned to it when he polished it. Monty denied loving it more than Belle, of course, but it was a pretty close thing in my opinion.

The caress of Belle's spell faded, and she turned, walking toward us. Her face was drawn and her silvery eyes flat, without their usual sparkle—both a sign of just how much energy she'd used. Monty immediately jumped up and went to her side, catching her elbow and helping her up the slight slope to where we'd been sitting.

I rose. "We need to get you back to the café—"

She raised an eyebrow. "So you can feed me one of your terrible potions? No way."

"The poor woman is so weary she's getting confused," I said to Monty. "It's her potions that are foul. Mine at least contain honey to sweeten the experience."

"Sorry, my love," Monty said, his grip on her tightening a little as she briefly wavered. "But I've tasted your energizing concoctions and, trust me, she's underselling their hideousness."

"Ungrateful, the pair of you." She reached for her pack, but I picked it up before she could. She sniffed but didn't otherwise object. "I take it we're going back to the café because of the portents of doom you had moments ago?"

I nodded. "I just ... need to be sure you're both safe."

"And Aiden?"

"After the whole not-really-a-dream confrontation with Marie this morning, we'd already decided to temporarily relocate."

"And won't that please his fucking mother," she said. "I daresay she'll use it as more ammunition against you."

"Yeah, but she can't do anything about my presence there now."

"She can still make your life there unpleasant, and remember, not all the pack was behind the decision to approve you living amongst them."

"No, but enough did to matter. Time will take care of the rest."

Presuming we all *had* time.

Goose bumps stole across my skin again. I picked up my pack, slung both over my shoulders, and then said, "Let's get going before you can't."

A smile ghosted her lips. "To quote a phrase used all too often by someone else here, I'm fine. I'm not going to collapse on you."

And I will draw on your strength if I feel that might happen.

And absolutely not a heartbeat before, I returned wryly.

Absolutely.

I chuckled softly, then turned and led the way toward the main exit tunnel. Ashworth was just making his way back down.

"All safe up there?" Monty asked.

Ashworth nodded. "That vibration we sensed was a proximity spell. Nothing dangerous and easy enough to disable. I've also dismissed our caging spell, given the beastie is no longer a problem."

"When you get home," I said, "can you and Eli ramp up the protection spells around your house?"

His gaze narrowed. "You've seen something?"

"Nothing definite, and it might turn out to be nothing at all—"

"When has that ever been the case?" he cut in. "I'll call Eli immediately and get him to start. With what we're facing, it's probably prudent, even without your instincts twitching."

"Thanks."

As he pulled out his phone to make the call, we continued on. Monty escorted us all the way down to the truck, kissed Belle, and then watched us leave before retreating.

"Hope he finds his way back," she said, amused. "His trail craft is not the best."

I grinned. "No, which is why he was sprinkling magical markers about the place."

Her eyebrows rose. "He was?"

"That right there is evidence of the fact you're almost out on your feet."

She laughed, though it was a pale echo of its usual robust self. By the time I'd driven through the forest and back onto the road, she was asleep and didn't stir until I'd parked at the rear of the café. Once I'd stored the ring in the glove compartment, I gently prodded her awake, then helped her into the café and up the stairs leading to the first-floor accommodation. There wasn't a whole lot of floor space up here, but it had two decent-sized bedrooms, as well as a separate toilet and bathroom. The living room was tiny, but had enough room for a kitchenette, an under-bench refrigerator, a small coffee machine to save us heading downstairs all the time, and a microwave, as well as a two-person sofa and a TV stand. Double glass doors led out to a balcony that extended out over the footpath, providing us with enough space for a table and four chairs while giving those in the café who wished to have their coffee and cake in the fresh air some form of weather protection.

It was perfect for two people, but with four of us, it was going to be tight.

"Bathroom rather than the bed," she said as we reached the top landing. "I can smell the dead on me."

I could smell it on us both.

And it wouldn't be the last time, either.

I shivered but shoved the premonition aside and helped her into the bathroom. Once I was sure she wasn't going to fall asleep or fall down, I ran back downstairs to tuck the backpacks away and make an energizing potion for her. The café was open and relatively busy, but Penny, Celia, and Ari —the twenty-year-old part-timer we'd very recently employed for the summer period—had things running smoothly.

"We're out of salted caramel and chocolate tart again," Penny said as she scooted past me and over to the coffee machine.

I blinked. "We only made it yesterday, and it's barely past one—how the hell could we have gone through two tarts so fast?"

She grinned. "The gossip brigade came in a day early, and apparently it's the new favorite."

I groaned. I loved the ladies—well, most of them—and their business was part of the reason we'd stayed afloat when we'd first opened, but damn, their appetites were ferocious when it came to desserts.

My expression must have been ... interesting, because Penny laughed. "I told them they've cleaned us out and not to expect another batch to be baked for tomorrow. They said they'd settle for the baked buttermilk donuts with whisky chocolate glaze instead. Which, I might add, they'd all but demolished by Friday last week."

Which was pretty good going, given the standing order with the specialist bakery over in Lyttleton Street was for fifty to come in on Thursday.

"Good, because I'm really not going to have the time to bake another batch of tarts tonight."

Penny made a face as she steamed the milk for the coffee. "Might be time to start ordering a few more commercial cakes in. I know we've a rep for home baked, but you haven't the kitchen space or time to keep up with demand at the moment."

I switched off the blender and poured the green concoction into a glass. "We're already buying in enough. If push comes to shove, Belle will swing full-time to baking."

"Which might need to happen sooner than you think." She swirled the milk into the coffee cups, spooned in the foam, then carefully decorated the top. "Oh, before I forget, there's a woman who's been waiting here a while for you. Says she has to talk to you. Privately."

I raised an eyebrow and glanced past the counter, but couldn't see anyone who looked like a rep of some kind. "Did she say what she wanted?"

"Nope, but I have seen her around. I told her I wasn't sure when you'd be in, but she said she could wait. I tucked her in the nook."

The nook was a table tucked behind the kitchen wall, right next to the line of windows that ran along the lane section of the café, and it was the only table not visible from the counter.

"Tell her I'll be there in fifteen," I said. "I've got to run this up to Belle, and I desperately need to shower."

She wrinkled her nose. "I wasn't going to say anything, but ..."

I laughed. "Yeah. Not the best way to meet a rep."

"Unless you want to run them off, never to see them again."

"Depends on what they're trying to sell us this time, I suppose."

"Indeed, it would." With a grin, she picked up the two coffees and whisked them away.

I headed back up the stairs to find Belle out of the shower and stumbling toward her bedroom. I slipped my free hand around her waist, guiding her the rest of the rest of the way before handing her the drink. I didn't move until she'd finished the lot.

"See you in a couple of hours," she mumbled, and she slipped down under the blankets.

"If you wake any sooner than six, I will be cross."

"You're such a bossy witch sometimes."

"Wonder where I learned that from?"

She didn't reply. She was already asleep. I smiled, padded lightly from the room, and closed the door. After I grabbed a shower, I tugged on shorts and a singlet top and put my hair into a ponytail. Then, feeling cleaner if not more awake, I headed back down the stairs.

Only to discover the woman who waited wasn't a rep, and she certainly wasn't trying to sell me something.

It was Karleen fucking O'Connor.

CHAPTER SIX

I was tempted—very tempted—to spin on my heels and walk away. I wanted nothing to do with this woman. There was a part of me, a *big* part of me, that wished I could ban her from having any interaction with Aiden or me or our daughter. But wolf packs didn't work like that. Family was all, and no matter how furious Aiden was with his mom, he would never eradicate her from his life.

And I would never ask him to.

But that didn't mean I had to be polite to her.

Her gaze met mine as I approached, her blue eyes and her expression carefully neutral. I pulled out a chair and sat down, my back to the window but feeling no warmer for the heat already radiating from the glass.

I raised a privacy screen to ensure our conversation wasn't overheard by the nearest gossip brigade members, who were already casting speculative glances our way, then crossed my arms on the table and leaned forward casually.

A movement that belied the tension radiating through me. "What do you want, Karleen?"

She smiled, though it was a flat, thin-lipped thing that

never touched the corners of her eyes. "I came to offer you a deal. A truce, if you will."

"What makes you think I'd ever be interested in anything you could offer? What makes you think I would ever trust you—" I cut the rest off and sucked back the anger. I couldn't release it. Not here. Not in front of all these people. Which was probably why she'd chosen to come here rather than do this at the compound. She'd already done enough damage to her reputation in the eyes of the pack. Now she was trying to ruin mine.

It was possible I was being too harsh on her, but ... I doubted it.

"What makes you think I want a truce?"

"For the sake of our family, I think it is needed."

"You're not my family. You will *never* be my family."

"My dear girl, you are marrying my son. Whether I like it or not—and I certainly don't, as you're well aware—that makes us a family in pack eyes."

I opened my mouth, then snapped it closed again and leaned back in the chair and studied her for a minute. I could see the tension in her. See the displeasure. "Ciara made you do this, didn't she?"

Surprise flicked through her expression before the neutral mask settled back into place. "She cannot *make* me do anything. Aside from the fact I am—*was*—alpha, I'm also her mother."

"And yet you're here because of her."

Her nod was a short, sharp, angry motion. "We had a discussion."

The emphasis she placed on "discussion" suggested it had more than likely been an argument. "About what?"

It wasn't hard to guess what it had been about, but there

was a vicious little part inside of me that wanted to hear her say it out loud.

And the angry gleam that flared briefly in her eyes suggested she knew it. "About you. About my ... attitude to you."

Oh, to have been a fly on the wall for that one.

"Which attitude are we talking about? The one that hates all witches because some psycho witch bastard raped your sister when you were both teens and she subsequently died in childbirth? Or the one that believes our daughter will be born an abomination?"

"I never said—"

"Yeah, you did. Maybe not so much to anyone beyond the confines of your pack, but you certainly thought it." I gave her a sweet smile that was anything but. "You forget how very well Belle reads minds."

Her gaze narrowed. "I thought there was some sort of code amongst telepaths not to randomly read minds?"

"Depends on the telepath and the mind. It's much like the whole 'threefold' rule that applies to us witches. For some, on rare occasions, the cost of spell bounce back is worth the price of getting a little retribution."

The flicker in her eyes suggested she hadn't missed the implication. But then, while she was many things, she wasn't dumb.

She drew in a deep breath and released it slowly. "Listen, I no more want this than you do. But Ciara is right. We are family. We must find a way to make this work."

She might be right, but I wasn't in a forgiving mood. Maybe it was the tiredness. Maybe it was just the desperate need for a little payback, but I nevertheless rose and leaned forward until my face was inches from hers. I could smell the scent of the soap she'd used that morning—lilac, with just a touch of honey—and the lingering hint of coffee on her breath. Saw the brief flare of surprise in her eyes and the ripple of anger through her aura. She didn't like being challenged, not in any way, but she didn't rise. Didn't make any sort of move, in fact.

Ciara's words had had more impact than she'd admitted.

"We will find a means of making it work when you fucking apologize and actually *mean* it. Until then, neither I nor our daughter will have anything to do with you." I paused, smiled sweetly, and motioned to the empty coffee cup sitting to her left. "That's on the house. Feel free to have another or even leave. I don't care."

And with that, I dismissed the privacy screen and walked away from her. She picked up her bag and left.

As the small bell above the door merrily announced her departure, the anger and perhaps a little self-recrimination began. I shouldn't have said any of that really, but, damn it, this was too important to compromise. My *daughter* was too important to compromise. At the very least she owed me and Aiden a goddamn apology for everything she'd said and done.

I checked with the kitchen to ensure Mike and Frank—our chef and kitchen hand, respectively—had everything under control, and bolted upstairs to my bedroom, closed the door, and rested my forehead against it for a couple of seconds, until the anger and the pounding of my pulse had eased. Then I stripped off and fell onto the bed. I didn't dream, but that intangible feeling of approaching doom nevertheless made for a restless sleep.

When I woke, it was to the comforting warmth of a body pressed against mine and the whisper of breath against the back of my neck. He smelled faintly of the citrus-and-ginger soap I kept in the shower, and his skin was cool and damp, meaning he'd only just joined me on the bed.

I turned in his arms and smiled as he drew so close my breasts were lightly pressed against his chest. "Good evening."

"It is now that I have you in my arms." His lips brushed mine, a sweet caress that barely hinted at the fierce desire that burned through him, around him. It was a heady scent. "I hear you and my mother had words this afternoon."

"Good God, the gossip lines in this place really are impressive."

He laughed, a warm sound that vibrated delightfully through my breasts. "It wasn't them this time. Ciara rang me and said she'd had words with Mom—"

"From what I gathered, it was more a full-on argument. Your mother was most displeased."

"Yeah, she said that, too. And apparently her face was something of a picture when she returned to the compound. What did you say to her? More importantly, what did she say to you?"

I told him, and he laughed. "You seriously demanded an apology?"

"Well, don't we deserve one?"

"Yes. I'm just picturing her expression when you said that. Few have stood up to her—including me—for far too long. But I wouldn't be expecting my mom to apologize anytime soon. It's not in her nature."

"Hmm." I trailed my fingers lightly along his side to his hips, then slipped them down between us. His cock jumped under my touch, and desire curled through me, a hungry, low-down, burning ache that said, without even being touched, I was already ready for him.

He skimmed his fingers, with torturous slowness, down

the side of my neck and then across the right side of my breast. Delight shivered through me, and that spark of hunger deepened in his eyes.

"I'm not expecting anything from her," I said softly. "It's an entirely different matter when it comes to you."

He raised a lazy eyebrow as his fingers continued their journey toward my hip. "And what might that be?"

"To stop playing around and get serious about satisfaction."

"Says the woman who is driving me to distraction with her delightful caressing of my cock."

"Said cock is obviously enjoying the attention. My counterpart is feeling decidedly left out."

"Perhaps I should remedy that?"

"Perhaps you—" The rest of the sentence was lost to a gasp as he slipped a finger into the heated heart of me and lightly brushed my clit.

He chuckled softly, then rolled me onto my back and began to devour me with lips and tongue, until I was a shaking, needy mess, unable to do anything more than simply plead for him to end the exquisite torture.

He didn't. Not immediately. He simply held himself above me for several long seconds, his gaze devouring mine, hot and heavy and yet so filled with love my heart swelled.

"I love you, Elizabeth Grace."

"And I love you, Aiden O'Conner." I hesitated, but devilment rose, and I couldn't help adding, "I doubt I will ever love your mother, however."

Amusement twitched the corners of his lovely mouth. "A normal man would find the specter of his mother being raised at such a critical moment in proceedings rather deflating."

I wrapped my legs around his hips and drew him down,

shivering in delight as his body slipped into mine. "Just as well you're no ordinary man, then, isn't it?"

He laughed, kissed me, and then drove me to heaven.

The dream came again.

I walked barefoot through the forest, the air alive with luminous threads of moonlight, some far older and more powerful than others. Unseen shadows paced me, but there were only four this time, rather than five.

In this version of the dream, no one paced beside me.

Trepidation stepped into my soul, but the dream pulled me on.

Up ahead, the mage fire pulsed, its deep purple glow staining the trees once more, curling the leaves with its force. It seemed to dance from tree to tree, briefly reminding me of the way flames leapt.

It is what comes, instinct whispered, though whether it was mage fire or real, it wasn't saying.

As before, I left the trees and came out into the clearing.

As before, Roger lay between me and Marie. This time, there were only three stakes. I guess there was no need to pin what remained of his right leg.

Instinct twitched again. I narrowed my gaze and studied his heavily bandaged knee stump. Perhaps it was my imagination, but the rest of his leg *did* appear to be present, even if in a ghostly form.

Only it was different—more muscular.

Which made absolutely no sense.

"You may be wondering why I called you here again." Marie's melodious voice held just a hint of amusement. "And perhaps even how."

"Given I've changed location and you cannot possibly have gotten through the wild magic that protects the café so easily—not without me being forewarned—I would hazard a guess that this is some form of lucid dreaming or astral projection. As to how ..." I shrugged. "While I would like to know, I'm thinking you won't tell me simply because you have no desire for me to prevent future occurrences."

"Oh, while it is true you are physically safe in your fortress, little witch, you could never prevent these meetings. Those who play with darkness can sometimes get leashed by it, however innocuous it might have seemed at the time."

I frowned. "I don't understand—"

"Oh, I think you do. Or at least, you will if you cast your mind back to a certain spell you once performed. One that involved several drops of your own blood?"

Ah, *fuck.*

I closed my eyes and scrubbed a hand across eyes that didn't physically exist in this plane. I'd known at the time how dangerous that spell was. Had even been warned in a note Nell—Belle's grandmother—had left in an unfinished book called *Spells from Uncertain Times.*

I foresee a need for this in the distant future, it had said, *but be wary of its use, dear witchling. The spell lies in the gray zone; it will not draw the ire of the council but it will make you more susceptible to the darker forces of this world.*

I'd understood the danger of using a blood spell even without that warning and had accepted the danger it represented in order to protect Belle. I just hadn't understood the implications within that warning. Hadn't understood that, by performing that spell, I'd opened my spirit or astral being or whatever this was to being called into the *presence* of darker entities.

Marie laughed. "I can see from your expression that you have indeed remembered."

"Yes, and I take comfort in the fact that while you can call me, you cannot control me."

The fact that I'd moved against her will in our first meeting, utterly surprising her, suggested her control was at best partial rather than complete.

For now, that annoying inner voice whispered again. *But that could so easily change ...*

I shivered and flexed my fingers, trying to ease the wave of trepidation. As usual, it failed.

"In some respects, you are right," Marie drawled. "But also, very wrong."

"I see that you and Maelle share another trait—you both love avoiding straight answers."

She laughed. "Why would I want to provide you with any real information when it is far more satisfying to see your confusion and taste the delicious acceleration of your heart?"

Did that mean she was as much an energy vampire as a blood one? Was that the danger these astral meetings presented? I didn't know, but I seriously needed to find out, and fast. "And yet you do provide real information when it suits you. So why did you call me here, Marie?"

"Perhaps I am simply charmed by your sparkling personality and scintillating conversation, and wish to hear more."

"And perhaps you wish to distract me from events happening elsewhere."

"Perhaps." Her smile flashed, all white teeth and sharp canines. "And perhaps I wish to emphasize the warning given to you yesterday, but in terms you may respect a little more.

Place yourself in the middle of this fight, and I will destroy all that you hold dear. The fire that surrounds us is not real in this plane, but it could so easily become so in yours."

And with that, I was cast back into my body.

I woke with a gasp and sat bolt upright. The sudden movement woke Aiden, and he shifted and sat up with me, his arm slipping around my shoulders and tugging me against him.

"Another dream?" When I nodded, he added, "How? I thought this place would protect you from her?"

"So did I. I was wrong." I pulled away from him and climbed out of bed, tugging on a T-shirt and a pair of sleep shorts. "I need a coffee. And possibly pancakes. And bacon."

He rolled out the other side of our bed and pulled on his jeans. "You make the coffee; I'll do the rest."

I shot a narrowed gaze at him. "Can you be trusted with pancakes?"

"Hey, they're only flour and milk, right? Can't be too hard."

Right. "We'll switch roles. I need decent pancakes right now."

He smiled, though it failed to chase the concern from his eyes. "You're going to have to teach me to cook your favorite foods properly—if only for those pregnancy hankerings that apparently hit at the most inconvenient hours of the night."

"Keep a steady stock of chocolate and several packets of white chocolate caramel popcorn in the pantry, and we'll be just fine."

He blinked. "Caramel popcorn? When did that become a thing?"

"Monday. Discovered it in the Christmas food aisle at the supermarket."

"And you didn't share? I'm outraged."

"You were working." I padded lightly down the stairs. "And it was very moreish."

I flicked on the kitchen light, lit the stovetop, then got out everything I needed to make the pancakes. With the bacon frying in one pan, I poured the mixture into two others. Aiden came in, handed me a mug of coffee, and then leaned back against the metal prep counter. "So, tell me what happened this time in the dream."

"It followed much the same path as the previous one, but it's not a dream. It's"—I flipped a pancake and wrinkled my nose—"more an astral travel thing."

"How is it happening, though? I thought the reason we moved here was to prevent it."

"She confirmed the fact she can't physically access this place, so staying here remains prudent." I flipped the pancakes onto a plate, slipped it into the warmer drawer, and threw more butter into the pan followed by the mix.

"That only answered part of my question."

I flashed him a smile, though it was a little more tense than I would have liked. "Apparently, a spell I did a few months ago to protect Belle allows darkness to call on my spirit."

"Were you aware of this at the time?"

"Sort of? There was a warning that using the spell would make me more susceptible to darkness, but it was the only spell I could find to protect her from Clayton's very obvious intent to rape her." I flipped the next lot of pancakes and checked the bacon.

"Meaning you didn't care."

I certainly didn't. And I'd do it again in a heartbeat to

protect her. I slipped the next batch of pancakes onto the plate, put the cooked bacon on another, and shoved both into the warmer drawer before making a final batch of pancakes. He and I couldn't possibly eat everything I was cooking, but I was betting Monty's nose for bacon would see him coming down the stairs sooner rather than later.

Aiden contemplated me for a second. "Can she control you in these dreams?"

"Not at the moment. But I need to ring Mom, so I might ask her to do some research."

He frowned. "Ashworth has more experience dealing with vampires than she does."

"Yes, but this is something else, and that spell—" I grimaced. "It was a blood spell, Aiden. A gray one, but nevertheless blood based. Ashworth might have contacts in the HIC, but Mom, as a member of the high council, has access to the restricted section of the National Spell Archive. That's where information will be found about it, if anywhere. Even Nell's book didn't really flesh out the implications."

When the last batch was done, I put all the warmed plates on a tray, gave it to him to carry out, then headed to the fridge to grab the toppings—raspberries, cinnamon butter, and maple syrup—then picked up the cutlery and my coffee, and followed him out.

Once we'd both filled up our plates, he said, "You said it followed much the same path, so what changed in this one?"

I hesitated. "There's a fire coming, but I'm not sure whether it's mage fire or real. The trees were certainly being hit by the former, but I just have this horrible conviction it might be the latter."

"Nothing much we can do about either until it happens. We're as prepared as anyone can be for a real fire."

Footsteps clattered down the stairs, and I looked around with a smile. "Well, that didn't take you very long at all."

Monty bounced down the last step and strode toward us. "And I do hope there's enough left to share, because otherwise I'm going to give you sad puppy eyes until you take pity and give me some of yours."

I laughed. "It's a brave man who'd take the food off a pregnant woman's plate. How's Belle?"

I knew she remained asleep, but I couldn't tell any more than that because of all the spells I'd woven around both our bedrooms to give Belle some privacy from the constant barrage of my thoughts. While both of us could raise a shield against the other—an ability that was definitely becoming stronger in me—it was nice to have an area where we didn't have to worry about shielding and could just let it all hang out mentally.

Monty grabbed the spare plate and helped himself to the extras. "She's sleeping easier, and the gauntness has all but gone. Why are you up so early? Dreaming again?"

"Yeah." I quickly filled him in, omitting the whole bit about the dark spell for the moment, because I didn't want to worry Belle. "I thought I'd ring Mom and ask her to—"

I cut off the rest as Aiden's phone rang, the sound echoing sharply and sending my pulse into overdrive. While it might have nothing to do with any of our current problems, instinct was twitching, and that was never a good thing.

"Ranger Aiden O'Connor," he said. "How can I—"

The woman on the other end didn't let him finish, and while she didn't in any way sound panicked, she was speaking so fast I didn't really hear much more than blood and bodies.

I sighed, gulped down my coffee, and rose. "We're up, Monty."

He blew out a breath. "It always happens when I'm enjoying good food."

"Then grab a container to take it with you. In the meantime, we need to get ready."

As Aiden continued talking, Monty and I ran up the stairs. After a quick wash, I exchanged my sleep shorts and old T-shirt for a pair of jean shorts and a supportive tank top, then grabbed a pair of socks and sat down on the bed. Aiden returned as I was pulling on my boots.

"What's happened?"

"Lynette was going for an early morning run and stumbled upon what she said could be a multiple murder scene."

"I take it you know her?"

He nodded and grabbed his socks and boots, sitting down beside me to put them on. "She's with the SES and has some experience with body retrieval."

The State Emergency Services was a volunteer organization that provided emergency help in natural disasters, road crashes, and rescues. And some of those definitely involved deaths.

"Did she say how many bodies we might be dealing with?"

"She's not sure. She peered through a broken window and saw at least one, but believes, given the amount of blood visible in the hall beyond, there were more."

"Did she recognize the victim she saw?" Castle Rock was at its base a country town, and most of the older residents did know each other by sight if not by name.

"No, though she did say the house was a rental and had only been recently leased."

"You think it could be our vampires?"

He glanced at me, his eyebrows raised. "Do you?"

"Maybe." I grimaced. "I did ask Marie if she'd called me to her last night in order to prevent me sensing their planned violence and perhaps stopping it, and she certainly didn't deny it."

"If she *was* behind this slaughter, what are the chances of the victims being connected to Maelle?"

"Fifty-fifty. She needs to rile Maelle into attacking her, but she also has a bunch of hungry vampires to look after."

"If she's determined to rile Maelle into attacking, why then demand she meet them at the court of justice?"

"She gave Maelle twenty-four hours. That's now past."

"Only just, and from the sound of things, these murders happened well before the deadline ended." He pulled on a T-shirt, then swept his keys and wallet from the side dresser and tucked them into his jean pockets. "Ready?"

I nodded and accepted his hand, letting him pull me up. Monty met us in the hall. "I left Belle a message just in case she wakes up fuzzy."

She'd certainly woken up fuzzy more than once, but that had never stopped her from reaching out to me to see what was happening. Monty was well aware of that, which suggested his note was probably more along the lines of a love note—he knew she adored that sort of stuff. Hell, she'd kept all the notes and poems past lovers had given her over the years—and it had been one of them I'd used in the blood spell. Trepidation stirred through me again, thick with the warning that I needed to uncover more about the spell's consequences. And *fast*.

I followed Aiden down the stairs, ducked into the reading room to get my backpack while Monty grabbed his breakfast, and then we all headed out the back. Aiden opened the truck's passenger door and helped me in, then ran around to the driver's side and started her up. He drove out at speed but didn't turn on the siren until we were away from the café. Not wanting to wake Belle, I suspected.

"Where are we heading?" I asked, reaching back to snare a bit of bacon from Monty's container. He gave me two. Either he was feeling generous, or he'd taken the warning about a pregnant woman's plate seriously.

"Moonlight Flats."

I bit into the bacon and frowned. "That area is close to town, isn't it? Why would Marie and her people risk setting up another charnel house in a place like that?"

"It's an acreage area rather than a housing estate, but we are talking about vampires here," he said. "And old ones at that. I get the feeling they don't think or act like us ordinary folk."

"Speak for yourself," Monty said. "There is nothing ordinary about me."

I snorted softly and wished I had something other than bacon in my hand so I could toss it at him. But I wasn't about to waste good bacon. "Yeah, but it's also only a couple of kilometers from the compound's boundaries, and plenty of wolves move through that area. They would have smelled death had Marie and her team been using it to store their meals."

"Most likely." Aiden slowed the truck fractionally, turned left, and then accelerated again. "From what Lynette said, the deaths probably all happened within the last six hours."

"Lynette's a wolf?" Monty asked, shoving the container between the seats so I could grab a pancake.

I shook my head. As much as I might want more, my stomach wasn't the steadiest beast of late and I might well end up regretting eating anything else if what we discovered in this house in any way came close to the mess we'd found in the cavern.

"No," Aiden was saying. "SES. I told her to move back to the road and ensure no one else entered until we arrived. I've called in Ciara, Mac, and Tala."

Tala was his second-in-command and hailed from the Sinclair pack. Neither she nor Mac had been there at the cavern, so he was obviously sharing the trauma around.

He swung right, onto a dirt road, but didn't slow down. Dust plumed around the truck, falling onto the windows, making it difficult to see much beyond them. Not that there appeared to be all that much aside from trees and the occasional flash of a building.

He skidded onto another, smaller road and finally slowed. Up ahead, leaning against a mailbox made out of an old milk drum that had been painted red, was a tall, thin-nish woman wearing leggings, a tank top, and runners. Sweat still dripped from the ends of her brown ponytail, and her cheeks remained flushed from her run. Although it could just as easily be the heat. It might still be early in the day, but the air was already uncomfortably warm.

Aiden stopped beside her and wound down the windows. "No movement?"

"Nothing from inside, and nothing along the road. You want me to stay and help?"

Aiden shook his head. "I suspect what we'll find inside is something the SES can't help us with."

She nodded, her nose wrinkling. "I forgot to mention earlier that I turned off the gas—got a big whiff of it through the window, so you'll probably find my prints on the meter."

"Thanks. I'll send Jaz to get your statement later, so you can head home before the heat really hits."

"Awesome. Talk later."

As she turned and jogged down the road, Aiden released the brake and continued on slowly up the curving stone driveway. The house was a surprisingly modern-looking, L-shaped building with a pale green tin roof and matching metal window frames. A wide veranda ran along the building's front, and two large windows sat on either side of the overly grand-looking front door. The window on the right had been smashed, though if the amount of glass glittering on the veranda's concrete base was anything to go by, it had been broken by someone inside the house, not outside. A freestanding carport sat at the end of the driveway, just behind the house, and had one of those large people-mover vans parked underneath it. On the other side, only partially visible, was a large machinery shed half-filled with round hay bales.

Aiden stopped the truck at the front steps, and we all climbed out. The air was hot and still, and cicadas sang, but there was little other sound and no immediate indication that death and destruction awaited. Even the broken window didn't tell us much, as there was no indication of what had caused the breakage and certainly no sign of blood. I couldn't smell it either, but that could just be because the air wasn't moving enough to trail the scent across my nose.

But then, my nose was nowhere near as sharp as Aiden's, and given the flaring of his nostrils and the brief flash of resignation through his expression, it was certainly there.

"I'm not sensing any form of magic," Monty said, and glanced at me. "You?"

I shook my head. "Which is odd when you think about it. Even if this had happened hours ago, restraining and silencing multiple people takes a good amount of magic. There should be at least some remnants floating about."

"For us normal witches," Monty noted. "Not for someone like Marie."

Aiden handed us both silicone gloves and some of those pull-on boot protectors. "There's also the point that many of the bodies we found in the cavern had been bound by ropes and gags rather than magic. It's quite possible that's what happened here."

That had obviously been discovered after Belle and I had left, and it somehow made the whole situation even more appalling.

Aiden led us up the steps, his boots echoing on the old wood as he strode toward the door. He pulled on the gloves and booties, then glanced at me. "Nothing on the doorknob I have to worry about?"

"No."

He opened the door and warily pushed it wide, but didn't immediately enter. The air that stirred sluggishly past us—suggesting there was an air con on somewhere in the house—was filled with blood, death and, to a lesser extent, the eggy smell of gas. Weirdly, unlike in the cavern, there was no cloud of fear or pain, which was decidedly odd given the heaviness of the first two scents. But maybe there was some sort of magic at work here, even if I couldn't immediately sense it.

The hall beyond was wide and relatively short with a left turn at the end, which no doubt led to the longer L section. There were two doors, one on either side, and the flooring was tiles rather than wood. White tiles, which made the thick smear of blood that started on the wall itself and then continued to the end of the hall and around the corner starkly obvious.

Either someone had dragged his or her bleeding body away, perhaps in a desperate last attempt to escape, or whoever was behind this destruction had dragged them away. But why only one? Why not move the person who lay in the room to our right? I didn't know, but I suspected we'd find out soon enough. I shivered and rubbed my arms.

Aiden glanced at me sharply. "Are you okay?"

I nodded. "Unlike the cave, there's no shroud of emotion here."

"Which is another oddity," Monty said. "Whoever that smear belongs to had to be feeling something pretty damn powerful."

"Unless they were already dead when they were moved."

"The bulk of the blood scent *is* coming from deeper within the house," Aiden said. "But we keep together until we know what else might be waiting."

We both nodded. Once Monty and I had gloved up and put the boot protectors on, we cautiously moved on. The room to our left was a study lined with bookshelves, though most of the shelving was empty. The large antique-looking desk sitting under the front window was dust-covered, and the chair tucked in underneath it looked to have seen better days. What was interesting was the two mattresses sitting on the floor, both of them neatly made up. Maybe whoever had rented this place had been expecting guests.

Had those guests come bearing a grudge rather than gifts?

Instinct whispered no.

Instinct was fucking annoying.

We moved on cautiously toward the room on the right. I wrinkled my nose against the sharper smell of blood and

Aiden reached into his pocket, handing me the tub of mentholated ointment without comment.

We skirted around the smear and went into the other room. It was a living area, though there was no TV or sofas, just a couple of mattresses on the floor. The body of a man lay sprawled face down on the carpet halfway between the door and the window. His hand was outstretched above his head, suggesting he might have been throwing something—maybe the something that had broken the window. There was blood in his hair, blood down his neck, blood on the back of his shirt, and ... horror surged, and I couldn't help but step away from him. A large hole had been punched right through his body. I could see the bloody carpet underneath him. See the shattered remnants of bone, the torn lines of muscle and veins, and the streaks of yellow that looked like fat, both within his skin and without.

This hadn't been done with a gun, a shotgun, or even magic.

This had been done by someone powerful enough to *physically* punch a hole right through flesh. The imprint of a clenched fist had been burned into the carpet, and the blood that had leached from the victim's body had not fouled or hidden it. It was as if that imprint somehow repelled any attempt to do so.

This body—that imprint—was a warning.

For several seconds, none of us moved.

Then Monty sighed and said what we were all thinking.

"Well, for fuck's sake, the last thing we need to be dealing with is another goddamn monster."

"What kind of fucking monster can punch a hole through the middle of a man's body?" Aiden asked. "Are you sure this isn't the result of magic?"

"There's no magical residue, though it is possible it

simply faded away." Monty squatted next to the body, carefully avoiding anything that might be evidence. "It has to be a monster of some kind—look at the size of that imprint. None of our vamps have hands like that."

"That we're aware of," I said, remaining right where I was. My stomach was behaving itself, but I wasn't about to push it. "We haven't seen all of Marie's crew, remember."

"True." He rose. "I'm thinking we need to see the rest of the bodies before we can make a judgment call on our killer."

Aiden nodded and led the way out. We followed the bloody smear down to the end of the hall and around the corner and found a second body. This one was a woman, and though she had a cleanish hole punched through her torso, her head was twisted at a strange angle and her face was visible. Her expression was one of horror.

So why were there no emotions staining the air? I really had no idea, and that was scary.

I gulped but nevertheless looked at the hole in her body, and the tile visible through it. Unlike the carpet under the first victim, there was no shadow of a fist here, but the tile had been smashed. Anything that could do *that* with a mere punch without doing serious damage to its hand and leaving at least some blood behind very definitely wasn't human.

As Aiden moved on, I dragged out my phone and took a quick photo so that I could ask Maelle if this was one of her people or not. Because if she was, then it was likely the rest were, too.

There was a bathroom next to the study, a toilet next to that, and at the end, before the hall turned right, a laundry. The door leading outside had been smashed off its hinges and lay in pieces on the floor.

Monty frowned. "They must have heard this thing

enter, so why didn't they run? None of this is making sense."

"The other thing that's not making sense is the position of her body," I said. "If our monster came through this door, why was the woman running toward it rather than away? If she's lying where she fell, then she was hit from behind, not in front."

"It could be that we're dealing with two killers." Aiden said. "Let's check the rest of the house, because the crew will be here soon."

We moved on. The short hallway opened out to a kitchen-dining area, beyond which was a large, open living area. There were no bodies here. No smears of blood. Nothing to indicate anything monstrous had even passed through.

Another hallway lay opposite the kitchen, so we headed over. There were five doors along the corridor, along with what I presumed was a double closet about halfway down. The other doors led into bedrooms and all of them held bodies. There were five split between the first three bedrooms and one in the fourth. All of them had holes in their bodies.

But in the fifth ... I sucked in a breath and retreated.

The fifth was an overly large bathroom that held God knew how many, because there was little more than bits of limbs, flesh, muscles, and bloody strings of intestines scattered all over the floor.

And obvious evidence that someone had rolled through the middle of it all.

"Whatever else might have been in this house, *that* is evidence that one or more of our vamps also were," I said, throat burning with the bile threatening to rise. "Maelle isn't the only one who loves swimming in the remains of her victims. Marie and Jaqueline apparently do, too."

Outside, sirens wailed, a sound that matched the scream in my head. It would get worse before this was all over. Much worse.

I gulped and backed away a little more. "I think I'll head outside, get some fresh air, and check the outbuildings, just in case."

Aiden's swung around, his gaze studying me. He didn't say to be careful, but the warning nevertheless glinted in his eyes.

I nodded at the silent request, then turned and got the hell out of there, leaping over the remnants of the laundry door and landing well past the two short steps leading out into the yard beyond. I stopped, rested my hands on my knees, and simply breathed deep in an effort to calm everything down. My stomach eventually settled, though the acidic taste remained in my throat. It wouldn't take much for my stomach to rise again.

I pushed upright, took the booties off, then walked around to the front of the building to grab some water from the back of Aiden's truck. He didn't have it on ice, so it'd be warm, but right then, I didn't particularly care.

An SUV stopped beside Aiden's truck, and Mac climbed out of the passenger side. He had the typically rangy build of a werewolf, with brown skin and hair. His gaze swept me briefly but assessingly. "You're looking rather peaked."

I half smiled. "Peaked is such a polite way of saying I look like shit."

He grinned, white teeth bright. "I am nothing if not polite. The boss inside?"

"Yeah, and so are a shit-ton of dead bodies."

"Just what we need on such a glorious day like today."

As he moved around to the back of the vehicle, Tala walked around the front and stopped beside me. She was about my height, with dark skin and silver-shot black hair. "Are we dealing with death by vampire or beastie?"

"A bit of both, unfortunately."

"Never a good thing." She glanced at me. "Congrats on the engagement, by the way."

"Here I was thinking you'd be in the against camp."

I couldn't help the surprise in my voice, and she raised an eyebrow, amusement lurking in her dark eyes. "Just because I thought you might have been a con woman when you first appeared doesn't mean I can't also believe you and Aiden are good together. And what is good for him is also good for us, because that man was a *bear* when you two split."

I laughed. "So Jaz said."

"Jaz probably understated it because she managed to be on patrol most of the time. I take it you're remaining out here?"

"Thought I'd do a sweep of the van and the outbuildings to see if there's anything untoward in them. My psi senses were getting a little overwhelmed by the bloodshed inside."

She made a low, somewhat growly noise in the back of her throat. "The sooner we get rid of these damn vampires, the better. And *that* should include Maelle, in my humble opinion."

"It's an opinion more than a few of us now agree with," I muttered. Question was, did the council dare do anything against her and risk retaliation?

Because she *would* retaliate, especially if things went

badly for Roger and her mind—and impulse control—slipped any more than it already had.

Mac returned, handed Tala a pair of gloves and booties, then headed toward the front stairs. Tala gave me a nod and followed. As they disappeared through the door, I capped my drink, tucked it into the backpack's side pocket, then walked around the side of the house to check the van. I didn't open the front doors because a quick look into the cabin said there was no one in there, and it wasn't my job to be going through the glove compartment or center storage well for clues. But the rear section of the people mover had all the windows blocked out, and that very much suggested it had indeed been used as a mode of transport for vampires.

I guess the question was, whose?

I gripped the van's handle and carefully slid the door open. No stench of blood or flesh rushed out. The air wasn't pleasant, and oddly reminded me a little of the slightly sweet but musty scent that sometimes came from older people. Which, given the vamps we were dealing with were very old indeed, made sense. And it was certainly better than the scent of decay some fiction would have us believe they smelled like.

I closed the door again then headed around the back of the van and across to the machinery shed. The right half was filled with closely packed hay rounds, but the left was empty aside from a ride-on mower that didn't look as if it had been used in months—which meant someone else had to be looking after the lawns and gardens surrounding the house, because they were pin-neat—and an odd selection of rusted gardening tools.

I did a circuit around the accessible bits of the interior just in case I'd missed something, then headed out again, stopping to study the yard and the tree-lined fence to my right. Instinct twitched and I resignedly turned and headed down that way.

The huge old gum trees were in full flower, their pale creamy flowers contrasting sharply against the green of old leaves and the coppery bronze of the new growth. Their lemony scent filled the air, and I drew in a deeper breath, hoping to wash the lingering remnants of death from my lungs.

And smelled, underneath the lemony divineness, the hint of wrongness. Magical type wrongness.

I swore and scrubbed a hand through my hair. It seemed fate hadn't yet finished handing out clues, because that wrongness suggested someone had performed a spell somewhere nearby, even if no magical threads lingered in the air. It was probably the source of the punch beastie, but until I followed that faint scent, I wouldn't know for sure.

There was a part of me that really, *really*, didn't want to follow.

But that was cowardice speaking, or perhaps even the natural desire of a mother-to-be not to take risks.

And yet if I didn't, we'd all pay the price. Or so instinct was saying.

Instinct could be a real pain in the ass sometimes.

Most times.

I blew out a breath and swept my gaze left and right. There was very little grass growing under the trees, thanks no doubt to the fact they were too close together and the shadows under their canopies rather dense. The fence dividing the home paddock from the sloping incline of the next one was a basic three-strand wire. The grass on the other side was far longer than it was here, making it difficult to see if anything or anyone lurked. If something did, it probably wouldn't be a vampire, given the sunshine, but until we had some idea what the beastie with the lethal punch was, it also had to remain a possibility.

I ducked under a low-hanging branch and stopped close to the fence. That's when I spotted the trail in the grass. Someone—something—large had run through this field fairly recently, heading toward the top of the hill.

It didn't take much of an effort to guess it had been our monster.

I climbed through the fence and walked over to the crushed grass. It was a wide, flat trail, and while I was no tracker, I was pretty damn sure it hadn't been made by anything human. Not given the way the footprints had impacted the otherwise hard soil.

I swung my pack around to tug out a bottle of holy water, and then spun a repelling spell around my other hand. I hoped neither would be necessary, but I'd learned the hard way it was always better to be safe than sorry.

I walked into the long grass, keeping to the right of the trail and damnably glad I was wearing boots. It'd be nigh on impossible to see a snake in this stuff before you stepped on the thing.

The wide line of trampled grass continued up the slope, but the closer I got to the top, the more instinct twitched.

I'd just about reached the crest when I spotted the large circular section of flattened grass and stopped. The feeling of wrongness swirled around me, and while there were no spell threads evident here, there *were* candles. Melted black candles, the type used in darker magics and summonings.

My grip momentarily tightened on the holy water, even though I had no immediate sense of danger. Nor could I see any indication of a pentagram on the ground, though the candles were sitting at what would be the five elemental points. There was blood here, too, I realized after a moment.

I couldn't smell it from where I was standing, but the grass in the middle of the pentagram was stained with what instinct and experience told me was dried blood.

I carefully walked around the edge of the circle, looking for any indication the thing I'd been tracking had simply pounded through here and run on down the other side of the hill.

It hadn't, because there was nothing but an undisturbed sea of yellowed grass that swept down the hill to what looked to be a dry creek bed.

Whoever had summoned the demon had also sent it back to whatever hell it had come from.

Which was good but a little puzzling. I mean, why not simply leave it unleashed to cause havoc and keep us away from the fight, as Marie had tried with the basilisk? Did that mean she'd changed tactics after we'd dealt with her snake? Or that Marie wasn't responsible for the presence of *this* monster?

Once I'd returned to my starting point, I put the holy water back into my pack—though I kept the repelling spell twisting around my fingers, just in case—and rang Monty.

"I guess you found something," he said, by way of hello.

"A pentagram. Or, at least, the remains of one."

"Where?"

"In the paddock behind the house yard. You can't miss the trail."

"Be there in five."

He hung up. I tucked the phone away and squatted down, studying the stained area of flattened grass through narrowed eyes. While it was not unknown for dark sorcerers to use their own blood in a summoning spell—hell, we'd used Mom's up in Canberra to catch and question a demon —for the most part, an animal of some kind was used. The bigger the spell, the bigger the animal. When Marie had summoned the basilisk to cause chaos and distract us, she'd used a sheep, but there was nothing here to indicate any sort of sacrifice had been used. Not even feathers, and chickens were, for the most part, the animal used the most in summoning ceremonies.

At least, they were if the little I'd read about these things was true.

I rose and glanced around at the sound of movement. Aiden and Monty were striding up the hill, following my trail through the grass rather than the monster's. They stopped either side of me, Monty with his hands on his hips.

"Well," he said, after a minute, "that definitely looks like the remnants of a pentagram, even if we can't see any evidence of it other than those candles."

"Why would they leave the candles there if they've erased all other evidence?" Aiden had his phone in his hand, recording the scene as he spoke. "That's not usual behavior, is it?"

Monty grimaced. "Depends on the mage and what the intent of the circle is. In this case, it was probably used to summon and then dispatch our fisty demon."

"That still doesn't answer the question."

"It's possible she wanted us to find it," I said.

"Yeah, but which 'she'?" Monty glanced at me. "You've done a safety check?"

I nodded. "I haven't stepped inside yet, though."

"Caution from you?" Monty raised a hand and touched my forehead. "No temperature ..."

I laughed and smacked his hand away. "You're the reservation witch and the one with all the training. I figured that maybe you could sense or see something I can't."

"Yeah, we both know how unlikely that is." Monty

leaned past me to look at Aiden. "You finished? We safe to enter and trample all over the scene?"

Aiden half smiled. "Trample away."

Monty warily stepped into the crushed circle of grass and approached the nearest candle. He squatted down beside it, brushed his fingers across the flattened grass, then rubbed them together. "No indication of ash or chalk used to mark out the pentagram."

"Both of those might be practical on solid ground but not here," I said. "She could have used her athame or even her index finger to draw it in the air, calling out the five points and then activating them." It did take more time and energy, which was why most of us didn't do it, but maybe that wasn't such a problem for a blood mage.

"It's generally a process used more for personal pentagrams rather than ritual ones, though," Monty said.

"Which does not discount the possibility of it being done here."

"No, but I wouldn't have thought a pentagram created in such a manner would be overly safe in a demon-summoning situation." He rose and moved around the circle, examining the other candles, with the same result. "What about the blood? Have you done a reading of it?"

The ability to sometimes touch blood and gain information or "see" who or what it had belonged to was a recent mutation of my psychometry ability, and one I tended to avoid using unless absolutely necessary, if only because touching blood somehow sharpened the connection and ultimately made it more dangerous.

"No, I have not," I replied.

"Do you *want* to do a reading of it?"

"That would also be a very sensible no, but I will, as it may be our only way of getting any sort of information." I wrinkled my nose. "But don't get your hopes up. Given how dried it now is, it's likely too much time has already passed for me to gain anything useful."

"Still worth a try, because right now, we've got nothing else."

I'm back online came Belle's still somewhat weary comment. *I'll drag you back if anything untoward happens.*

Why the hell are you awake? You need more sleep.

I needed to pee more. Amusement ran down the line. *Never fear, I will stagger back to the bedroom once you're finished. Unless, of course, the blood leads to Maelle, and then I will grab a strong coffee to wake myself up, because we both know you will immediately go and talk to her.*

I'm doing that anyway. I need to know if any of the dead are her people. But Monty can come with me.

Monty won't be allowed inside, and we both know it.

Yes, but it won't hurt to have him there.

It wouldn't hurt to have Ashworth or Eli there, either.

Aside from being overkill, Maelle could see that as a threat. I drew in a deeper breath and then returned my attention to Monty. "Belle's awake."

"Ah, good. Well, good for this process; not so good for her."

"She promised to go back to sleep once we're done."

She did not.

I ignored her, stepped closer to the stain, and squatted down. It was only then that I spotted the small, yellow, coin-sized charm almost hidden by strands of bloody grass. I pointed at the thing. "What is that?"

"Don't know." He squatted opposite me and held out a hand, letting it hover an inch or so above the token. "There's a vague pulse of magic coming from it."

"A spell?"

"Not any kind that I've come across, but we are dealing with a dark mage, so that doesn't mean anything. It could be just residue from whatever spell was used."

"Why would a blood mage need to use a charm in a summoning ceremony?"

"You're asking me that like you expect me to know the answer." He glanced up at Aiden. "You want to take a photo before I examine the thing?"

Aiden stepped forward, took several photos from different angles, then squatted next to me. "There's some sort of image etched on the surface of it."

"There is?" I squinted at the thing, but between the grass half covering it and the blood smudged over a good portion of the visible surface, it was hard to see anything else. But his eyes were far sharper than either mine or Monty's.

"Yeah, though it's faint." He opened one of the photos and enlarged the image and showed us both. On the visible part of the charm—the section not covered by the grass—was a faint, partial figure of a man-like creature with dispro-portionately large fists.

"What that image means," Monty said, his voice grim, "is that this charm is a demon summoner. They're suppos-edly very rare, not only because the fuckers are extremely dangerous but because few people actually have the skill or the magical power to create them."

"Maelle and Marie would have both, I'm thinking," I said.

"Yes, but the question is, which one of them created this thing?"

"If there's magical residue sitting on the thing," Aiden commented, "it likely won't be safe for Liz to touch it and find out."

Monty wrinkled his nose. "Possible, but from the little I know of them, they're inert unless activated and generally are only one-use items. But I don't know enough about them to be certain."

"What about Ashworth or Eli?" I asked. "Is it worth contacting them?"

"I'll ring them while you check the blood." He immediately rose and stepped away to make the call.

I tugged off a glove, then, after checking Belle was ready, warily brushed a finger across several strands of blood-stained grass. Nothing stirred across the psychic lines. I frowned and pressed a section of bloody grass between two fingers, but the result was the same. As I'd suspected, too much time had passed to get any sort of sense of who or what might have shed this blood.

I hesitated, and then shifted my fingers, letting them drift across the grass covering the charm. Energy burned across my skin, the pulse so bright and powerful it rocked me backward. I would have landed on my ass had Aiden not moved with lightning speed and somehow steadied me.

"You okay?" he asked. I nodded and, after a slight hesitation, he released me and then added, "What the hell was that flash?"

"A warning not to touch the charm."

"Meaning it's *not* a one-off charm."

"Definitely not." I rubbed my fingers together. Though the flash hadn't burned me, a slight residue remained, and my psi senses stirred. While I couldn't be absolutely certain, that residue felt more like Maelle than Marie. Which might not mean anything, given one was the fledgling of the other, but still ... I glanced up as Monty came back. "Anything?"

"Yeah, they said not to touch the thing."

141

His voice was dry, and I gave him a lopsided smile. "Technically, I didn't."

"Technicalities often don't matter when dealing with this sort of shit. Ashworth's on his way with the appropriate tools to disarm it."

"Meaning he's come across them before?"

"Once, apparently. I described the image that appears on it, though, and he wasn't familiar with that type of demon. Eli's going to do a search to see what we might be dealing with."

I frowned. "We're not dealing with it, though. It was sent back to wherever it was summoned from."

"That's what we're presuming, but not necessarily the case."

"Huh." I pushed to my feet. "Did he say if he needed us all here? Because I have to go talk to Maelle."

"Is that really a good move?" Aiden said, rising with me. "If those are her people inside that house, she's going to be in a foul mood."

"I doubt her mood could get any fouler, given what is happening with Roger."

"Then wait for either Monty or Ashworth to go with—"

"Monty won't be allowed inside," I cut in. "And if she did decide to attack me in there, it'd take him too long to break through the magic protecting her place to be of any use."

"That's presuming I could break through in any meaningful amount of time," he said. "And to be honest, it's likely that she's ramped up the protections since we were last there. I suspect it'd take a concerted effort by all of us to break in. By the time we did, Maelle would be gone."

Aiden's frown deepened. "I still don't think it's a wise move."

I leaned toward him and dropped a kiss on his cheek. "Whatever else Maelle is, she's not a fool. She may want to taste the wild magic in my blood, but right now she needs me to help her eradicate Marie and her crew. She won't do anything until after this fight is done."

He grunted, not sounding in the least convinced. But he dragged his keys out of his pocket and held them out to me. "Let me know when you're going in and safely out."

"Will do. And I'm not going in there alone—Belle is with me mentally, remember."

"I remember."

And still wasn't comforted.

With a quick grin, I dropped another kiss on his cheek, then turned and headed back down the hill, climbing through the fence before making my way around to Aiden's truck. After carefully reversing out, I drove out of the property and back into town. Once at Maelle's, I parked the truck and then reached down for the pack, pulling the silk-wrapped ring from the side pocket and tucking it into my jean shorts. I might yet need to find Roger, but instinct was twitching, and I wasn't about to gainsay her.

As I climbed out of the truck, a soft but luminous glimmer caught my eye.

Wild magic. *Katie's* wild magic, rather than the older wellspring's. And it struck me then that I really hadn't seen many threads from her wellspring over the last few days, and that was extremely unusual given she was usually right on top of anything bad happening in the reservation.

I held out a hand, and it wrapped around my wrist. While it was totally possible for me to contact Katie—or vice versa—without using the wild magic, we both tended to default to its use simply because it eased the drain on our strength.

Everything okay? I asked.

The old wellspring's influence spreads. The Fenna have been in contact with me. Us.

I blinked, even as unease stirred. Not for me, not even for the reservation, but for her. She and Gabe had sacrificed everything to become the newer wellspring's guardians, and it would really suck if, in an effort to protect the O'Connor compound and my daughter, I'd jeopardized their position.

What did they want?

To judge me. To judge my ... suitability, I suppose.

They'd judged me, too, and while it now appeared I hadn't been totally rejected, I also hadn't been fully accepted. But Katie was in a totally different situation. She existed because of the wellspring—because her soul had been basically fused to it.

And?

And they offered to teach us to control and protect this place in the same manner as a full Fenna if I am willing to let you step into my spring.

If they're asking rather than demanding, that surely has to mean they can't break the hold you and Gabe have on the spring.

They never said that.

Well, they wouldn't, would they?

No came Gabe's comment, his tone deep and warm, *but in many respects, they didn't need to, as that was the implication of them seeking permission. Katie is this spring's protector, and I'm hers. She might not be Fenna, but our dual presence gives us Fenna-like control over our clearing. But while we can watch over the greater reservation, we have no means to protect it. That is what they offered to teach us.*

It would be brilliant if that were true, because it would definitely take some of the pressure from me, at least until my daughter was old enough to step into the position. Presuming, of course, that she *wanted* to step into it. Between my stubbornness and her father's alpha, often single-minded tendencies, it was always possible she'd refuse the life I'd committed her to. God only knew what would happen then, but I would back that choice if she made it. No matter what it might cost me.

Because there would be a cost. The Fenna might not be gods, but they were powerful, omniscient beings, and probably the closest we got to them these days. I rather suspected they would not appreciate a promise broken.

Did they say why they want me to step into your spring?

This spring is newer, fresher, and far less powerful than the main one, Gabe replied. *They said you cannot control the old, that you are too old, too untrained, and it would destroy you. But that would not be the case with ours, apparently.*

They also said, Katie added, *you will need every ounce of power you can muster if you wish to defeat that which infests this place.*

Oh, that was fucking good to know. *Would me stepping into your spring mean I usurp your position and become its defender?*

It hadn't with the older wellspring, but possibly only because they'd rejected me as unsuitable for all the reasons Gabe had mentioned, although at the time that hadn't really been clear. I'd just gotten stuck on the whole rejection point of it.

No, Katie said. *It will simply allow you to use this one in the same manner as you do the older, but without the immediate danger of being consumed.*

"Immediate" meaning it remained a threat if I overused it. I frowned. *But I can already call to your spring's power.*

Not to the same extent. That which entwines through your magic has mostly been old.

I leaned back against the truck and contemplated the building ahead, though I wasn't really seeing anything other than the multiple layering of bright magic that sparkled like a dark and dangerous rainbow in the heat of the day. That rainbow was definitely more intricate—more deadly looking —than it had been earlier.

Belle, what do you think?

Does it matter what either of us think? If you don't do it, the Fenna will throw another tanty.

I mentally snorted. *You can hardly call threatening to destroy the whole compound a mere tanty.*

Perhaps. Doesn't alter the truth of the comment, though.

Frustration and no small amount of angst stirred through me. While the thought of having the younger well-spring's power at my call—without fear of refusal or a personal physical cost—was undoubtedly tempting, I couldn't help but worry what it would mean for my daughter. I'd already bound her to one. Dare I risk further consequences—to her life, and to her freedom to choose what she wanted—by stepping into a second and possibly binding her to it? Because I suspected that's what might lie behind this request, even if it was couched as a means of helping me. *What's your feeling on the whole thing, Katie?*

I don't like what is gathering in this place. These vampires do not care for anything or anyone other than their own wants and desires. The killings will not stop no matter who wins their war. Their darkness will spread. I can see it, hear it, in the faint voices that rise from my wellspring.

Could the voices be telling you what you fear in order to get you to do what they want?

She hesitated. *That's possible, I guess.*

Gabe? Your thoughts?

I think we need to know more about the Fenna and their power before any further decisions are made, he said gravely. *For what it is worth, though, I do believe they intend to help you.*

I believed that too, but like he'd already said, we just didn't know enough about them to be certain we weren't causing future problems.

Tell them I'll think about it. I hesitated. *Tell them to talk to me if they want me to do this, not you.*

Katie's chuckle ran softly around me. *Oh, I pity my mother. Between you and Aiden, your child is going to have one hell of a wild and stubborn streak.*

That's presuming your mother is allowed to have anything to do with her, I said bluntly. *Right now, that's not looking good.*

When she sees your daughter, she will mellow. I promise you that.

I sniffed, unconvinced. Katie had been promising a change of heart almost since day one, and it still hadn't happened. As her threads unwound from my wrist and drifted away, I returned my attention to the club.

To see the doors open and Maelle standing inside the foyer, just beyond the creeping reach of sunshine.

CHAPTER SEVEN

For several minutes, neither of us moved. We simply stared at each other across the heated expanse of road tarmac. She was barely discernible from the shadows that surrounded her, but her eyes gleamed with a molten, silvery fire that boded no one any good.

I'm thinking she doesn't want you inside that club for a reason we really don't want to know about, Belle said.

And I'm thinking I sure as fuck don't want *to go inside that club, no matter what the reason.*

Belle snorted. *You really are on a roll today with this whole sensible thinking thing.*

Don't worry—I'll be back to my usual "fools rush in" modus operandi any moment now.

As her laughter rolled down our line, I checked for cars and then crossed the road, stopping again once I reached the pavement. Though there was a good eight feet between me and those open doors, the magic protecting her building was a dark wave that made my skin jump and tingle—and not in a pleasant way.

I crossed my arms, hiding my hands and the instinctive

press of inner wild magic at my fingertips. "I need to know, Maelle—were you responsible for the slaughter in that house up in Moonlight Flats?"

She smiled, revealing canines that we just a little longer than normal, which generally meant she'd just fed or she was anticipating a feed. Unhappily, instinct was suggesting that in this case, both might actually apply.

"What makes you think I had anything to do with that?" Though her tone was lightly amused, the molten gleam darkened.

It was not an amused sort of gleam.

"You mean aside from the summoning charm we found in the field next door that has the feel of your magic? Those murders have the thick taste of revenge." I somehow kept any sign of nervousness from my voice, though given she was a vampire and my heart beat rather erratically, it was a pretty pointless exercise.

"And my, it does indeed taste *so* good."

Which was confirmation enough for me. "What sort of creature did that charm summon, Maelle?"

A smile touched ruby red lips. She'd moved closer, I realized, though I hadn't actually seen her do so. Sunrays danced only millimeters away from her bare toes ... I blinked. She wasn't wearing boots. My gaze jumped upward. Or indeed clothes. She was naked and bloody, and there were bits of flesh and God only knew what else smeared ... My stomach heaved, and I looked away, swallowing unsteadily. I hadn't vomited earlier, and I would not do so now. Not in front of her.

This bitch really isn't running on a sane playing field anymore, is she? Belle said.

I think it's more that the combination of Roger's kidnapping and his subsequent leg loss has finally torn away the

149

thin veneer of civility. What we're seeing is the reality rather than the sophisticated projection.

"That was an Átahsaia," Maelle was saying, "a creature I am particularly fond of."

"I thought you were fond of snakes?"

"I have an affinity with them, yes." Her eyes gleamed. "But the Átahsaia? Ah, he is a grand one, a demon the likes of which is rarely seen."

My gaze skimmed the blood covering her torso, and I couldn't help but wonder if her "grand demon" had survived its recall. "Were the people killed Marie's? And isn't using such a demon overkill, given you were there with it and are more than magically capable of taking them all out?"

"I am not one to take chances, and I dare not overestimate my abilities when it comes to matters such as revenge, especially when it comes to a coven I am no longer a part of or indeed familiar with. Precautions are only sensible when you are unfamiliar with your foe's depth of skill. Where is Roger?"

I blinked at the abrupt change of topic and tone, the almost teasing lightness replaced by a deep and dangerous flatness. "Hard to say, given the ring you gave me was yours rather than his, and it wasn't his echo I was sensing. You led me to that place, Maelle, because you wanted me to kill your demon and unleash the tidal wave of his negative energy in the hope it would take out at least some of Marie's people. But she was one step ahead of you."

"I led you to that place because I truly believed he was *there*. I had no awareness that only a ... portion was." Her anger swelled, briefly burning the air. "You should not have banished my demon. The cost of that one action will be high."

For her, *and* for me. She didn't say that but that's exactly what she meant.

"It will indeed, especially if you don't start being honest with me, Maelle."

"So, you wish honesty?" She shifted again, her toes pressing against the streaks of sunlight invading her sanctuary. Her skin did not immediately burn, though a pale pink flush appeared at the tip of her big toe, and a glimmer of pleasure briefly danced through the dangerous glint in her eyes.

The woman was mad. Utterly mad.

And getting madder, if we're using the insane definition of the word rather than the angry, Belle growled. *Do not, under any circumstances, step closer. It would be just like that bitch to lunge forward, sun-be-damned, and attempt a sip.*

Trust me, I have absolutely no intentions of giving her any opportunity to take a bite.

Not now, not later.

Because there would be a later, I was sure of that. Even if we somehow saved Roger, I doubted his presence would calm her inner monster now that it had been fully unleashed.

"Do not believe Marie's silver tongue," she said in that same flat but chilling tone. "Do not believe that she will not harm you and yours. Do not believe that she will leave if she is the victor, and do not think this reservation will survive her celebrations if she does."

"Oh, I don't believe her any more than I believe you truly meant your vow not to harm anyone in this reservation."

"I vowed I would not feed on the unwilling or shed the

blood of those who lived and worked here. I have kept that vow."

"Perhaps to the letter of the vow but not the spirit. There's an entire fucking cavern of bodies to prove it."

"Those bodies were not from this reservation, and you are clever enough to have guessed that. And that means the reservation council cannot legally evict me, because I have harmed no one from *this* reservation."

A big fat "yet" seemed to hang over that declaration. "Aside from the fact no court of law will uphold your contracts, given the circumstances, you fucking murdered dozens of people. Since when has that ever been acceptable?"

Her smile was ... well, freaking scary. "It is not murder if they wish the death."

"And it's not a wish if it's enforced by magic. Besides, there was no magic in that place. You simply tore them apart and swam in their misery, their pain, and their remains."

"Perhaps that is so, but neither you nor your wolf can prove that I am responsible. And we both know the reservation's council would not want this matter to reach the courts. The publicity alone would make this place a tourist ghost zone."

Her toes, I noticed, hung further into the sunshine and her canines were now protruding. She wanted to feed. Badly. I clenched my fists against the wild magic aching for release, but was nevertheless comforted by its presence. If she lunged, it would shield me. However much stronger she was than me magically, she would not get through such a shield. Not before the sun crisped her flesh and the gentle breeze blew away her ashes, anyway.

"Of course," she continued, "legalities will not prevent

them attempting to evict me physically or perhaps even magically, but there are few here, beyond yourself, who would in fact have any hope of besting me. And it would certainly be an interesting and desirable experience for us both if you did indeed try."

A tremor ran through my soul.

Maelle didn't just want to taste the power in my blood. She wanted *me*. Sexually.

Never fear, Belle said. *I'll fry her brains out if she so much as lays a finger on your lady bits.*

A laugh bubbled through me. I somehow managed to keep it in, but the tension that had been gathering eased a fraction.

"Jaqueline told me that you've always known how to find Roger—that your connection to him makes it impossible for you not to know. Is that true?"

She considered me for a moment. "To some degree."

"Then why haven't you simply gone and gotten him?"

"That is an inane question and one that is beneath us both."

Bitch, Belle muttered.

Yeah. But I guess the answer is *obvious.* Because he was both bait and a trap. She'd much rather I spring it than her.

"Then why go through the rigmarole of handing me the ring when you could have just given me directions?" I paused, realization finally dawning. "Or was the ring a means of keeping track of me?"

Her too-toothy smile flashed. Instinct was right again.

I took the silk-wrapped ring from my pocket and tossed it at her. It hit the ground several feet my side of the doorway, and the ring rolled free of its wrapping, scurrying toward her like it had a life of its own. She bent and picked it up, her fingers briefly caressed by sunlight. Again, there was little reaction from her skin and nothing but the flick of pleasure through her eyes.

I shivered. "You need to tell me where he is now, Maelle, and stop playing these games."

It was an effort to keep the internal anger from my voice when I wanted to do nothing more than scream at the mad bitch.

"It is not that simple, Elizabeth. The white ash embedded in flesh diminishes our connection."

Hence her creeping insanity. "That didn't stop you knowing he was in that cavern."

"I am familiar enough with that cavern to recognize it even with the briefest glimpses through his eyes."

"Then what are you getting from him now?"

"He lies in darkness, on dirt, and he is ringed by magic. I cannot say whether it is a house or a shed of some kind because his eyes have been bound and I cannot see through them. I suspect the latter, however, because I have a sense of restriction rather than space." She paused briefly, her gaze inward-looking, her eyes unsettling slits of silver. "Something scrapes across its roof, though it does not feel close. Trees, I think."

"Anything else?"

"He is within town, I believe. I can hear traffic and dogs barking excitedly. There are at least eight animals, and they are not close, perhaps across the road."

A dog park? Belle asked.

Either that, or absolutely every dog in that area has gone off at the same time. To Maelle, I added, "Are there any voices? Dog owners shouting at their pets or something?"

"No." She paused. "Some of the dogs are terriers from the sound of it. Their blood, I must say, is surprisingly sweet."

Well, fuck, Belle said, *like we needed to know that.*

She's trying to unsettle us.

She's succeeding. Can't see the purpose of it, though.

Hesitation at a vital moment. Like her lunging at me. My gaze automatically dropped. Her toes remained past the edge of that sunlit line, and while her skin was definitely redder, it wasn't burning up like the vampire who'd met his demise on the café's rear steps. Was the dark wave of magic somehow protecting her? Or did vampires gain some sort of immunity as the centuries rolled by?

If the latter is true, then that might mean this bitch can move about in daylight without major protection.

If she can, then Marie and Jaqueline probably can, too.

What a thought. I might hunt through our index of Gran's books and see if she has anything on the subject.

Worth a shot. I returned my attention to Maelle. "Can you feel the magic that's protecting him?"

"Yes."

"And?"

"And do have fun dismantling it." She paused. "And do watch your back. Marie has a habit of layering and disguising trigger spells into her protective ones. Hitting one might summon something nasty into your presence. Bring Roger here when you free him."

And with that, she stepped back into the shadows and disappeared. A heartbeat later, the doors slammed shut, the sound ringing loudly across the hum of traffic behind me. I stared at the club for several more seconds, then swore softly and retreated across the road.

The truck's seats were hot despite the fact it hadn't been sitting there for very long, so I reached back and grabbed a sweater from the back seat to sit on. Bare legs and black leather were not a good combination in summer.

I started the truck up, did a U-turn once there was a gap in the traffic, and headed back to the café. Belle was upstairs and had a pot of my favorite green tea and a large slab of banana cake waiting for me when I arrived. There was also a half-finished revitalization potion sitting nearby on the coffee table and a laptop sitting next to it.

"You're a doll." I tossed Aiden's keys onto my bed, then walked over to pour myself a cup of tea. The sweet scent of melon and jasmine teased my nostrils, and I sighed happily. The only thing better than this stuff was chocolate. And cake. And possibly bacon ... I shook my head. It seemed that no matter how many atrocities I stumbled across or how bad the bloodshed, my touchy stomach wasn't about to let them get in the way of food.

I took a drink and then added, "Did you run down any leads on vamps and sunshine?"

She wrinkled her nose. "There's one book that apparently discusses myths and facts regarding vampires, but it's at the storage unit rather than here or at Monty's."

"Why didn't we find that one when we had our first vampire problem?"

She snorted. "You've seen Gran's index, haven't you?"

I grinned. "Meaning it wasn't actually listed."

"No, it was not. We caught it when we were doing the redo, though it's not been scanned yet."

"We" being her and Kash, the rather delicious-looking man we'd hired to help us convert Nell's books into digital format, and who'd turned out to be a bit of a bastard. "You heard anything from Monty?"

"He rang about ten minutes ago to say he and Ashworth were finished and were on their way here." She paused, her expression going inward as she reached out mentally.

"They're just parking out the back now, so will be here in a couple of secs."

"It didn't take them very long to take care of the charm, then."

"No, because the thing disintegrated just as Ashworth arrived."

My eyebrows shot up. "It *disintegrated?*"

"Yeah, and from what I could gather, that happened just after you and Maelle began talking."

"She deliberately destroyed it."

"Or destroyed the monster attached to it."

I remembered all the blood and gore covering Maelle and shuddered. If she'd swum in her monster's remains, well, she was further out on the insanity limb than we'd thought. And that meant we needed to find Roger before the disintegration could get any worse.

I scooped up more cake, then reached for my phone and did a search for dog parks. There was one, according to Google, and it was only a few minutes away from here. I flipped the phone around and slid it across the table to Belle. "If your guess is right and the barking was coming from a dog park, then it's possible he's located somewhere near this one."

"Finding him will be the problem. We can hardly go knocking door to door asking if they're harboring a vampire's one-legged thrall."

"Not unless we want to cause the wave of panic the council is trying to avoid," I replied dryly.

"It might be the one way to save more people getting dead, though."

"The only way of doing that," Monty said as he bounded up the last of the stairs, "is to get rid of all the damn vampires."

"Easier said than done when we can't find hide nor hair of one lot." Belle motioned toward the small kitchenette. "Kettle's boiled, and there's cake in the fridge."

"Excellent." He glanced around as Ashworth appeared. "Something to drink? Eat?"

"A coffee would be grand." Ashworth continued on to the patio doors, opened them up, and dragged two of the plastic outside chairs back in. "So, what's this about dog parks?"

I quickly explained the conversation I'd had with Maelle about Roger's location. "Given the dirt floor, I'm thinking we're probably dealing with some sort of shed at the back of a house."

"The house would have to be empty, though, surely? They couldn't risk the owners randomly walking in and discovering him." Monty handed Ashworth his coffee, placed a second mug on the table, then headed back to collect his cake.

"She did say he was well protected with spells," Belle said. "It's possible one of those is a redirect."

"Redirects are notoriously unreliable," Ashworth said. "I think the bigger worry is the summoning spells interwoven through the protection ones. If Maelle mentioned them, you can bet your ass they exist."

"Which is why I think we need all witches on hand," I said. "Two of us can dismantle, and three can guard our backs."

Ashworth nodded. "It'd also be wise to grab Aiden or at least one of his people, so they can evacuate the house if it's not empty."

"I'll call him—"

"He likely won't answer," Monty cut in. "He muttered

something about having to report to the council. Ring the station instead."

I did so and got Jaz. I explained our situation and what we needed, and she agreed to meet us in twenty minutes. Which at least left time for both Monty and me to finish our cakes.

Once Ashworth got off the phone to Eli, I asked, "What do you know about vampires and sunshine?"

"Aside from the fact it ashes them, you mean? There's a theory in some quarters that the very old do gain some immunity from it, but I've encountered no evidence that supports it." His expression was speculative. "Why?"

"Maelle stuck her toes and fingers into sunlight, and she did not go up in flames. Her skin barely even turned pink."

"Like we haven't already got enough fucking problems," Monty muttered.

"'Barely' means her toes *did* turn pink, laddie, and that suggests she isn't immune, just ... resilient." Ashworth's gaze returned to mine. "Or was she perhaps using some sort of magical shield to ward off the worst of the effects?"

I wrinkled my nose. "She could have been, but it was hard to tell because the whole building was wrapped in protection spells, and all of them were stained with darkness."

"Is it possible she was merely trying to scare you?"

"She was achieving that well before her toes decided they needed to sunbathe."

He shook his head. "Then I'll add it to the ever-increasing list of things we need to research."

"Perhaps jump it to the top of the list," Monty said, "because if Maelle is resilient, you can bet the other two will be as well."

Ashworth nodded, then drained his coffee and rose. "I'll go pick Eli up and meet you at the park."

As he left, Monty asked, "What about the demon? Did you ask her about that?"

"I did, and she said it was a grand beastie she was quite fond of." A smile twitched my lips. "Given she was naked and covered in gore when I questioned her, I'm not sure if she meant that in a rhetorical, 'I just loved swimming in its remains' manner or not."

Monty just about choked on his cake. "God, things just go from bad to worse."

"Well, look on the bright side," Belle said dryly. "If she did swim in its remains, then it's one less monster we have to worry about."

"I'd like to think so, but given she wasn't letting you into that club and she was naked, maybe swimming wasn't all she was doing with it."

"Eew," I said, and tossed my spoon at him.

He laughed, caught it, and dropped it back onto the table. "We should get going. We can scout the area out a little before the others arrive."

I picked up the teapot and rose, transferring the remainder of the drink into a travel cup, then sent a message to Aiden telling him his truck was at the back of the café and the keys in my room. After grabbing my pack, I followed Belle and Monty out and jumped into the back of the SUV.

Monty reversed out of the parking spot and drove toward the dog park, Belle giving him directions via Google Maps on her phone. Monty's old station wagon came from the era that had cassette players rather than Bluetooth and GPS—and, like many other things in his car, said cassette player did not work.

It only took five minutes to reach the park. Monty swung into McGrath Street, then parked under one of the old trees that ran along the verge on the right. I took a final sip of tea, then tucked it into the middle console for safe-keeping and climbed out, swinging my pack over my shoulders. A couple of dogs were barking in the park behind the trees, though the thick greenery lining the dividing fence made it impossible to see what they were. They did sound like yappy little terriers, though.

"According to Google's satellite map," Belle said, studying her phone's screen, "all the houses in this area have some kind of shed."

I wrinkled my nose and glanced at the house directly opposite. Like many of the houses in the street, it was an older-style brick building that wasn't overly large, and the shed—which I could see from where I stood—was the type that stored tools. It would barely be big enough to stand upright with your arms outstretched in let alone lie on the ground pinned by stakes.

"We're after something larger than a common garden shed," Monty said, moving around the car and stopping beside us. "We're probably looking more at a garage-style one."

"I'm not seeing anything like that here." She paused, moving her fingers over the image, enlarging one area. "There is, however, an old house back on the main road, with a factory on one side and the dog park right behind it. There are a couple of outbuildings to one side of it that might fit the bill."

"We might as well check it out from the safety of the footpath, before the others get here," Monty said, and grandly waved us forward. "The ladies with all the appropriate skills should go first."

I left the shade of the tree and wished almost instantly I'd thought to bring a hat. It was damnably hot, even though we were barely past lunchtime. As we reached the end of the street, Ashworth arrived and swung in behind us, parking illegally on the footpath.

"Discovered anything yet?" he asked as he and Eli caught up with us. He was very sensibly wearing a floppy toweling hat, though it had very definitely seen better days. Rather like his rock 'n' roll T-shirt and grungy jeans, really.

"No, but there's what looks to be an abandoned house round the corner that holds possibilities," Monty replied.

"An abandoned house is a more likely holding cell than a shed in someone's yard, no matter what our resident vampire might be sensing through her creature," Eli said. He was a tall, well-built, and very handsome man in his late sixties, with thick salt-and-pepper hair and bright blue eyes. And, unlike his husband, was impeccably dressed even if he was only wearing cargo shorts and a short-sleeved shirt.

"He's pinned to dirt though," I said. "That suggests he's not in the house."

"Unless the house has no floors," Belle said. "Or perhaps he's simply been shoved under them. That would also explain her sense of restricted space."

"Possible." The sound of an approaching siren had me looking around. A ranger vehicle raced toward us. "That'll be Jaz."

We stopped near the old house's gate, and she swung in beside us, braking hard enough to send dust flying. She bounced out of the SUV, her grin wide. "Sorry for the noise, but the traffic wouldn't get out of my way fast enough without it."

"And besides that, you like going fast with all sirens blazing," I said, voice dry.

"There is that." She stopped beside me and studied the old house, her golden eyes bright in the sunshine. "That's the Hargraves' place. The old girl who owns it was moved into aged care some ten years ago but refused to sell the place. Insisted her son still lives there."

"And does he?" Monty asked.

Jaz shook her head. "He died fifteen years ago. Before my time, but apparently he was cleaning the roof, slipped off, and broke his neck." She sniffed and glanced pointedly at Ashworth "Older men and ladders are never a good combination, in my limited experience."

"Glad I'm not the only one who was casting him a disapproving eye," Eli said, his tone also dry.

"Hey," Ashworth said, raising his hands. "I had all the magical protections necessary, so was never in danger. Now, is anyone sensing anything untoward around that house?"

"Yeah," Belle said, "the old lady was right. Her son *is* living here."

Monty's gaze shot toward her. "We've got a ghost?"

"Indeed." She frowned. "A very pissed-off one, too."

"Because he's dead?" Eli asked. "Or because his mother no longer lives there?"

"Neither. He's been blocked from the house."

"By magic?" I studied the building with a frown. "Because I'm not sensing anything."

"Not magic." She wrinkled her nose. "It's a physical barrier of some kind, from what he's saying."

"What sort of physical barrier can block a ghost?" Jaz asked, her expression confused.

"Salt is most commonly used," Eli said. "But iron is also a well-known deterrent. It's also said that cat's eye shells can block them, though they're more commonly used in Europe and the Middle East for protection against the evil eye."

"The things you learn," Jaz muttered, amusement obvious.

I smiled and glanced at Belle. "Can you ask him if anyone has been going in and out of the building?"

She hesitated. "He hasn't seen anyone, but he's heard some activity both in the house and in the sheds."

"Has he been in the sheds?" I asked.

"No, because apparently they're full of snakes and he hates snakes."

Monty snorted. "He's a ghost. The bastards aren't likely to see him, let alone bite him."

"Becoming a ghost doesn't mean you lose all your pre-ghost prejudices and fears," Belle said dryly. "It just means you can't be hurt by them."

"Perhaps we should briefly split up," Ashworth said. "Eli and I will check the sheds, you three do a walk around the house."

"If you're opening and entering the sheds, I'll come with you to record it," Jaz said.

Ashworth nodded and the three of them headed through the broken gate and around to the left. We went straight on, following the rutted stony path toward the old truck parked at the end of the drive. It had a decided lean on it, suggesting the tires and possibly even the springs on the driver's side had gone. It was also covered in bird crap, cobwebs, and dirt. I suspected the last person to drive it was the man who now haunted the place.

The house itself was an old miners' cottage with a rectangular section built onto the back that jutted out an extra ten feet from the end of the main house. The red tin roof on the original part had partially collapsed, but all the windows remained intact and there was no graffiti to be seen anywhere, which was unusual in this day and age.

Maybe our ghost kept both taggers and vandals away. Fifteen years was certainly long enough for a more determined spirit to gain some skill in interacting with this world, even if it was nothing more than unleashing a moan or shifting random bits of furniture.

We moved around to the back of the building. A covered veranda ran its length, with two smallish square windows sitting either side of a wooden door. Monty jumped up onto the veranda, the wood under his feet bending alarmingly as he walked over and checked the door. The handle turned, but the door itself didn't budge.

"According to our ghost," Belle said, "there's a metal bar jamming it from the inside."

"Explains why it isn't moving and why he can't pass through it." He walked over to the nearest window and cupped a hand against the glass to peer in. "There's salt on the windowsill and along the base of the external walls."

"No surprise, though it doesn't explain why he can't get in through the roof," I commented.

"It's probably corrugated iron." Monty checked the other window, then turned and headed down the other end. "These days, it's usually powder-coated steel."

He checked the final two windows, then jumped off the patio and continued around the building. When we neared the end of the building, my senses burned to life and the faintest wave of agony rolled over me but just as quickly disappeared. I stopped. "Unless there's someone else being pinned by ash stakes that we don't know about, then he's here."

Monty swung around. "You can't tell if it's him or not? Isn't that unusual given you've Maelle's ring and have some sense of his—or at least—Maelle's emotional and psychic energy?"

"I'm afraid I threw the ring back at her."

"Why? I mean, I could understand throwing a pointy ash stake or holy water, but that ring—"

"Was being used to track our movements."

"Ah."

"Yeah." I motioned toward the house. "As for the wave, I didn't have time to examine it—it simply hit and then disappeared."

"Did you have a chance to pin a location at all?"

"It was close, but more under the house than in." I squatted down, peering through the gaps between the boards screening the house's stumps. Despite the brightness of the day, it was as dark as hades under the house. I tugged my phone from my pocket, flicked on the flashlight app, and shone it through. The light hit an impregnable wall of darkness three feet in. "Whatever—whoever's—emotions I sensed, they're lying behind those shadows."

Monty squatted beside me and studied the shadow wall. "And they are definitely caused by magic. It's just of a frequency so low it wouldn't register along regular sensory lines unless you're close. I suspect the threads are also dark, so wouldn't stand out against the shadows."

"All of which would no doubt take some serious magical nous," Belle said.

Monty rose and walked around to the front of the original section of the house. It was smaller than the extension, with only one window on either side of the old wooden door. He stopped abruptly at the halfway point between the house's end and the steps and squatted again. "There's something here—a pin of some sort."

"A pin?" I squatted beside him, my hand briefly brushing the ground to balance. In that instant, a thick wave of emotion rolled through me, singeing my senses and sucking the breath from my lungs. I jerked my fingers away, and instantly the wave stopped. I hesitated, then warily ran my fingers across the dirt. Emotion chased after the move-ment—and so too did power.

The wild magic.

It was here, in the ground, responding to my touch and somehow enhancing my ability to see and feel past that dark veil.

Or perhaps, Belle said, *it's the Fenna doing what they can to help you stop the stain of darkness pressing into the ground and subsequently them.*

Maybe. I'd certainly formed a direct connection with the earth's power before by being barefoot, but this was the first time it had happened by merely brushing my fingers across it. And it made me wonder if, perhaps, it was a more direct way to converse with the Fenna—*not* that I was going to attempt that here, with all that emotion building up behind the shadow wall.

I ran my fingers across the ground a third time, this time asking what lay beyond the shadows ahead. The whispers rose, speaking of foulness pinned to the earth and blood staining.

"And just what might you and Belle be silently discussing?" Monty asked, breaking my concentration and making me jump.

"Sorry, I was just caught off guard by another surge of emotion." I lightly touched his arm. "What is a pin?"

"Nice redirect, but I'll play along. It's generally a single spell stone that is used as an anchor point for minor spells like the shadow wall we're seeing."

I frowned. "Why would a shadow wall spell need an anchor point? Spells like that usually don't."

"Pins are generally used in enclosed spaces and tend to

make the spells harder for passing witches to spot." He waved a hand toward the house. "Case in point."

"I wouldn't call under the house an enclosed space, though," Belle said, then cocked her head sideways, obviously listening to our ghost. "And I would be wrong. There's an old root cellar positioned just behind that shadow wall."

"Is a root cellar any different to a regular cellar?" I asked.

"Only in that they're generally roughly constructed from earth, and used for storage of vegetables, fruits, nuts, or other foods," Ashworth said as he, Eli, and Jaz came around the corner. "They weren't used much here in Australia, though. They're more an English and American thing. I take it you've found one?"

"Our ghost confirms its presence," Belle said.

"And so does the wild magic," I said." Or rather, our Fenna whisperers."

Eli squatted beside us. "Have you tried taking out that pin? It should dismantle the shadows."

"Having only read about pins rather than having dealt with them, no I have not," Monty said, then added with a grin, "Thought it best to wait for the more ancient members of this investigative team to dispense their wisdom."

"That would be Eli you're talking about, then," Ashworth said, with a grin at his partner.

"Oh, he definitely was." Eli's voice was droll. "He did, after all, mention wisdom."

"Rather than simply knocking the pin out of alignment," I said, rolling my eyes at the two of them, "can you retrieve it? I might be able to track the current location of whoever it belongs to."

"The last time you tried that," Ashworth commented,

"Jaqueline attacked you through the connection and then set the basilisk after us."

"She caught me unawares that time." I squinted up at him. "And this might be our only chance to ferret out the location of Marie and her crew."

"Of which there are now far less, thanks to Maelle's actions," Monty said.

"Indeed, but that's likely to have only made them angrier, laddie."

"And an angry vampire might be more prone to make a mistake," Monty replied. "Right now, we've nothing much else to work with."

Ashworth made an "indeed" sort of movement with his hand, and Eli got down to business. After studying the shadow wall through narrowed eyes for a moment, he rose and moved closer to the front stairs. Squatting once again, he started to spell. Magic rolled around his fingers, forming a glittering thread of ever-increasing length. Then, with a short, sharp flick of his fingers, he sent the thread whipping through the baseboards into the darkness. There was a brief flash of purplish light, then the shadows fell away, revealing a solid wall of stone around five feet in length that ran from the ground to the floor joists.

A heartbeat later, the whip curled back and dropped a rounded black stone into Eli's hand. Even from where I was, I could feel the residual pulse of darker magics emanating from it, but I had no idea whether it belonged to Jaqueline or Marie.

"Well," he said, "the stone certainly has the deep stain of blood magic on it, but I'm not sensing anything active."

"It's still worth trying to maintain the pulse that remains," Monty said.

Eli nodded in agreement, wrapped the stone in a

protective spell, then glanced up at Jaz. "You got a glove on you?"

"I do indeed," she replied, handing him one. "It might be an idea if I held it while you lot concentrate on whatever else lies under the house."

"*That* appears to be a stone wall built between joists," Monty said.

"According to our ghost, that's a stairwell link between the house and the cellar," Belle said.

I glanced up at the building. "So, we're looking at the kitchen? At the front of the house?"

"Given the positioning of the wall," Eli said, "I think it more likely we have a small living or bedroom at the front, then the cellar stairs—which usually have their own entrance—and then the kitchen at the back."

He rose, jumped up onto the steps, and walked across to the door.

"He also says there's another iron bar across the door," Belle said.

"Easy enough to deal with." He pressed his fingers against the door, and his magic rose again. After a brief moment, there was a heavy thump. Eli twisted the handle and opened the door. Air brushed past me. Our ghost, rushing back into his home.

He's missing his favorite soap, Belle said, her amusement running down the mental lines. *Which is, in case you're curious,* The Young and the Restless.

Meaning his mom or whoever handles her legal affairs must have ensured electricity remains connected to at least the TV room. But the bigger question is, how on earth is that soapy still running after all these years?

Belle's amusement increased. *There's a surprising number of people who love that show. Apparently, he got hooked when he brought lunch home for himself and his mom. They used to sit down to watch it together, and it's a ritual he likes to continue now that she's not here.*

That's lovely.

He's a lovely ghost. He was just angry at being locked out. She waved a hand. *I promised we'd break the salt lines so he can move around freely.*

Nice idea. I followed Monty up the steps and, after Jaz had taken the required photos, we warily stepped through the door. The TV room door was closed—our ghost obviously wanted privacy to watch his show—but the door to our left was open. The room was empty aside from the framework of a dismantled bed leaning against the outer wall.

Eli and Monty had stopped at the next door along, which was open. The scent drifting past spoke of musty darkness, dank earth, and blood. I had my shields locked down tight, but could still feel the distant caress of agony.

"The cellar is practically writhing with protection spells," Monty said, his expression grim. "It's going to take us fucking ages to break them."

I stopped and peered past his arm. Steep wooden steps led into a deeper darkness lit by a thick, twisting mess of spell threads that glowed either a deep purple or ghastly green, two colors synonymous with darker spells.

"Those spells aren't covering the stairs," I noted. "I'll climb down—"

"I'm thinking that's probably a bad idea," Ashworth said from behind me. "Just because we can't see any triggers on the stairs doesn't mean they're not there."

"But if I'm touching the earth, it will warn me about them."

Eli glanced at me, eyebrows raised. "Is this a recent

development? Because it's not something that's happened before, is it?"

I hesitated. "I've certainly used the earth to find someone before. I just didn't really understand the reason for the connection."

"What you're about to do sounds more a direct interaction, though."

"Because the Fenna want Roger and the stain of his blood gone from the earth, so they've decided to help me."

"The book hasn't mentioned that as a possibility. Not so far, anyway."

"It didn't mention the wellspring's source being the cumulus of past Fenna souls either, so maybe whoever wrote the book didn't know about it."

"Possible." He studied the darkness for a second. "It still might be best to test the waters first, so to speak, and send something else down those stairs."

"That won't help if the triggers are set to react to flesh," Monty said. "Besides, if there's something lurking we can't see, it'll just give them warning we're on our way."

"Laddie, if there's something lurking, then its already aware we're here," Ashworth said. "We haven't exactly been quiet."

"Besides," I said, taking off my pack and handing it to Monty. "If we start worrying about everything we can't see, we'll get nowhere fast."

"And the 'fools rush in' mode of operation returns with a bang," Belle said dryly.

"Yeah, but that doesn't alter the fact I'm the best choice to do this. I have both my inner wild magic and the wilder stuff looking out for me. Everyone else here does not."

"I'm not arguing. I'm just pointing out a fact."

"And the fact is, she's going anyway," Monty added.

I grinned and stepped down. The wood bowed under my weight. I froze, but there was no indication it was about to give way. I took another step, then placed one hand on the stone and earth wall and created a repel spell around the other, just in case.

The whisperers stirred and then fell silent. Other than expressing a desire that I hurry up, they obviously had nothing else to say. I continued on warily, moving past the stone wall and into the actual ground, but the whisperers remained silent, and the only magic that burned my senses was the tumultuous swirl of threads that lay to the right of the bottom step.

I paused on the final step and scanned the earth. I couldn't see anything that suggested there was any sort of trap—magical or otherwise—and the air was still and dank. The thick weave of magic to my right flickered briefly as I stepped down, but otherwise, didn't react. This close, it was possible to see past the ribbons of darkness, though the figure lying a few feet beyond the barrier was little more than a ghostly shadow. A shadow missing the bottom part of his right leg.

Unless Marie had decided to amputate someone else's leg for the sheer hell of it—and right now, I wouldn't put anything past her—it had to be Roger.

He wasn't moving. Wasn't breathing. Not that I could see, anyway. But then, as Belle had noted, he was a thrall and probably didn't really need to.

I glanced up and gave the all clear. Monty immediately clattered down, followed by Ashworth.

"There's definitely a number of trigger points built into those protective layers," he said after a moment. "And given their weight, I suspect we wouldn't be dealing with a lesser demon."

"No surprise, given Roger isn't just bait but a means of weakening Maelle," Monty said. He squatted down and motioned toward the ground. "The spells don't cover the earth. Maybe we—or rather, Lizzie—can use that to our advantage."

"How? It's not like we can tunnel—" I stopped. We might not be able to—not without the right equipment and the possibility of destroying a good portion of our ghost's house—but maybe the wild magic could.

"Exactly," Monty said, obviously guessing where my thoughts had leapt. "If the wild magic intended to consume the entire damn O'Connor compound, that surely means it can shift a few meters of dirt and create a tunnel for us to drag Roger out."

"It would certainly be one way of skirting the protections," Ashworth said. "If—and that's a big if—they haven't countered the possibility. They're obviously aware of Liz's ability to use the wild magic."

"In her spells, yes, but why would they suspect she can use it to manipulate the earth itself?" Monty countered.

"Right now, we dare not discount *any* possibility."

"Rather than us standing here arguing, let's just ask." I bent and pressed a hand against the ground. Power spun about my fingertips and the whispers immediately started, once again urging me to remove the stain on the earth. I cut through the noise and asked the question. There was a brief moment of silence, then they started again. Giving directions—orders.

As I withdrew my touch, another pulse ran through the dark weave of magic, and concern stirred. I frowned and wondered if it was a warning. We hadn't touched the magic as yet, but that didn't mean it wasn't primed to react to proximity.

"Anything?" Monty asked.

I jumped a little and glanced up. "They'll help, but have warned the ground here has become unstable thanks to the press of the magic and blood, and they cannot guarantee it will not collapse and take out some of the anchors."

"We have to at least try," Monty said. "There's no guarantee that us attempting to dismantle the weave won't set something nasty off anyway."

"Might be wise if you—" I stopped and tilted my head to one side. A high-pitched, almost inaudible whining had just started, and it rather oddly seemed to be coming from the deeply threaded spell mass ahead *and* from somewhere beyond the house. "Do you hear that?"

Ashworth frowned. "Hear what?"

"I do," Jaz said. "There's a soft whine coming from the cellar and a louder response from somewhere outside."

Another flicker ran through the tightly woven threads, a gentle pulse that suddenly reminded me of a beacon.

Oh, *fuck* ...

"If there's something here making a noise that's beyond regular human hearing," Monty was saying, "I'm thinking it's not going to be a good thing. Maybe we should err on the side of caution and just—"

"Out," I cut in abruptly. "Everyone get out of this house. *Now*."

No one argued. They just turned and ran. I bolted up the stairs after Monty, my heart beating a million miles a minute as the high-pitched whine grew closer, stronger, fiercer.

The protective net around Roger—or rather, the pulse running *through* the net—was calling to whatever the hell was speeding toward us.

And we'd set that beacon off when we'd flicked aside the shadow pin.

Fear lent my feet wings. I leapt over the final couple of steps, grabbed the doorframe to steady myself as I spun around the corner, and then bolted for the front door.

But the magic below was stirring, the whine now accompanied by a wave of magic that was much deeper and darker in intent.

Jaz leapt from the front door, clearing both the veranda and the steps. Belle, Ashworth, and Eli followed her through, racing down the steps and then on toward the front gate.

The whine was now so fierce it hurt my ears, the magic below stirring with enough force that it was shaking the house. Boards cracked under my feet, and I swore, reaching for more speed, racing down a hall that now seemed impossibly long.

But it wasn't the hall.

It was me.

I was slowing. The thick waves rolling up from below were somehow snaring me, making it feel like I was running through glue. Magic flared within me but before I could react, Monty spun, tore the pack from his back, and drew his silver knife. Then he threw it, as hard as he could, into the floorboards. The magic recoiled, and I stumbled forward briefly. Monty caught my hand, and as one, we raced through the door and leapt off the veranda.

Just as the whine reached its peak and the goddamn house exploded.

CHAPTER EIGHT

The force of the explosion tore Monty's hand from mine and sent us both flying through the air. I hit the ground with a grunt and slid forward several feet. I swore, but nevertheless twisted around to see what had happened. The front corner of the house—the section containing the smaller bedroom and the stairwell down into the cellar—no longer existed. There wasn't even the skeletal remains of joists or wall, though, rather weirdly, the roof remained intact. The stumps supporting that section of the house were also gone, as was the stone wall link. In their place was a crater.

Fuck—Roger.

I scrambled upright just as Ashworth and Eli reached me. "I'm fine."

"You're bleeding," Ashworth said, "so that's obviously not true."

I glanced down and saw that I'd skinned not only my palms but also my knees—the latter fairly badly. I accepted Eli's offer of a handkerchief and wiped away the worst of the grit. It hurt, but it could have been far worse—*would* have been far worse—had Monty not thrown that knife and saved my ass.

I motioned toward the house. "Where the hell is Roger?"

The two men studied the remains, their expressions grim. "Well," Ashworth said, "if he *was* in that cellar, we'll probably find bits of him scattered all about the yard."

"Why would Marie kill him like that, though, when him being alive and slowly draining Maelle of strength plays to their benefit?"

"I would think the explosion was aimed more at you than Roger, given only you and Jaz even heard the incoming spell," Eli said. "They gave you just enough time to get out."

"Um, no, they didn't," Monty said, returning my rather beaten-up pack to me. "The magic in the cellar was somehow thickening the air and slowing her movements."

"And I'm only standing here thanks to my clever cousin's quick thinking."

"I can do quick when the occasion calls for it," he said with a grin.

Belle dropped a kiss onto his cheek. "From the bottom of both my heart and hers, we thank you."

His eyes twinkled devilishly. "You can thank me in a more appropriate manner later."

"Now that Monty has his evening activities booked," Jaz said, her tone dry, "is it safe to approach that house and examine what's been done? Or is our ghost going to retaliate, given what's happened?"

Belle's gaze went to the house and after a moment she said, "He's pissed about the destruction but he can still watch his show, so he's not going to lash out at us."

"Well, I'm glad he's not been put out at all." Jaz's

expression was amused. "Though how on earth did the explosion not affect the wiring?"

"Apparently his mom had things rejigged when she went into the nursing home so that the electricity is only connected to the front room," Belle replied. "She didn't want to risk kids or mice causing damage in the disused portions of the house and causing an electrical fire."

"Sensible mom," Jaz said. "What about the magic?"

I scanned the broken remnants of the house. "I'm not feeling anything. Anyone else?"

"There's a bit of broken thread floss floating about, but nothing active," Ashworth said. "It'd still be worth approaching cautiously."

I refrained from saying my usual "cautious is my middle name" because it was very blatantly obvious that cautious was the one thing I hadn't really been here.

You can't hog all the guilt on this one, Belle said. *This explosion is a result of inattention from us all. Maelle warned us there would be traps and concealments layered within the spells surrounding Roger, but none of us for a moment considered that might mean a simple shadow spell pinned onto a solitary spell stone.*

I guess I can't argue with that logic. Which didn't, of course, in any way ease the sense of guilt.

We walked across to the ruined house and stopped just short of where the corner section had been. The crater was twice the width of the cellar, and from where we were standing there didn't appear to be a bottom. It looked for all the world as if a monster had risen out of the earth and taken a bite of the end of house.

And maybe it *had*.

It would certainly explain the high-pitched screaming and the way the house had begun to shake.

"That's a bloody deep hole," Jaz commented. She had her phone out again, recording the scene. "I'm not smelling much in the way of blood, but there's definitely a faint whiff of mustiness coming from that crater."

"What sort of mustiness?" I asked. "Animal type?"

"More snake."

My gaze shot back to the hole. "If we were dealing with another basilisk, surely there'd be bits of it scattered all about."

"Basilisks are demons and can't be killed by an explosion," Eli said. "This was more likely to have been some sort of caged spirit."

I frowned. "Spirits are no more killed by explosions than demons, though."

"Depends on the type of explosion, and what else was contained in that weave of threads," Ashworth said. "Given there's no trace of either spirit or thrall, I'm thinking erasure of both was included."

"With me as the side bonus if I happened to be caught," I muttered.

"Indeed, lass."

Monty glanced at Jaz. "Have you any objections to us going down there to investigate?"

"Not as long as you're wearing booties and gloves," she replied. "Hang on while I go retrieve them."

"If you've any climbing gear in your SUV," Eli said, "it might be worth grabbing that as well."

Jaz nodded and left. I bent and pressed a hand against the ground. The whispers responded immediately. The blood had gone. The body had gone. The earth no longer held the taint of either.

Which basically confirmed that Roger had indeed been killed.

I drew in a breath and released it slowly. "I'm thinking I might need to ring Maelle."

"She would have felt Roger's death if he was caught in that explosion," Monty said. "Why poke the crazy vampire any more than necessary?"

"Because the crazy vampire is crazy, and we need to do as much as we can to stay in her good books. We don't want her coming after us, rather than Marie and Jaqueline."

"Good point."

Jaz returned with the promised booties, gloves, and also a couple of ropes. As Monty and Ashworth kitted up, I tugged my phone from my pack—noting that only one bottle of holy water had survived being thrown onto the ground—then made the call.

It rang on and on. I was about to hang up when she finally picked up.

"He is dead."

Her voice was cold. Unemotional. As scary as fuck.

"Yes."

"She took Augustine from me, and now she has taken Roger. She will pay. Everyone will pay."

I had a bad, *bad* feeling that "everyone" might well include us. "Who is Augustine?"

"My great-great-grandson—the one Marie turned against his will."

"The one who triggered the coven's destruction, in other words."

"Yes." She paused for a long moment. "What happened exactly?"

"We unwittingly triggered an explosion." I hesitated. "I'm sorry, Maelle. We tried."

"Indeed." The silence that followed was so long that I started wondering if she'd forgotten I was still on the phone.

"I am not surprised, and it is for the best. I would most likely have had to dispose of him myself had you succeeded in rescuing him, and that would have been ... hard."

Hard, but not impossible. God, this woman ... "Because he was a drain on your strength?"

"It is more what they did to him. For one such as he, a wound made of white ash is unhealable. His existence would have been one of never-ending agony."

"Ah. Sorry." I hesitated again. "Does his death release you from the bonds of your vow not to attack her?"

"If I could attack her, I would not be standing here talking to you."

"It's daylight—"

"That is no impediment for the likes of me and her."

"Sunning your toes is a far different prospect to stepping fully into sunlight, though. Not even the most ancient vampire can survive that."

"The most ancient vampire probably couldn't," she replied, tone coldly amused. "But we are more than merely ancient vampires."

Ah, fuck ...

I opened my mouth to reply, then stopped, unsure what to say, and in that brief silence, I heard it.

The rattle of chains. The shuffle of feet. A low rumble rising from a throat that wasn't human.

The hairs along the back of my neck rose. "Maelle, what's that odd sound?"

"That is my vengeance." Just for an instant, there was a crack in her coldly calm tone, and I very much suspected it was the *only* sign we were ever likely to get that her sanity had well and truly tumbled. "It will be unleashed on all eventually."

Dear God, no ... I swallowed heavily and somehow said,

my voice thankfully void of the horror churning through me, "You've got the Átahsaia leashed at the club?"

"Where else could I keep it? I can hardly send it back when its work here isn't done."

I closed my eyes and wearily rubbed my forehead. We needed to end this, quickly, before things really got out of hand—and certainly before she could unleash her monster on all of us.

On *me*.

I shivered, but did my best to ignore the trepidation tripping through my soul.

"Now, dear Elizabeth," she continued, "do please find Jaqueline and bring her to me. I will not be best pleased if these delays continue."

The restrictions that apply to you hunting Marie do not apply to your daughter, so why don't you damn well do it, I wanted to say but wisely didn't. The truth was, she basically had us over a barrel. We would do anything in our power to keep the reservation safe, and she was well aware of that. She'd always had the capability to cause havoc, but had been held at bay by her vow to the council not to cause harm to anyone living in the reservation. And while she might have inferred that breaking the vow would have dire consequences to herself, I suspected that, with Roger gone, she was no longer overly concerned about repercussions.

"I will try, Maelle, but—"

"Don't try. Do."

"Why?" I asked. "What do you want with her? I would think it's far too late to get back into her good books now, especially if, as you say, she has inherited your ability to hold a grudge."

"What I intend with my daughter is none of your business."

183

"It is if I'm leading her to her doom."

"Her doom and her fate have always been mine to decide. She knows this—why do you think she wishes me dead? It is a desire that stems not from the need to avenge a lover, but rather a need to shatter an agreement made before she was born."

"What sort of agreement?" I asked, even as something within me twisted. In very many ways, there were echoes of my own situation in Maelle and Jaqueline's. I just had to hope that the resentment the daughter had for her mother wasn't one of them.

"That is also none of your business."

And with that, the bitch hung up on me again.

My grip tightened on the phone, and it was all I could do *not* to throw it in frustration. I swung around and returned to the house, stopping beside Belle. Ashworth and Monty had descended into the pit, with Eli and Jaz manning the ropes.

I stepped forward carefully and peered over the edge. It really *was* a long way down. "Anything?"

"The remains of some sort of snare down at the base of the hole, which suggests we were dealing with some sort of spirit." Eli grimaced. "But aside from a few bits of hair and bones, there's nothing left of Roger. How did Maelle take the news?"

"With scary-as-fuck calm. Our next mission—which we have no choice but to accept—is to find Jaqueline. Or else."

"She can't do 'or else' or she'll break her vow to the council," Jaz said.

I glanced at her, surprised. "You know about that?"

"Aiden told us some time ago. He believed we needed to know."

And they definitely did. "Well, I'm afraid Roger's death

means any governance she'd had over her impulses went with him."

"In normal circumstances, I'd suggest we go in there and arrest her ass, but that—"

"Will likely end in bloodshed," I cut in. "The punch monster that did all the damage up in Moonlight Flats is currently residing in her nightclub."

"*What?*" Jaz and Eli said as one.

"Yep. It's chained, but I'm thinking it will be a quick-release system." I grimaced. "And with all the protections she's now got ringing that place, I very much doubt the five of us could break in."

Eli scrubbed a hand through his hair. "Maybe it's time it stopped being just us. Maybe we need to call in the high council."

"*Our* council won't ever agree to that," Jaz said.

"And besides," I added, "we dare not risk them learning about the wild magic. It may be protected but it's certainly not restrained, and we can't let anyone from the council know its sentience is growing."

"I know that." Eli's expression was grim. "It's just that I'm not sure the five of us can withstand what's coming."

"But it's not just the five of us, is it?" I said.

"I wouldn't be relying on the wild magic or the Fenna," he said grimly. "I suspect their agenda has nothing to do with the safety of this reservation."

"No, but by necessity, they have to help protect it because I live here and I'm carrying the very first Fenna to be created in God knows how many centuries."

"What the hell is a Fenna?" Jaz asked, confusion evident.

"Long story," Belle chimed in. "Best told over several long beers. Or, in Liz's case, several hot chocolates."

"We're coming up," Monty called from the bottom of the hole.

Eli and Jaz braced, and the two men climbed up. Both were sweating by the time they were hauled over the edge, but that wasn't surprising given the depth of the hole and the fact the wind—what little was stirring—wouldn't have reached that far.

As they climbed out of the harnesses and ropes, Ashworth said, "There's nothing down there that we can use to trace our vampires."

"But the spirit or demon or whatever the hell was doing that screaming is definitely gone?" Jaz asked.

He nodded and glanced at her. "Sadly, it won't stop them conjuring another."

Jaz glanced at me. "We can still use that pin stone we found to track them down, though, can't we?"

"We can."

"I'm not sure that's an entirely good idea," Eli said. "Given what happened the last time we used one of Jaqueline's spell stones to find her, it's likely that she'll be waiting for such an immediate response. Better to wait a day, and let her think the stone either didn't survive or that we didn't find it."

I frowned. "If it doesn't belong to an actual spell stone set and is just a solitary pin, why would she feel me trying to trace her through it?"

"Technically, she should not, but I don't think we can take the chance."

I hesitated. "Tomorrow morning, then, nice and early."

He nodded. "You can make the attempt in your reading room and then we can all head out to hunt her."

"Plan," I said. And it would give me time to do some much-needed paperwork for the café and also ring Mom to ask what she knew about astral connections, if indeed that's what Marie's nightly summonings were. The more I knew about that, the easier it would be to turn it to my advantage.

Easy being a relative term only when compared to all our other problems.

The wail of sirens grew louder than the gentle groaning of the building and the nearby hum of traffic. Jaz looked around "That's probably the SES and Mac."

"There's no need for all of us to remain here," Monty said. "I can stay—"

"It's probably best if I do, too," Belle cut in. "Just in case our ghost decides he doesn't want all these people sniffing around his house."

"I'll drop by later to grab your statements, unless the boss decides they're not necessary," Jaz said, then held up the glove containing the solitary spell stone. "You want me to keep this safe?"

I hesitated and then nodded. "There's a very minor chance the stain of darker magic we sense is some sort of locator spell, so it's probably best she believes it's in the hands of you rangers rather than me."

"Will us holding on to it present any danger?"

"Unlikely," Monty said. "Spell stones like that are a dime a dozen, so even if there is a locator spell, they're unlikely to attempt retrieval."

"Ah, good." She tucked it back into the evidence bag.

I glanced at Eli. "Do you mind dropping me off at the café?"

"Of course not," he replied, then hooked his arm through mine. "We have a few things we need to discuss anyways."

"We do?"

"Indeed, lass," Ashworth said, as he fell in step beside

us. "We're needing a date, you know, because we need the roses to be at their peak when you get married."

I laughed. "Your garden is pretty with or without the roses in bloom."

"Aye, but you canna beat a rose for the romance of the whole thing."

"Does that mean you and Eli got married in a rose garden?"

"Not just *any* old rose garden, but the one at the Werribee Mansion," Eli said, voice wry. "It would be fair to say there was rose overload."

"What can I say?" Ashworth's amusement was evident. "Under this weather-beaten, grungy exterior there beats a romantic heart."

"Grungy being the operative word there." Eli's voice was dry, and I laughed.

"We've made some enquiries, and it's looking likely to be either New Year's Eve or Valentine's Day, but we wanted to check both dates with you first before we decided."

"Valentine's is always a romantic choice," Eli said. "But the roses will likely be at the end of their blush by then."

"We're good with either, lass, but you'll likely struggle to book a celebrant at such short notice, though."

"We've already spoken to a couple and have an appointment with one on Friday."

If, that is, all this vampire shit didn't get in the way of it.

"Let us know what you decide, but in the meantime, we'll start tidying the gardens in readiness."

"That would be awesome. Thank you."

"It's our pleasure, lass." He paused and opened the rear door of his car for me. "Never thought I'd be having the pleasure of walking a daughter or granddaughter down the aisle, so it's an honor to be doing so for you."

"As granddads go, you two are the best." I dropped a kiss on his cheek before climbing in, and saw him blink rapidly. He really was an old romantic.

Back at the café, I checked in with Penny to ensure everything was okay and to grab a list of what we needed, then headed upstairs to do the ordering and accounts. It was close to six when my phone rang, the tone telling me it was Aiden.

"Hey," I said, by way of greeting. "That was one hell of a long council meeting."

"It was actually over in a couple of hours, which is quick in the scheme of things according to Rocco. Apparently they do all like waffling on."

"So, you're at the station?"

"No. We got a report of a fire over Joyces Creek way as I was heading back, and we ended up having to block some roads while the brigade dealt with it."

"Was it deliberately lit?"

"Uncertain at this stage, although there was some evidence people had been camping at the reservoir there, so it could simply have been a campfire that hadn't been put out properly. Anyways, I'm ringing to see if you're hankering for something particular for dinner."

"Aside from you, you mean?"

He laughed. "We both know which hunger has priority these days, and it isn't the sexual one, even if it's a close second."

That was a truth I couldn't deny. I considered my options for a moment then said, "A burger with the lot, sans beetroot. And chips, with chicken salt of course."

"Of course." His voice was dry. "I'll be there in about half an hour."

"I'll have a cold beer waiting for you."

"*That* would be appreciated."

He hung up. I shut the computer down, checked there were indeed a couple of beers in the small fridge up here, then grabbed a quick shower. After dressing in a loose shift dress rather than my usual shorts and tank top, I grabbed a cold bottle of water, then settled back on the sofa and rang Mom.

She answered almost immediately. "Lizzie," she said, her voice warm. "This is a surprise—is everything all right?"

"I'm fine, but unfortunately, the reservation has been infested with vampires and they're looking at going to war."

"And you're ringing for help?"

"God, no—the last thing this reservation needs is to be inundated by the high council."

"My fellow councilors would never venture far from their lofty halls without good reason, and they would never consider a vampire war that."

Surprise flickered through me. "They never asked you about the wild magic I unleashed up there?"

"Oh, they asked, but I feigned ignorance. It is best the council be kept in the dark when it comes to your control over the wild magic, Elizabeth. Such knowledge would not only mean too much attention being placed on yourself, but also our family in general. And with your father the way he is ..."

I was well aware she never meant that last bit to sound like she was once again putting my father and family fortunes above—or at least, at the same level—as mine, but that's nevertheless how the inner me, who hadn't one hundred percent forgiven, read it.

"He's seen no improvement then?"

"No." She hesitated. "I personally believe what the wraith stole will never be returned, but he refuses to accept that."

Because, for a man like my father—who'd bathed in the glory of being one of the most powerful witches in Canberra —the loss of his magic would be a bitter pill to swallow.

I had no idea what Mom actually thought about his loss —even now, her voice gave very little away—but I continued to hope he remained without magic. He'd spent most of his life belittling me and walking over others for their so-called magical "lack," so this bit of karma was very well deserved. And if you asked me, a year—which was how long the few doctors he had seen believed it would take for his magical prowess to be restored—was certainly *not* punishment enough.

An absence that stretched over the rest of his lifetime might not heal all the harm he'd caused over the years, but it would at least go some way to satisfying the ghosts of pain and heartache, be they within me or others.

Of course, there were plenty of people who'd consider *that* a horrible thing to wish on a parent, but my father hadn't really been much of a parent.

"What I'm actually ringing to ask is a couple of questions—first, what do you know about gray-area blood spells making you more susceptible to the call of dark witches or mages?"

She sucked in a sharp breath. "This has happened to you?"

"Sadly yes, though it appears that while they can summon me, they can't control me."

"That is at least something." She paused for a second. "I'm not personally familiar with the implication of gray blood spells, but I know someone who is. I shall ask him and get back to you."

"Thanks."

I could almost hear the smile in her voice as she said, "And the second?"

"Do you know anything about astral summoning?"

"Other than what is taught in university, I take it?" She was obviously forgetting I'd never finished high school, let alone gone to university. "As it happens, I did dabble in the practice when I was much younger."

"You did?" I asked, surprised.

Her soft laugh ran down the line between us, briefly stirring memories of Christmases when I was a kid. Not all of my childhood had been bad, and I needed to start remembering those times more.

"I was once a bit of a wild child, though many might find it hard to believe these days."

"Well, I had to have gotten my rebellious streak from somewhere, because it sure as hell didn't come from Dad."

"No, although he did have his moments before we were married." Her soft sigh spoke of gentle regrets. "My dabbling involved a boy I was rather attracted to. I would have been only nineteen or twenty, so well before your father came on the scene."

They'd met in their third year of uni, I knew, and while their marriage had definitely been a financial arrangement designed to benefit both families, there'd also been a deep attraction, even if it had now devolved into nothing more than a working partnership.

"And was this boy someone you shouldn't have been associating with?" I asked, my smile growing.

"Oh indeed, my parents would have been mortified." She lowered her voice, sounding conspiratorial and so much like Catherine—the sister I'd lost when I was barely sixteen, and who was now a spirit guide-in-waiting—that tears stung my eyes. "He was a Sarr, after all."

And *that* probably went a long way to explaining why she'd never held the same prejudices as either her family or my father's when it came to Belle. She'd been in lust with a Sarr. Who'd have ever guessed that?

"So how did the whole astral summoning come about?"

"Our ... liaisons were by necessity rare, but he was not only a spirit talker but a spirit walker. Which meant he could astral travel and fully interact with those who joined him on the plane."

"Fully interact, as in sex?"

My voice was somewhat incredulous and her soft laugh decidedly wicked. "Indeed, and astral sex is ... well, quite satisfying."

"Well, that's good to know, but I have absolutely no intention of fucking this vampire, astrally or not."

She laughed again. "Of course not. The point, though, is that while I couldn't initiate an astral session, once I was summoned, I could fully interact with those on the plane. Rodrik theorized the skill had to lie in my bloodline some-where, even if somewhat diluted. That would make sense, given the psi skills you inherited, which certainly did not come from your father's bloodline."

And *he'd* certainly made his opinions about those psi skills very clear over the years. I couldn't help but wonder if he'd have ever married Mom had he been aware that the "stain" of humanity—the only way psi talents could enter a witch bloodline was via a witch either marrying or having a child with a psi-gifted human—was in her family's past.

"Astral travel isn't one of them, though."

"It could be latent, or it could be reactionary, like mine."

"How do I stop it?"

"If it is reactionary, you probably can't. Not unless you uncover how you are being called."

I frowned. "Meaning?"

"Rodrik summoned me via a lock of my hair. When our relationship ended, I took that lock back."

"I don't believe any of them has something like that."

"A personal item is not always necessary. Sometimes, all it takes is an understanding of a person's resonance."

"Resonance as in magical or spiritual being?"

"Either. Were you placed in a situation recently where the vamp that calls you was able to taste the rhythm of your magical or psi aura?"

I frowned again. "I did get caught by one of them when I used psychometry to track her down via her spell stone, but she isn't the one calling me out."

"If she is closely connected to the vampire who *is* calling, then it's possible they could have shared the information."

"Would a master and her fledgling be considered close enough?"

"I would think so."

"Damn." I blew out a frustrated breath. "What if it's a latent skill? How would I go about initiating an astral journey?"

She hesitated. "According to Rodrik, one must travel with intent. So, visualize where you are and what you want to achieve on the plane, then relax your body and gain a meditative state. Once your energy has been centered, imagine a rope hanging from the ceiling and use it to pull yourself out of your body. If successful, you will be able to see your body beneath you."

"And to get back?"

"Imagine your body, feel the weight of each breath, and express the wish to return."

Seemed easy enough and was no doubt the exact opposite. "If I can't stop the summoning, what do you suggest I do?"

"Control the direction of the astral meeting."

"How? She's a blood mage and far stronger magically than me."

"You have wild magic in your very DNA. There is *no one* stronger magically than you."

"Yes, but using the wild magic in real life is very different to using it on the astral plane—especially when I'm not the one in control of the whole thing."

And yet, I *had* used it, if only very briefly, in that first dream to move myself against her orders. If I could do that, I could do far more.

"Astral walking is not so much about power but will," Mom was saying. "You might never have been the strongest magically, Elizabeth, but you were always the strongest of our children both physically and mentally."

"I had to be, didn't I?" I couldn't help the trace of bitterness that crept into my voice, and I hoped she didn't catch it. She might have been somewhat absent when it came to parenting me—at least, that's what it had seemed to the younger me envious of the attention Cat and Julius had been getting—but she had never been uncaring.

"Perhaps," she was saying, "but that does not alter the fact that you and Belle, two somewhat naive sixteen-year-olds, managed to outsmart and outrun all the forces that your father and Clayton could bring to bear for over twelve years. If the younger you could achieve that, the older you can certainly beat a couple of vampiric mages."

Again, those silly tears touched my eyes. Being pregnant was really playing havoc with my emotional equilibrium. "I like the confidence with which you say that."

"Given you outwitted a wraith who'd been plotting his revenge for over a decade—a creature who killed your brother and destroyed your father—I have every reason to be confident."

I wish I shared that confidence but then, lack of said confidence in my own skills was definitely one of my stronger traits. "So, how do you suggest I take full control of these astral meetings? Our tête-à-têtes to date have been nothing more than her warning me to not get involved and me throwing sass back at her. She's not going to answer any questions she doesn't want to, and I can't force her—"

"Actually, you probably could."

I blinked. "How, when I'm not the one initiating the meetings?"

"Initiation doesn't mean control. Rodrik always initiated our meetings, but I more often than not led proceedings afterward. You simply have to bring the force of your will to bear, and if it is stronger than the initiator's, you will gain control."

"Meaning I could force her to answer my questions?"

"Possibly, though if I were you, rather than verbally ask, I would use your psi talents. It is a far subtler approach."

"Subtle is not a word many would associate with me," I said dryly.

She laughed again, and again memories stirred. Perhaps one day, my memories would be dominated by the good times more than the bad. "Then do unsubtle."

It was certainly something I'd try if Marie did drag me back onto the astral plane—though with Roger now dead, there was no real reason for her to do so. Unless of course she was using the meetings to somehow keep tabs on me …

I frowned and asked, "Could she use these astral meetings to gain information about me? Without actually questioning me, I mean?"

Mom hesitated. "Is she psi capable?"

"I don't think so."

"Then it is unlikely. However, please do ensure that your physical body is well protected when these events happen," Mom said. "It's possible she could use them as a means of distraction—with your spirit on the astral plane, your physical self has no means of reacting to any sort of threat. Being killed in the astral plane is rare and difficult, but your spirit's absence leaves your body entirely too vulnerable."

"Oh, trust me, not only does the café have more protections around it than the high council's chambers, there's my werewolf to contend with."

There was a brief moment of silence. "How goes the relationship? You never said anything while you were here, but I got the impression that things were ... unsettled."

"They were, but we finally sat down and talked." I paused. "He asked me to marry him."

"And you said yes?"

"I did. I love him, Mom."

"Which is all any mother could want for their child, and I am extremely happy for you both." She paused. "When is the big event?"

"We haven't decided between New Year's Eve and Valentine's Day yet, but I'll let you know as soon as we do." I paused. "Father is *not* invited."

"Utterly understandable." She paused again, this time longer. "I would also understand if you do not wish me—"

"Don't be daft, Mom," I cut in.

She laughed, though it was a slightly relieved sound.

"It's not daft, Elizabeth, given you have reason enough to ostracize me for what I *didn't* do or see—"

"We can't change the past, but we can at least move beyond it. I want you there."

"Then I will look forward to hearing more—and to finally meeting your wolf."

Awareness shivered across my senses, and I glanced toward the stairs. "Speaking of which, he's just arrived home with dinner, so I will say goodbye and speak to you later."

"I look forward to it. Goodnight, be careful, and remember I'm here if you do decide you need extra magical help. It is not a long flight down to Melbourne."

"Thanks, Mom."

She hung up. I rose and walked toward the kitchenette to grab the tomato sauce and Aiden's beer. He appeared a few seconds later, looking tired, sweaty, and smelling faintly of smoke. "You look like crap, Ranger."

He laughed. "It's been a bit of a crap day. One thing I had not considered about being an alpha was the tedium that comes with council meetings and policy discussions. I'm not sure how Rocco has stood them for so long and remained sane."

"Rocco's made of stern stuff." I grinned. "Just as well I met you first because, hey, he's definitely worthy of attention."

"Hmm" was all he said to that.

Grin growing, I sat down beside him and plucked a chip free from its packaging. "Did Jaz update you on Roger and the explosion?"

"Yes." He handed me my burger. "What sort of retribution can we expect from Maelle?"

"Well, for one thing, she has the thing that punched the

holes through those people up in Moonlight Flats leashed in her club."

"Of *course* she does." He shook his head. "I'm gathering there's nothing any of you can do about that?"

"Getting through all the protections she's ringed the club with might well take all our time and magical energy, and that would leave us wide open to an attack by either her monster or her."

"Well, that's off the table then. I take it we concentrate on finding Jaqueline instead?"

"That's our best option. Jaz has the spell stone we found in evidence at the station, so I'll need you to grab it for me in the morning."

He nodded and motioned to my burger. "Eat before it gets cold."

"Well, if you'd stop asking questions, I would."

He nudged me lightly with his shoulder. I laughed, picked up my burger, and ate. Over dessert—banana bread with cream-cheese frosting for me, a brownie for him—he drank his beer and updated me on the council meeting. Then, when his beer was gone, he offered me his hand and said, "I need a shower."

I ignored his hand, amusement twitching my lips. "And this concerns me how?"

"I want you in the shower with me."

My pulse rate leapt in anticipation, but I didn't move. "Sadly, I've already had a shower."

"On days such as this, one can never have too many showers. Besides, hot sex and cold water is a delicious combination."

I laughed, placed my hand in his, and let him pull me to my feet. "I thought cold water was detrimental to certain parts of male anatomy?"

"It is unless there happens to be a hot naked female in the near vicinity. Lust will always win out in such a situation."

"I believe this is a theory we need to check out."

He grinned, swooped me up into his arms, and carried me into the bathroom, where we did prove that cold water was no impediment to a man's capabilities of getting an erection, or indeed hot sex.

We spent the rest of the evening snuggled on the couch, watching TV, then went to bed. But as sleep descended, I was once again called onto the astral plane.

Not by Marie.

By Jaqueline.

Once again the summoning followed the same pattern—I walked barefoot through the forest as the wild magic spun around me. Figures I couldn't see walked either side of me, but once again I was alone when I entered that forest clearing ringed by purple mage fire. In the middle of the clearing lay a body. This time, it wasn't staked, and it wasn't Roger. It was just an insubstantial, indistinguishable figure that was neither male nor female. A ghost of what might yet be.

Jaqueline stood on the far side of the clearing, in the same spot that Marie had been.

"Stop," she said, her voice holding the whip of command backed by magic.

My magic stirred in response, and her order skated over my skin with little impact. Mom had been right—they might be able to summon me, but my actions on this plane remained my own. Relief stirred but I clamped down on it, wary of it showing in my expression, and stopped as ordered. There was little point in revealing their lack of control just yet.

"Why have you summoned me, Jaqueline?"

"To pass on a message."

"I'm not your or Marie's personal postal service," I replied evenly. "If you've a message for your mother, pass it on yourself."

"Given she wishes to kill me, that would be unwise."

"She's your mother. She does not wish to kill you." And had indeed almost leapt across a table to rip my throat out when I'd asked why she'd bother leaving her daughter alive. That definitely wasn't the action of a woman who planned to kill her offspring.

But even as I thought that, doubt stirred.

Jaqueline waved a hand, the movement eloquent. "Perhaps before the madness descended that might have been true."

"Then why ensure that descent happened?"

"Because disorder is something she abhors, and it is delicious to watch her unravel."

Maker, mother, daughter—they were all certifiably crazy. "Maelle told me that your doom and your fate were always hers to decide—what did she mean by that?"

A frown flickered across Jaqueline's almost too-perfect features. "I could not tell you."

"Then perhaps you had best ask Marie."

"And perhaps you interfere in business you should not."

"You fuckers made it my business when you came to this reservation and decided to go to war. I didn't start this shit, but I will—"

"Finish it, blah, blah, blah," Jaqueline cut in, in a bored sort of tone. "It is no truer on this plane than it is in real life."

I called to the inner wild magic and imagined myself standing in front of Jaqueline, inches from her face. Before I could even blink, it happened. I reached out and wrapped a hand loosely around her throat. My psi talents roared to life, and I caught a glimpse of a street, a building, a room. Of her, lying in bed alone, though the dented pillow beside hers suggested that until very recently that had not been the case.

Grabbing her by the neck definitely wasn't subtle, but it had certainly worked.

"Well, well," she said, her voice even despite the startlement that briefly flickered through her expression. "Aren't you full of surprises."

"More than you will ever know." I let my hand drop and stepped back. I had what I needed. Now I just had to keep her from realizing that. "What do you really want, Jaqueline?"

"As I said, I'm here to pass on a message, but not, as you presumed, to my mother."

"Then to whom? Because really? These little tête-à-têtes that do nothing more than give me warning not to interfere are getting a little tedious."

"Then you will be pleased to know this will be the last of them."

"Oh?" I raised a casual eyebrow even as alarm ran through me. "Have you finally accepted their uselessness?"

A vicious light ignited in her eyes, and the alarm boiled over to fear.

"No. They simply end because you will no longer exist to call onto this plane. Enjoy your final minutes on this earth, Elizabeth Grace."

And with that, she flung me off the plane, back into my body.

Straight into chaos.

CHAPTER NINE

I woke with a gasp and sat bolt upright in bed. Aiden wasn't beside me, but I could hear him speaking in the living area, his words urgent but barely audible against the cacophony of sound coming from the street beyond the café —alarms, explosions, and screams.

I flung off the sheet, climbed into my shorts and a T-shirt, and then ran out, barely avoiding Monty as he stepped from Belle's room.

"What the hell is going on?" His gaze shot toward the glass sliding doors, where the night sky burned bright with smoke and fire. "Ah, fuck."

"Yeah." I ducked past him and ran into the living room.

Aiden was on the phone but swung around as we entered. "The station was hit by a fireball. A *purple* fireball."

Meaning it was mage fire, not regular. "Anyone hurt?"

"Don't know. Ric had patrol duties tonight, but it's close to knock-off time, so I have no idea if he was there to sign off or not."

Ricardo Pérez was the newest of the reservation's rangers and had come here under the reservation's exchange program—a program designed to prevent inbreeding—as a replacement for Byron, who'd been murdered by one of our "monster of the month" invasions.

It would be the mother of all ironies if Ric had also been killed by one of them.

I moved past Aiden and headed for the glass sliding doors and the patio beyond, Monty and Belle two steps behind me. The night was stinking hot and filled with not only the acidic scent of burning plastic but the foulness that came with a spell created from blood. I stopped at the balustrade and stared in horror at the chaos in front of me.

It wasn't just the ranger station that had gone up in flames; half the damn block was little more than fragmented bits of burning rubble. And visible through the sweep of smoke and fire were the broken remnants of a spell.

Even without knowing mage fire had created this mess, those remnants were evidence enough this hadn't been an accident.

Monty stopped beside me. "Why on earth would they hit the damn ranger station?"

I glanced at him grimly. "I think you'll find they believed they were hitting the café."

"But why—" Belle stopped abruptly. "The pin. They thought it was *here*."

I nodded. "Jaqueline called me onto the astral plane again tonight, and it was obviously meant to distract me while Marie launched her destruction spell."

Monty's gaze was on the burning mess ahead of us. "Given the damage they've done, I'm thinking it was designed to break through the protections ringing this place."

I nodded. "Jaqueline was pretty damn sure she'd just seen the last of me."

"And with good reason," Belle murmured. "I'm not sure even the wild magic could repel such a spell. It's certainly not infallible."

"No, but there's a reason few witches dare mess with it. We're just going to have to boost the protections around the place to counter that"—I grimly waved a hand toward the destruction—"happening to our block."

"What we're going to have to do is get on the front foot with these bitches," Monty growled. "Maelle must know where to find them. Punch monster or not, we have to confront her and demand she give up any and all information she has—"

"While it may yet come to that," I cut in, "it's not necessary right now. I know where Jaqueline is, and I believe we need to hit her hard and fast, before she can move again."

"And before she realizes their ploy has failed," Belle said.

Monty frowned. "How did you uncover that information? I can't imagine she'd have willingly given that sort of information out."

"I used my psi talents while threatening her. She didn't really react to said threat, and now we know why."

He nodded. "We'll need Eli and Ashworth in on any attack—even if we have the element of surprise, any place Jaqueline and her mad maker are in will be ringed by protections. It might be wise if we go to their place rather than convening here."

"It's far safer here, what with all the—"

"Not if Marie's people are watching the café," he cut in. "The last thing we need is to give them additional targets."

"Monty, we're already all targets. Aside from the fact

Marie and Jaqueline did their research before they arrived, they tore all the pertinent information from Roger's mind."

"Yes, but at this point, they're focused more on you than anyone else. Hate to say it, but it's probably best it remains that way."

His words had me remembering the hazy figure on the astral plane. Were my psi senses warning me that while fate had yet to be decided, someone I cared about *would* take Roger's place if I wasn't very careful?

Possibly. *Very* possibly.

"Fine. We'll go there."

"And just to be safe, I'll weave a concealment spell around the SUV before we leave. Even if Marie's people are watching this place, they won't have time to counter the spell or place a tracker before we're gone."

"Good idea." I glanced around as Aiden came through the door. Fury dominated his expression but there was also relief. "Is Ric okay?"

"A few cuts and scratches, but alive. Apparently he was waiting for the gates to open so he could get into the rear yard when the fireball hit the station. The force of the explosion sent the vehicle tumbling, but he managed to crawl clear before the thing caught fire."

"And the nearby buildings?" Monty asked. "Any casualties there?"

"Won't know until we get the fire out, but Ric's vehicle wasn't the only one caught in the explosion." He glanced at Monty. "I've ordered everyone to keep out until we know it's safe. I'll need you to come down there to check the place over magically."

Monty nodded and glanced at us. "It shouldn't take me more than ten or fifteen minutes to do the check. If I do happen to find anything, I'll give you a call and meet you over at Ashworth's."

"Ashworth's?" Aiden asked sharply. "Why? What's happened?"

"We've a possible location for Jaqueline," I replied. "We're going to hit her tonight."

"Then you should probably contact Maelle. As much as I don't want her roaming around the reservation willy-nilly, she should be involved in any hunt for her daughter."

"I'll contact her once I know for sure Jaqueline is there." Calling her before we were certain risked making the crazy vampire even crazier.

"Be careful, then, okay?" He glanced at Monty. "Ready?"

Monty nodded again. Aiden dropped a kiss on my cheek, then turned on his heels and ran back inside, grabbing a T-shirt and his shoes on the way through. Monty followed him down the stairs, and the two of them appeared on the street below a few seconds later, running toward the wreckage of the station.

"I'll go collect our gear," Belle said. "You'd better call Ashworth and warn them we're heading over."

I nodded and followed her inside, locking the sliding door, then heading into my bedroom to grab my phone. It rang just as I was reaching for it—and it was Ashworth.

"Is everything okay, lass? We heard the explosion, and from where we are, it seemed a little too close to you and the café."

"Marie hit the ranger station with mage fire, and it's taken out half the block."

He swore. "Any casualties?"

"At this point, no rangers, but until they put out the fires that started after the mage fire hit and get into what remains, no one can be sure if there was anyone in the other buildings."

"At least it happened at midnight. Had it been midday, it would have been far worse." He paused. "Why hit the ranger station though?"

"They thought they were hitting me—"

"The magic on the pin," he cut in with a groan. "It was a tracker."

"Yep. You want to put the kettle on? Because we're planning a little vengeance and we're coming over there to plot."

"Putting it on now. We'll see you all soon."

I hung up, swapped out the shorts for jeans and boots, then grabbed my purse, keys, and phone and headed downstairs to wait with Belle. Monty appeared nearly twenty minutes later.

"Sorry," he said, sweat trickling down the side of his face and staining his T-shirt. "Most of the spell had disintegrated, but there was a tiny kernel of magic left in the remains of the ranger station, and it took me a while to dismantle it."

"Any idea what the kernel was?" I asked.

He caught the bottle of water Belle tossed him and opened it up, taking a long drink before answering. "It was some sort of 'Eye' spell, designed to send images back to whoever spelled it."

"So that they could admire their handiwork, no doubt," Belle said. "Although if you killed it, they'd know their destructive efforts failed."

"Maybe not, because they'd have seen me rather than Liz or you, so it's possible they could still believe their plan worked."

"At least until I start spelling again," I commented.

"Indeed, so hold off doing so until we're ready to hit them." He drained the bottle, then tossed it into the bin. "Let's get out of here."

He grabbed our packs and led the way out. After opened the passenger doors for me and Belle, he tossed the packs into the back, then wrapped the SUV in what I presumed was an invisibility spell—from the inside, it was hard to tell, because the spell was external and the vehicle visible for us—then climbed into the driver's seat. After starting her up, he reversed out, then switched over to drive and hit the accelerator. Tires squealed as we shot toward the street. Thank God no one happened to be walking across the entrance to the lane at that particular moment, because they'd have been mown down.

As he swung right, I twisted around and looked out the rear window. I couldn't see anyone—or anything—obviously following us, but tension nevertheless rode me. The streets remained empty, though, and we reached Ashworth's in good time, parking out the front.

After Monty had dismantled his spell to ensure no other car would crash into it, we grabbed our packs and headed through the gate and up the rose-lined path to the front door. Ashworth quickly ushered us inside, the house delightfully cold compared to the night.

Eli placed the teapot and a jug of milk on the table, then went back for the cups and a packet of Scotch Fingers. "Sorry, Monty, we're out of cakes."

"Anyone would think I am nothing more than a walking stomach," he said, even as he reached for a biscuit.

"Well, not entirely a stomach," Belle noted, a teasing light in her eyes. "You do have one other notable attribute."

A smile twitched his lips. "A biggus dickus?"

"Biggus feetus."

He laughed and nudged her. "With one comes the other, I'm afraid."

I rolled my eyes. "When you have finished the sexual byplay, we have a raid to plan."

His amusement instantly fell away. "Where is Jaqueline holed up?"

"In a house on View Street, about five minutes away from here."

"Is she alone?" Ashworth asked. "One or two additional vamp mages we can probably deal with, but if it's the lot of them, well, that'll take more planning."

"The pillow beside her was dented, so there's possibly one other person there, at least."

"Could it be Marie?" Belle asked.

I wrinkled my nose. "I'm not sure they'd risk cohabitation, given what Maelle did up in Moonlight Flats. Besides, Maelle said that she forbade Marie from taking Jaqueline as a lover."

"After what Maelle did to the coven," Monty said, voice dry, "I'm thinking any agreements the two might have had were rendered null and void."

"The one preventing Maelle from attacking her maker still holds, so it's likely the others might, too."

"I'm also thinking there's plenty we haven't been told about that particular agreement." Monty got out his phone and brought up Google Maps. "What's the address?"

I gave it to him and reached for a Scotch Finger before he could snaffle them all.

"I'm guessing the place would have been unoccupied," Eli said, pouring the tea while Monty googled. "Because vamps wouldn't be able to enter it otherwise. Not without a freely given invite to step over the threshold, anyway."

Belle frowned. "I thought residences, even if empty, were a tricky prospect for vamps? Isn't it more usual for them to use commercial properties or even ones that are mixed?"

"It's something of a gray area," Eli said, "and generally depends on the length of time it's been vacant and whether there's a lingering connection to past owners."

"They got into our ghost's place, though," she said, "and he definitely had a lingering connection to it."

"As I said, it's a gray area."

"Got it." Monty put the phone down so we could all see it. "From the look of things, it's a pretty standard triple-fronted brick house from the seventies."

"It's also on a big, raised triangular block with nothing more than grass between the street and the house," Ashworth noted. "They're going to see us coming."

"They're more likely to hear our heartbeats before they ever see us," I said. "And that, combined with the fact we're dealing with vamps who have shown a penchant for spelling in and out of locations, is going to be a problem. We need to find a way to stop them transporting away."

"What about the wild magic?" Monty said.

I picked up my cup and took a sip. "What about it?"

"Well, it's basically immune to dark magic, is it not?"

"If it was immune," Ashworth said, "history wouldn't be littered with fresh wellsprings being stained by the influence of evil and the town and people surrounding them destroyed."

Monty waved a hand. "Fresh isn't what we have here, though. It's partially sentient thanks to the hundreds of souls it's got lurking within it, and it's very determined to get rid of the evil that has now infested the reservation. And it has a means of directing its power, thanks to Liz's connection to it."

"You did use it to contain those vampires who attacked the O'Connor compound," Belle said. "That isn't much different to what we need here."

"Except it is, because I could feel the weight of those vamps on the earth, whereas here"—I waved a hand to the image still on Monty's phone—"we're dealing with a vampire hiding in a house. The house has the connection, not the person, if that makes sense."

"Can't you just send the wild magic in to investigate?" Monty asked. "It's not like it doesn't float about everywhere anyway."

"It doesn't go inside as a general rule, though. Not unless it's the café or it's directed to do so by me or Katie. Besides, Jaqueline is well aware of my control over it and will bolt the minute she sees it." I half shrugged. "What about a regular old cage spell? They're designed to imprison all manner of beings, supernatural *or* witch, so surely a combination of all ours will prevent her transporting out and hold her in place long enough for Maelle to get here."

Especially given it now appeared Maelle was as capable as her maker and her daughter at creating and using transport spells.

"Cage spells are not instantaneous," Eli said. "The minute we start raising one, she'll run."

"The wild magic *is* instantaneous, though," Monty said. "Why can't you just wrap the wild magic around the entire house and cage the bitch inside that way?"

"If that is possible," Ashworth said, "it's a rather good idea."

"I do have them occasionally," Monty said, amusement evident.

A smile touched Ashworth's lips, but he didn't make the very obvious reply and glanced at me instead. "*Is* it possible?"

"Probably?" I wrinkled my nose. "I'd have to check, because the Fenna did make a point of saying my usage would be restricted to what I could physically handle, and raising enough power to encompass such a large building might push those limits."

"Caging those vamps didn't pull on your energy, though, did it?" Monty asked. "The wild magic doesn't actually run through you, does it?"

"It generally doesn't for the smaller stuff, but I still have to connect to it and *that* is what pulls on my strength." That, and having to envisage what I wanted and then direct it into being.

"It's still worth checking whether it is a viable option or not. Otherwise, we'll have to switch to plan B." Monty paused, a smile twitching his lips. "Which, of course, has yet to be developed, because plan A is simply brilliant, even if I do say so myself."

I rolled my eyes. "There is one other problem—Maelle's not going to get past a wild magic barrier, and if we do anything more to Jaqueline than capture her, Maelle will be pissed."

"And given she's already sliding off the edge of sanity," Belle murmured, "that would not be a good idea."

"Could you retract it once she's locked inside the house?" Eli asked. "That will allow Maelle to confront her daughter without having to breach the wild magic."

"Retracting it should also cut down on any pull the bubble has on your strength," Ashworth added.

"In theory, yes." In reality? Who actually knew. But I could at least get an answer on that one. I finished my tea and rose. "Mind if I head out the back to see if I can commune with the wild magic?"

"Go right ahead," Eli said. "Spotlights are to the right of the door."

I grabbed another biscuit and headed out. Their rear yard was on the narrow side but very long, consisting of a decked patio area with steps leading down onto a white stone path that wound its way through a series of garden beds, roses, and Japanese maples, in all of which small lights twinkled and shone. There was a lawn area three-quarters of the way down, and beyond that lay a small wildflower area. I couldn't help smiling. It was pretty enough in the daytime, but at night, with the spots and all the fairy lights in the flowerbed and winding along the path, it was pretty damn special. And absolutely perfect for a night wedding.

Aiden and I hadn't yet discussed the timing of our marriage, but seeing this ... it had to be at dusk or night. *If* we could get the celebrant to agree.

I headed down the steps, munching on my biscuit as I followed the pretty path down to the lawn area. Once there, I brushed the crumbs from my fingers, then knelt and pressed them into grass that was thick and lush despite long days of heat. Ashworth had a number of water tanks installed along the left side of the house and was obviously using them to keep everything green.

I closed my eyes and reached for the wild magic. Unlike previous occasions, there was no immediate connection, making me wonder if perhaps I needed to directly touch the earth rather than having anything—even grass—between us. Or maybe it was simply that, at this point in time, they could not sense the presence of darkness or evil in my location, and simply weren't responding.

It's not like any of us really knew how this stuff worked.

Then a tiny, luminous thread—something I saw more through my mind's eye rather than real—floated toward me and twined itself around my wrist. The connection instantly flared to life, and the whispers once again filled my mind. I posed my question, and their voices retreated. I waited for what seemed an interminably long time, but was in reality probably only a few seconds. When the whispers returned, it was with an affirmation but also with the warning that I would need a direct connection to the ground to ensure the power I was drawing didn't remain in my body, but could loop back out.

Meaning, basically, they wanted me grounded, in much the same manner as electricity was grounded.

Was that why I'd been walking unshod through the forest in those astral dreams? Had my subconscious realized it was a means of curtailing the danger the wild magic presented to me personally?

More than likely. It did have a history of recognizing problems before my conscious self did, after all.

I thanked them and withdrew. The tiny thread unleashed from my wrist and floated away, though it didn't venture too far. Which was a good thing, given I had no idea what state the earth around Jaqueline's retreat was in, and I might yet have to draw on that thread to enhance my connection and create the sphere cage.

I returned inside, scooting through the rear glass sliding doors quickly and sighing in relief as the colder air hit.

"How'd it go, lass?" Ashworth asked.

"They agreed it was feasible." I sat down, picked up my tea, and took a sip. "No guarantee it'll stop a transport spell, though. Apparently, none of them have ever had to deal with such a situation."

"Which I find rather hard to believe, given there are

centuries of souls down there," Monty said. "One of them surely would have at least come across a blood mage before."

"Yes, but said mages are generally intent on claiming the wellsprings, rather than transporting to and from them. Did you figure out a plan of attack while I was gone?"

"Given the position of the house, our best bet is to come in from the side street." Eli, who was sitting the closest to me, slid his phone toward me and pointed to the street in question. "If the satellite images are correct, there's no front fence and the corner point of the block has been planted out with a gum tree and some shrubs, which should hide your presence while you raise the magic."

"Our main problem still remains, though," I said. "It may be faster to raise the wild magic than a spell, but she'd still have a second or two in which to flee."

"Which is why Belle will create a distraction here." Ashworth leaned past his partner and pointed to a gravel driveway. It belonged to the house next door and ran all the way up to the back of the property. "She'll raise a protective circle and start a snare spell, which should keep Jaqueline's attention long enough for you to raise the wild magic."

"The minute she senses the snare, she's going to react," I said. "And, more than likely, attack."

"Yes," Belle said. "But even if she hits me full force with her magic, the protection circle will hold long enough for you to lock her down. Besides, your personal wild magic runs through our charms now and that might prove to be the best protection yet."

I hoped so, especially given that insubstantial figure I kept seeing on the astral plane. I hadn't noticed if he or she had been wearing the charm, but with the wild magic woven into it, darkness shouldn't be able to take it or break it. Not without major effort anyway.

Of course, you didn't have to break the protections to kidnap someone. All it would take was catching them unawares and knocking them out.

"Monty and I will sneak in through this yard—" Eli pointed to the white house behind our target. "And deal with any guards or spells they might have. Ashworth will shadow you, protecting your back as you raise the wild magic."

Trepidation shivered through me, but I did my best to ignore it. "Sounds good."

"Then give us a few minutes to gather all our gear, and we'll get going."

Ten minutes later, we were back in the SUV and heading for View Street, Monty driving at a far more genteel pace this time around. I dragged out my phone and sent Maelle a quick message, giving her the heads-up that we might have located her daughter.

Where? came the immediate response.

I'll send the address once we know it's not a trap.

Send it now.

Can't. There're several possibilities. Better to lie than having to deal with her unstable presence, especially when I was trying to raise wild magic.

When you know, do not delay.

The "or else" remained unwritten, but it was neverthe-less there.

I blew out a breath and shoved the phone away. Once we reached View Street, we dropped Belle off a few houses down from our target house, then continued on around the corner. Monty swung in behind a lovely old paperbark tree, killed the engine, and took out the keys. "I'll tuck these in the center console storage, just in case things go wrong and someone needs to grab the SUV in a hurry."

"Hopefully, things will go as planned for a change," I said. And having said that, it probably wouldn't.

I opened the door and climbed out. The night was still and clear, the storm that had looked so promising earlier having passed us by without providing any relief. I couldn't see Jaqueline's hideaway from where I was standing, just the end of her block and the thick mat of shrubs that hugged the area. That hopefully meant she wouldn't see or hear us. Not until it was too late, anyway.

Ready when you lot are, Belle said.

Are you sensing anyone lurking in the shadows?

She hesitated briefly. *I can't get a reading on our target's house, which suggests they've got some sort of telepathic barrier in place.*

Makes sense given they know you're telepathic. What about the surrounding area?

There're five people asleep in the house below me, and three in the house behind our target's. She paused. *There's also someone in the yard of the house on the other side of the street, but he's right on the edge of my telepathic range and I'm not getting much information from him.*

Meaning if he is a guard, he might also be wearing a protective device.

Possibly. I'll keep an eye on him, because if there's one guard, there might be more.

I think "will be more" is more likely than "might." I returned my attention to the men. "Belle's in place and ready to go. She said there's a man standing in the yard directly opposite our house, but he's right on the edge of her range, so she can't tell if he's a problem or not."

"And at Jaqueline's? How many are in there?"

"It's protected against telepathy."

"Damn," Monty said. "But I guess not unexpected. We should get going."

"Indeed," Eli said and glanced at me. "Give us a minute to get into place."

As he and Monty grabbed their packs and headed in, I took off my boots and socks, tossing them into the back of the SUV before grabbing my pack and slinging it over my shoulder.

Once Ashworth had shouldered his own pack, he hit the button to close the hatch door and then glanced at his watch. "Let's go. Eli and Monty will be in place by now."

I nodded, and we headed down the slope, walking along the edge of the still-warm road simply because there were no footpaths. The street remained empty, and the only sound to be heard was the occasional hum of distant cars. Tension nevertheless crawled through me. I had absolutely no doubt there'd be other guards here somewhere, even if we couldn't see them—especially after the mess that was Moonlight Flats—but it was unnerving not to have any scent or sense of them at all.

When we reached the intersection, I padded across the prickly grass verge into the shrub-filled corner of the block. The second my feet touched the bare ground, energy stirred around me. A heartbeat later, a tiny luminous thread wound itself around my wrist.

The wild magic was ready and waiting.

The old gum tree that dominated the corner was ringed by bushy native brooms that almost entirely blocked the house from sight. Which, while necessary to stop any watchers within the house from spotting us, was also something of a hindrance. While I technically shouldn't have to see the house to guide the wild magic, I suspected things would go a little faster if I could. I shifted around and eventually spotted a small gap between the bushes low to the ground. After drawing in one of those deeper breaths that did nothing to curb the growing tension, I glanced at Ashworth. "Ready?"

He nodded, a cage spell already buzzing around one hand and a repel spell around the other. "Tell Belle to go."

I did so, and her magic rose, sharp and clear across the night. I knelt, dug my toes deeper into the dust and then pressed both hands against the ground. The Fenna's chorus briefly rose, but they already knew what I wanted and intended, and the wild magic responded instantly. Its force surged into my hands then up my arms, across my body, and back through my feet, before racing across to the house. Between one heartbeat and the next, a net of sheer wild magic crawled around the outside of the house, wrapping it in a pulsing, luminous sphere of energy.

A scream rose, fierce, sharp, and familiar. Jaqueline. We'd got her. We'd fucking got her ...

Her magic surged, a dark spell designed to destroy. It hit the sphere hard, and the wild magic rippled briefly under the attack, but held. Another spell rose, this one unfamiliar. The result was the same, and another scream rose.

"That," Ashworth said, "very much suggests your sphere was successful."

"Yes, though I can't guarantee how long it'll hold if she keeps hitting it magically." Because every time she did, it rebounded through my brain. I pushed to my feet and brushed the dirt and bits of pine from my hands. "I'll ring Maelle. You, Monty, and Eli had better—"

I cut the rest off as movement caught my eye. Two men, coming in fast from the right. Ashworth swore and unleashed his repelling spell, hitting one in the chest hard enough to knock him high into the air. The other neatly avoided the cage spell and kept on coming, but before I could react in any way, Ashworth flicked his cage spell around and snared the bastard from behind.

They weren't alone, however. There were others, but I couldn't tell how many because they were wrapped in shadows, making them invisible to regular sight, and I couldn't even feel their weight against the ground thanks to the thick layers of tarmac.

"Apparently the showers aren't working wherever these lads have been hiding," Ashworth said, voice wry. "You should ring Maelle, then go do whatever you can to keep that sphere up until she gets here. I'll deal with these bastards."

"Four against one isn't the greatest—"

"For them, not me, lass. Go, before Jaqueline calls in more reinforcements."

I hesitated briefly, then thrust to my feet and ran around the shrubs, the scattered pine bark digging into my feet but not really hurting. I dragged out my phone as I ran across the grass and made the call. Maelle answered immediately and I gave her the address. She didn't reply, didn't say thank you, didn't even say she'd be there soon.

She didn't need to, because I'd barely hung up and shoved the phone back into my pocket when the air shimmered on the footpath below and she stepped into existence.

Her face was pale and thin, her clothes black, and her eyes as luminous as the moon, with no discernible difference between their sclera and iris. Hell, even her pupils were almost nonexistent. It was a frightening sight, made more so by the darkly dangerous river of energy that rolled around her. It was a protection spell and something else. Something that wasn't so much a spell as a presence.

Goose bumps trailed across my skin, and I swallowed heavily. I had no idea what that presence was, but I had a very bad feeling it was something supernatural. It just felt ... wrong, in the same way demons felt wrong.

In the same way the basilisk had felt wrong, though not as foul as Maelle's leashed demon.

This insubstantial, ghostly presence wasn't a basilisk—it was far too small—but that didn't discount the possibility of some other sort of demon snake. She had admitted that they were hers to call, after all.

But why in the hell would she bring one here to confront her daughter?

I really didn't know—really didn't *want* to know—but feared I'd find out soon enough.

Her white gaze went briefly to the house and, just for an instant, a myriad of emotions flowed across her flawless features, the strongest being anticipation, determination, and perhaps a touch of fear. The latter surprised me. Why would she fear Jaqueline, given she was so sure *she* was the stronger mage?

Or was there something else going on? Something to do with that ghostly presence and her earlier statement that Jaqueline's fate had always been hers to decide?

She leapt lightly from the footpath to the top of the raised bank and strolled toward me, her movements elegant and unhurried despite the tension radiating from her. Once close, she motioned toward the house with a gloved hand. "I cannot step through your barrier."

"I know—I'm going to retract it." I hesitated as the sound of fighting increased. "You'll have to watch my back while I do so, though."

"Oh, trust me, any vampire foolish enough to come near either of us will quickly be apprised of their mistake."

She flexed her fingers as she said that, and it was then I noticed not only the length of her nails but how sharp they were. She wasn't intending to dine on them. She was intending to gut them, and no doubt swim in their remains at a later point.

I shivered again and pushed away the gory images my imagination was unhelpfully providing, then bent to press my fingers once again into the ground. As the looping connection reformed, I contracted the sphere. The glimmering weave of luminous energy pulsed and glimmered as it tightened in response, its light briefly caressed the red bricks before sinking into them, disappearing from sight but not from my inner eye. Though I couldn't feel the weight of darkness resting on the floorboards, as the sphere grew ever smaller, the thick wash of dark wrongness grew ever closer.

Another scream of frustration echoed, and once again, dark magic rose, the spell beating, tearing, at the luminous threads.

They held, but every blow shuddered through my brain and echoed into my body, and I wasn't sure how long I could ignore it before I was forced to break the connection.

"Jaqueline has definitely inherited my temper and my power. That is as pleasing as it is troubling." Her gaze came to mine. "Your power shines from you, Elizabeth. It is … tempting."

I pointed to the house. "I suggest we get in there and deal with your daughter, before that power fades and we lose her again."

Her too-sharp teeth flashed in what I presumed was amusement, then she nodded regally and led the way forward, moving fast and yet somehow gracefully across the remaining bit of grass before climbing the concrete steps. Her gaze briefly scanned the thick shadows to our right, and her amusement seemed to sting the night.

At that exact point, the shadows parted, and two vampires appeared, running straight at us. I stepped back automatically, forgetting where I was, and fell off the porch, arms flailing as I fought to keep my balance. I landed awkwardly but on both feet, felt the caress of air, and glanced up sharply. Saw the vampire in the air, coming straight at me. I swore, ran backward, and raised my hand, a repelling spell buzzing around my fingers. But before I could unleash it, Maelle lunged forward, caught the vamp by her feet, and hauled her back down onto the concrete patio with enough force to split the woman's chin open. Then she flipped her around, bent down, and casually sliced the woman's gut open with one clawed hand. Blood sprayed, but the woman kicked free of Maelle and scrambled upright, her wound opening up and her guts spilling out. It was almost as if she wasn't even aware that she'd been hurt ... My gaze jumped to her eyes. There was no life within them, just blankness. She wasn't in control of her body; her maker was.

Once again she tried to launch at me from the porch. Once again, Maelle caught her feet. This time, she threw the other woman hard against the corner of the building. Bones cracked, the sound as sharp as a gunshot.

Vampires were capable of many things, but even they weren't capable of movement when their back was shattered.

The blankness oozed from the woman's dark gaze, and awareness returned. Awareness and pain. Maelle drew in a deeper breath and sighed happily. Meaning the bitch didn't only draw enjoyment from swimming ...

I shuddered and walked back to the patio. The other vampire lay dead at her feet, his throat cut, and his head all but severed from his neck. The blood had sprayed across the nearby brick and door, and dripped from Maelle's dark clothes and face. As I climbed the steps, her tongue flickered out, tasting the dark liquid. Delight and hunger briefly touched her expression. I flexed my fingers, itching to unleash the spell that buzzed around my hands and send her far, far away, but didn't. She'd only come back, madder and nastier than ever. I motioned her to continue, then followed, but just as I was about to enter, Ashworth appeared. He had a bloody scratch along his left cheek and another down his right arm, but otherwise appeared fine.

"We're going to loop a protection circle around the house," he said. "So don't panic when you feel it activate."

I frowned. "There can't be too many more of Marie's vamps left, not if Maelle's estimates are right."

"And they are," she said from inside the house.

Ashworth cast a grim look her way. "I'm thinking more about Marie attacking us magically, now that you've retracted the wild magic."

"She will know I am here and will not attack me directly," Maelle said. "To do so would shatter the bonds preventing me from attacking her, and I doubt she is willing to do that as yet, not even for my daughter. You witches, however, have proven to be inconveniently resourceful and could certainly become a target."

"Then we'll definitely be raising the protection spell." Ashworth's gaze met mine. "Be careful in there. No heroics, okay?"

I nodded and quickly continued on. The entry hall was surprisingly wide, with three doors on the left, one on the right, and a bathroom directly ahead. The hallway went right, which was where the main concentration of wild magic was.

Maelle was just disappearing around the corner, meaning she must have been waiting for me. I hurried after her. There was a second entry point into the living room to our right, and the strong metallic scent of blood rolled from it, making me wonder if the person who'd shared Jaqueline's bed had ended up as dinner. I certainly couldn't smell anyone else in the house besides the three of us.

Down the far end of the hall was the kitchen ... and Jaqueline. She paced back and forth, her magic boiling through the air, powerful but impotent, held at bay by the sphere of wild magic encircling the entire room, not only preventing her escape but also curtailing her ability to hit us magically.

She saw us and stopped. Another spear designed to tear hit my barrier; the threads bowed against it briefly before snapping back into place. A red-hot lance of pain stabbed through my brain, briefly making my eyes water, and my knees buckled. I stopped and pressed a hand against the wall to keep upright, but ignored the growing ache in my head, all my attention on the two women ahead of me.

"Jaqueline, dearest," Maelle said, her tone low and warm, "how lovely it is to see you again after such a long time."

She stopped inches from pulsating threads of wild magic, but if their closeness in any way made her feel uncomfortable, I had no sense of it. All I could see, all I could smell, was the dark caress of the presence that swirled around her. Though it remained insubstantial, there was a purplish-green luminosity to it now that very much reminded me of the basilisk's scales.

Trepidation stepped into my heart, and the urge to get

the hell out of this house was so damn strong that I actually took a step back. I forced myself to stop. I couldn't leave, as much as I might want to. I needed to be here, so I could instantly react to protect the wild magic. I could not let it be stained by whatever was about to happen, especially if what was about to happen was a bloody brutal death within the confines of its net.

Though why on earth would Maelle want to kill her daughter? Especially when she'd been so adamant that *we* didn't kill her?

"Let's not pretend that you in any way care about me." Jaqueline's fists were clenched and almost invisible thanks to the storm of darker magic that swirled around them. "You were an absent parent at best when I was human, and that only got worse when I crossed over. You certainly offered little in the way of help or support."

Every word was filled with a bitterness centuries in the making. I couldn't help but wonder yet again if Jaqueline really *had* been a willing participant in the crossover ceremony.

Couldn't help but wonder if a similar bitterness was what I might yet face. I had no sense that the Fenna whose souls now haunted the wellspring regretted the decision that had been made for them, but that didn't in any way ease the kernel of fear.

I just had to hope that, by doing what Maelle obviously had *not*, and being by my daughter's side every step of the way to guide and support her, I would avoid this sort of confrontation. Because her resenting or hating me for the decision I'd had no real choice in would break me, I was sure of that.

"Because," Maelle said evenly, even as her creature continued to wind around her with increasing intensity. "It was not my duty or my job to care for or support you. You were Marie's creation, not mine. That is the way of our kind—"

"That is bullshit, and we both know it."

"I know many things that you do not, dear Jaqueline, and it is perhaps time you understood the true reason for your being." The insubstantial presence partially solidified. It was indeed a snake. A snake whose body was as thick as an anaconda's. "The lies have dripped from Marie's lips since your rebirth, and you have swallowed them all without thought or reason."

Jaqueline snorted. "She loves me in ways you couldn't even understand."

"She doesn't love you, my dear. She has never loved anyone in her entire life, not even me, and I was her consort for more decades than I care to remember. She uses you, uses your abilities and powers to benefit herself. Nothing more, nothing less."

"You lie. You have always lied. This is nothing more than a game to you—"

"And the biggest game of all is the quest for power, Jaqueline. You know this. It is the creed by which we all have lived."

"Until you fucking destroyed the coven and my life."

Meaning Jaqueline really *hadn't* gotten over Maelle destroying her lover. That was definitely something I could understand, because if any of these bastards threatened anyone I loved, I would hunt them down and kill them without a goddamn second thought.

"Marie crossed a line," Maelle replied, in that same calm and controlled manner. "She broke a promise and faced the consequences. By killing Roger, she broke it yet again."

"Roger was a thrall," Jaqueline bit back. "He was your strength and your sanity, and as such, always fair game in any revenge or war."

"Except our darling maker swore an oath never to turn or kill any of my line without my consent. She broke that oath with Augustine, and then with Roger." She paused, and just for an instant, her anger rose, so thick and heated it sucked my breath away. "He, my dear child, was Augustine's brother. Your great-great-uncle."

CHAPTER TEN

Holy fuck ... Roger had been one of Maelle's descendants?

That certainly explained her fury at Marie snatching him. It wasn't just the fact he was her thrall, but also a grandson a few times removed.

"That is impossible," Jaqueline said. "Augustine never had any siblings. He told us that many times."

"He told you that because he feared what Marie would do if she discovered his sibling existed. She has always had a taste for our bloodline. I was not the first, but I did all in my power to ensure Augustine was the last."

"By making his brother a thrall?" She snorted. "You are no better than Marie."

"Roger wanted revenge. He was a willing participant in the transition."

Jaqueline's fingers twitched, and the darkness boiled around them with greater intensity. "Even if that were true, why seek retribution for the wrong done to Augustine and not to me? Some would say the choice was not mine, either."

"Then some would lie. Magic did play a part in your ceremony, but the decision to turn was always yours. In truth, I wished you had not, but you were always an impetuous, foolish young woman and would not listen—"

Jaqueline made a low sound in the back of her throat and unleashed the spell spinning around her fingers. It hit the wild magic hard, splashing across its surface like paint, briefly staining the luminous threads. Pain shuddered through me, along with a warning; the sphere could not withstand too many more attacks like that without the stain becoming permanent.

"We will never agree on any of these matters, because our memories and experiences are very different," she growled. "What do you want, Mother?"

"I came to give you a choice. Leave this life of darkness Marie has pulled you into—"

"And what? Join your coven?" She laughed bitterly. "Why? So that you can use me as you believe Marie uses me?"

"You are of my blood, but will never be as I am. I have no desire for what you hold, because what you hold is less than mine."

Wow, I thought, *way to win back your daughter, Maelle.*

Jaqueline laughed again. "Oh, I do so love the way the endearments drip from your tongue, Mother. And my other option? Because the first is very unappealing."

Maelle remained silent for several interminably long seconds, but her creature was on the move. It swirled down her body to the floor, and just for a second, seemed to look my way. My breath caught in my throat. Death stared at me through eyes that were little more than pockets of shadows.

Maelle snapped her fingers, and it looked away, leaving me able to breathe again.

Liz? Belle's thought was somewhat fuzzy and seemingly coming from a long distance. *What's going on? The biggest rush of terror just hit me.*

I'm fine. It's fine. It sounded faint and unconvincing, even to me. Then I frowned. *You haven't been following?*

Haven't been able to, though I'm not sure if it's their shielding or the wild magic intervening again.

Well, let's just say the shit is about to hit the fan. Maelle has given Jaqueline an ultimatum and she's definitely not appreciating the choices. Make sure no one comes in here and if I yell run, get everyone away from this house.

As long as you run out as well.

Trust me, if she unleashes her snake, I'm out of here.

Snake? What the fuck—

The pulsing of the wild magic grew, and Belle's voice faded into static. I returned my attention to Maelle and her creature and saw the latter slithering back and forth along the length of sphere separating us from Jaqueline. The sphere pulsed—convulsed?—whenever the creature brushed across it, and the pain in my head and body increased each and every time.

"Maelle," I warned softly.

"I am aware," she replied, not looking away from her daughter.

"No, I don't think you are."

"You will hold your barrier. I will not be much longer."

"I am *not* your serv—"

"No, but you certainly have attachments. Do as I say, or they shall taste my wrath."

I clenched my fingers against the inner wild magic that flared, but it rather scarily held none of its usual power. It might not be connected directly to the sphere, but it was nevertheless being drained by it, just as my physical energy was now being drained, and at a far faster rate than before.

"When you decided to step into this life against my advice and chose Marie to be your maker"—Maelle's voice held just a trace of ... regret? Or was I reading too much into that very slight catch?—"I took steps to ensure that, should you ever wish it, you could leave this life."

Jaqueline stared at her mother for a second. "You would really kill your own flesh and blood?"

That was certainly the question running through my mind, though it wasn't accompanied by the same sense of incredulity.

"Flesh and blood has never been an impediment. Remember, dearest, that I did not falter to kill Augustine, or make Roger a thrall in an effort to not only protect him, but to one day, perhaps, give us both revenge. In that, I have now failed, at least where he is concerned. However, that is not what I meant." She paused, and the snake's actions became more agitated. An odd sense of anticipation rose from its smoky form, and a deepening sense of dread rolled through me. "When I agreed that Marie could turn you, I had two conditions. One, that should you ever wish to leave this life, you could."

"I do not wish," Jaqueline growled. "So, what was the other?"

"That I have the means and the power to return your humanity."

"That is impossible."

A statement that echoed my own, though mine was lodged somewhere in my throat. The pulsing in the sphere was reaching a critical point and the pain in my head was so fierce that I could barely even see. Weakness was a wave I could not fight, and my knees buckled. I hit the floor hard

233

and wrapped my hands around my waist, rocking back and forth and sucking in great gulps of air in an effort to stave off unconsciousness. I could not—*dare* not—let it take me while Maelle and her shadow creature were here.

Somehow, I croaked, "Maelle—"

"A minute. No more, no less." Her voice was sharp. Commanding.

Infuriating.

I glanced at my watch. A minute, no more, no less, just as she'd ordered.

"No one has that power," Jaqueline continued, the sneer I couldn't see thanks to the tears in my eyes so very evident in her voice.

"And in that, you would be very wrong." As my watch ticked over to the minute, she added, "Now, Elizabeth."

I immediately released my hold on the sphere, and the luminous threads disconnected and floated away. The pain eased—not much, but enough—and my vision cleared slightly.

Just in time to witness Maelle unleash her shadow creature.

It boiled through the doorway and straight at Jaqueline. Her eyes went wide, and she stepped back, her gaze cutting to the right, toward the spot where darker magic now pulsed, but before she could run, the snake cut her off.

"Mother, you can't—"

The words died as the snake flowed over her. Flowed into her. She made a garbled sound and dropped to her knees, her expression one of horror and pain. Maelle was spelling, and her power rose, though I had no idea what the spell was other than dark, because she wasn't speaking in any language that I knew. It didn't sound French, more Latin, I thought. As the force of it rose, the darkly lit shadows continued to boil around and through Jaqueline, though I suspected it was the spell rather than the snake that was causing the jerky movements and the shimmering in and out of existence. Her skin was stretching, changing, the bloom of youth fading into something more timeworn. Even her hair lost some of its shine and gained silvery streaks that glittered in the darkness.

The spell was *aging* her.

Or was this the doing of Maelle's shadowed demon? There were plenty around who fed on the life force of others, many of them leaving their victims as little more than aged husks. I hadn't gotten the impression that that was what Maelle had intended for her daughter, but who really knew? The revelations of the last few days had certainly proven just how little we'd really known about her.

Maelle's spell reached a pinnacle, and Jaqueline's body "solidified" once more. Though I really couldn't see her that well, she'd definitely aged. Just how much remained to be seen.

"Dearest Jaqueline," Maelle murmured, her voice now resonating with a power that crawled across my skin. "You are hereby once again made as you were born. Humanity is yours to use as you wish, one year given for each century you have existed. But you can never return to the life of darkness. What has been taken can never be returned."

And with that, Maelle's power snapped away, and her snake—bloated and luminous—left Jaqueline and returned to its mistress. Maelle reached out with one hand, running her fingers through its diaphanous form before murmuring what sounded like a spell. The snake flowed up her body, seemed to kiss her cheek, and then disappeared, returned to whatever hell it had been summoned from.

Jaqueline remained on the floor, her arms wrapped around her body in much the same manner as mine, though for a very different reason. The magic that had flown through me had never intended to hurt; my flesh was simply incapable of withstanding its force for too long. That was obviously not the case with the magic that had swept Jaqueline, and I was sure it had done far more than merely altering her being to dismiss her vampire-given immortality.

You want us in there? came Belle's thought.

No. Maelle is— I paused and studied her. Though I could see her face, I didn't really need to, given the myriad emotions flowing around her. While regret and fury were dominant, there was a deeper sense of instability radiating off her. It wouldn't take much to set her off, and I did not want to be anywhere near her when that happened. *On edge.*

That isn't exactly a new development.

No, but it has definitely gotten worse.

And Jaqueline?

Alive, and possibly human.

What?

Explain later.

I cut our connection as Jaqueline sat back on her heels and drew in a deep, shuddering breath. Her once-perfect face was lined and her skin a little paperish, but in truth, she still looked amazing.

"What in God's name have you done, Mother?" Her voice was hoarse and held more than a little trace of fear.

"I swore an oath to protect my line," Maelle said evenly. "Marie intended to use you—use your magic—to boost her own so that she could kill me. I merely thwarted those plans and, in the process, saved your life. She would have drained you unto death to defeat me."

"Making me human does not erase my magic."

"No. The Nakahi did that."

Was that why her shadow creature had looked at me so ... heatedly? It had wanted to feed, and I was a far closer meal possibility than Jaqueline? Thank God Maelle had called it away.

Jaqueline stared at Maelle for several seconds, her eyes wide, her expression disbelieving. Then she flung out a hand, as if casting a spell. Nothing happened. No magic rose.

She screamed in fury, pushed to her feet, and launched at her mother, her fingers curled into claws ready to rent and tear. Maelle calmly raised a hand and flicked a thin rope of dark purple magic toward Jaqueline, looping it around her daughter's neck and stopping her in her tracks.

"Do not be so foolish, dearest, as my patience has the thinnest of edges now that Roger has been taken from me. I suggest you step through your portal while it still lingers and then leave this reservation—and Marie—for good."

"Marie will help me." The comment came out even hoarser than before, no doubt thanks to the rope lashed around her neck. She was apparently human now, and humans did need to breathe. "She will find a way around what you have done—"

Maelle laughed, the sound low and derisive. "Oh, if you believe that, then you truly do not understand our maker. You have lost that which made you useful. You will be cast out, have no doubt of that."

"She would not—"

"Then go, discover for yourself."

"Maelle, no," I said. "We need her—"

"No, you do not," she cut in, and flicked her rope to the left, toward that hovering pool of darkness I could feel but not see. A heartbeat later, there was a sharp report, followed by an almost metallic scent, then that darkness was gone.

As was all sense of Jaqueline.

Maelle spun on her heels and stared at me for several seconds. Her eyes were flat and yet luminous and her expression remote, but her emotions nevertheless roiled around me. While anger and regret were definitely present in that turbulent cloud, it was for the most part something far more dangerous.

Hunger.

Even as I watched, the tips of her canines began to protrude over her thin lips.

I froze and somehow managed to keep my inner wild magic restrained. If it so much as flickered into existence right now, she would attack, of that I had doubt.

For several more interminably long seconds, neither of us moved. Then she blinked, and the danger retreated, even if its remains echoed in the turbulence that still surrounded her.

One day, all too soon, she would give into temptation and attack.

"I thank you for your assistance in this matter," she said, her voice soft and polite, showing little evidence of her ongoing battle against her baser instincts. "And I offer a word of advice. Protect those that you love, because Marie will be aware of the part you played in this evening's events, and she will seek revenge."

And with that, her magic rose and a vortex of dark energy appeared in the room behind her. She turned, stepped into it, and disappeared. A heartbeat later, the vortex did the same.

I briefly closed my eyes and rested the side of my head against the nearby wall. All I wanted to do was give in to the call of unconsciousness, but Maelle's words echoed and the urgency to get out of this house hit. Marie could and would visit hell upon this house that had cost her a trusted power source, and probably sooner than any of us wanted.

Coming out, I said to Belle.

Coming in, she replied, and a heartbeat later she appeared around the corner. And she wasn't alone. Monty was with her, and I could hear Ashworth and Eli on the porch. I pushed unsteadily to my feet.

"We need to leave. I think Marie—" I paused as energy prickled across my skin. Saw the consternation flicker across Monty's expression, suggesting I wasn't the only one sensing it.

"Run. *Now,*" I ordered, as panic surged.

Belle and Monty swooped in, each wrapped an arm around my waist, then lifted me between them and charged for the door. But the dark energy was drawing closer and closer, the wash of it burning across my skin so fiercely it felt as if I was being consumed by its fire.

As we raced out of the house, I looked up. Saw, in the starlit sky, a tumbling mass of purple fire arching toward the house.

"Fuck," Monty said as we leapt off the porch and raced after Ashworth and Eli.

Five steps. That's all we were able to take before that purple mass of fury hit the house and sent us all flying.

CHAPTER ELEVEN

As we were catapulted high into the air, I reached for my inner wild magic and imagined it forming a protective ball around the three of us. It flowed from my skin without its usual force and wove a net around us, though it wasn't exactly spherical in nature. It nevertheless provided a buffer between us and the ground as we hit hard and then rolled in an ungainly, tangled mess toward the street. We stopped just shy of the three-foot drop onto the pavement, but none of us moved as bits of wood and brick, roof tiles and glass rained all around us. None of it pierced my barrier, though. While it didn't hold any of its usual force, it certainly saved our lives.

It seemed to take forever for the deadly rain to ease, and every bit of me was shaking with exhaustion and pain by the time it did. I released the net, detangled myself from Belle and Monty, but didn't immediately move. I simply didn't have the energy to sit up, let alone stand. I sucked in a deep breath in an effort to stop the inner shaking, but the thick stench of smoke caught in my throat and made me cough. The pain in my head immediately intensified, and I closed my eyes, groaning. A heartbeat later, Belle was in there, dialing the pain sensors back to a survivable level.

"Better?" she asked.

I nodded weakly, but didn't open my eyes. "What about Ashworth and Eli? Anyone seen them?"

"I've contacted both and they're fine," Belle said. "Ashworth's gone to grab the SUV, and Eli is just about to call in the fire brigade."

"I imagine the neighbors have already done that," Monty said. "There's plenty of them peeking through curtains right now to see what the hell is happening."

"I'd rather them be peeking than confronting," I muttered. I really didn't have the energy or the patience to be dealing with questions from curious onlookers right now. "What about the house? Anything left of it?"

"The fireball hit the kitchen, and there's nothing left of it or the living room," Monty said. "But most of the bedrooms remain intact. I guess we were lucky that Marie didn't throw a fireball as big as the one that destroyed the ranger station. Otherwise, even with the wild magic protecting us, we might have been toast."

"She probably wasn't capable of throwing another fireball that big," Belle said. "Those things take blood and energy, and even a vampire has a finite amount of either."

"I doubt she's using her own blood." He glanced at me, something I felt more than saw. "You able to move yet, Liz? Because what remains of the house is on fire, and the grass is starting to catch. We need to move."

I finally opened my eyes. The night was bright with a mix of orange and purple fire, and the smoke rising from both smothered the brightness of the stars. Instinct stirred briefly, and I had a bad, *bad* feeling it was a phenomenon we would see again, and soon.

I pushed into a sitting position, waited until my head stopped spinning, then turned around on my butt and carefully slithered down the embankment to the pavement. Then, finally, I looked up at the house. Monty had been practicing the art of overstatement when he'd said most of the bedrooms remained intact, because that entire area had no roof, and two of the rooms were missing internal walls. The blast had also taken some tiles off the roof of the house behind, and there were bits of wood and bricks embedded in the sheds of the property next door. Overall, though, there hadn't been a lot of fallout damage—not when compared to the destruction surrounding the ranger station, anyway.

As our SUV turned the corner and headed toward us, my phone rang, the tone telling me it was Aiden. I dragged out my phone, hit the answer button, and said, "I'm fine."

"Fine as in alive, but the weariness in your voice suggests you're also dead on your feet." He hesitated, his concern evident. "Perhaps you should go to the hospital and be checked out. I know the Fenna said our daughter would indeed be born, but let's not take any chances."

"The last thing I need right now is to be sitting in the Emergency Department for hours. Trust me, there's nothing wrong that a good meal and twelve hours' sleep won't fix. How's things there?"

"Obvious change of topic, but I'll play along. The fire's under control, and two of the brigades that were here are now on their way over to you." He paused. "What happened to Jaqueline?"

"Well, she's still alive."

"Did you call in Maelle?"

"Yes, and she's the reason Jaqueline lives. We're about to head home—how far away are you?"

"Another hour, at least. Don't wait up for me."

"I doubt I could even if I wanted to." I hesitated. "Just be careful, okay?"

"As someone is prone to say, always."

I laughed, told him I loved him, and hung up. Ashworth stopped the SUV in front of us, and Monty opened the rear door and waved me in. I scooted all the way over so that he and Belle could sit next to each other. Eli climbed into the front.

"So," Ashworth said, once we were underway again, "what the hell happened inside that house?"

I quickly updated them and then added, "I had no idea it was possible to regain humanity after becoming a vampire."

"That's because it's generally not," Eli said. "But then, there are few witches or mages in this world that would have the power and the demonic contacts that Maelle obviously has. I suppose what magic gives, magic can also take away."

"And I'd place money on the fact that the registrar are well aware it is possible to undo vampirism with magic," Ashworth said. "They are undoubtedly the reason there's very little information about the possibility out in the wider world."

The registrar was a private vampire organization that supposedly held the record of every vampire created and which insisted that all vampires report a location change to ensure there was no overlap of territory. "Maelle mentioned the existence of the registrar, but I was under the impression few people knew about it."

"Few do, but the RWA has by necessity had some interactions with them." Ashworth grimaced. "They are not an easy organization to get information from, however."

"I'm surprised you get *any* information from them," Belle said.

"A rogue vampire is no more in their best interests than it is RWA's," Ashworth said. "For the most part, they deal with the situation well before whispers of vampire troubles ever reach our ears."

"To which the sane amongst us can only say, thank God," Monty said, voice dry. "I only wish they'd step in and take care of *this* situation."

"Maelle wouldn't want them here," I said.

"Doesn't mean we shouldn't contact them. Maybe they could help."

"And maybe that would just tip our insane vampire over the edge."

"She leapt over the edge a long time ago," Monty said. "But that being the case, it might be best if we all bunk in together for a couple of days at the café until we sort this mess out."

"Laddie, aside from the fact the café is not big enough for all of us, I'm way too old to be sleeping on the floor."

"Besides," Eli added, "it's unlikely she'll come after us before the three of you, or Aiden. As far as that lot are concerned, we're the spares rather than the main event."

"But," Ashworth said, flicking a glance my way, "we'll nevertheless ramp up the protections again, just in case."

"Good," I said, even though I suspected they were right about us being the targets more than them. If Marie or Maelle was going to kidnap anyone in order to take me out of the picture, it would be either Aiden or Belle, and instinct was leaning more to Belle. Maelle was well aware that she was my familiar and, thanks to her telepathic raid of Roger's mind, so was Marie.

Ashworth dropped us off at the café with the promise to

return the SUV later that morning. Belle made the three of us a strength and revitalization potion, which I gulped down without really tasting, then I staggered upstairs, grabbed a quick shower, and all but fell into bed. I was asleep almost before my head hit the pillow.

Dreams came and went, fragile wisps that held neither warning nor substance, but rather the desperate need to find Jaqueline. She was probably our biggest hope of ferreting out Marie's location before an all-out, all-consuming war started. Because that's what was coming if we couldn't find a way to stop it. We needed to find her. *Had* to find her.

As that thought echoed through my dream state, something within me shifted, and I once again found myself on the astral plane. This time, I caught a glimpse of my sleeping body first, before my astral being was swept away, not to a forest clearing, but rather a house. It was a two-story building with a steeply pitched roof and two dormer windows on the front side of the building that rather resembled eyes. Dark, broken eyes—as broken and as dark as the people who sheltered inside. It was surrounded by ancient trees that kept it shrouded in shadows despite the brightness of the sun, and the song of cicadas rode the air. There was no car, no van, and nothing to indicate anyone actually lived here, even if every sense I owned said there were at least three inside.

A flicker of movement through the trees to my right had me looking around.

A figure stumbled out from the trees, her clothes torn and dark with sweat, her copper-colored hair no longer in a ponytail but floating around her face like glimmering snakes.

Jaqueline.

My gaze darted back to the house.

This had to be Marie's lair. *Had* to be. And *that* meant this time, for the first time, I hadn't been called onto the plane, but had stepped onto it of my own free will. Excitement pulsed through me, but I resisted the urge to move. Jaqueline showed no sign of sensing my astral presence, but I wasn't about to risk changing that or drawing Marie's attention.

Jaqueline staggered toward the house and up the steps. The door must have been locked, because she raised a fist and hit the old wire screen several times. The sound echoed and, a few seconds later, the main door opened, and a man appeared, though I was too far away to see anything more than a vague, largish outline.

They spoke for a few seconds and then the door was opened, and Jaqueline stepped inside. I wanted, so wanted, to follow but caution held me in place. Better to be safe than sorry, even here on the astral plane.

A few seconds later, voices rose. One angry and yet oddly amused, the other bitter and filled with hurt. I had no idea what they were saying, because they were speaking French, but it was very definitely Marie and Jaqueline.

Then magic rose and, a heartbeat later, Jaqueline came flying backward out of the house. She hit the ground hard and rolled several times, then simply lay there, sobbing and cursing.

Maelle had been right. Marie had no use for Jaqueline now that she had lost her magic and regained her humanity. To be honest, I was surprised she'd simply been evicted rather than dined upon.

Jaqueline lay there for a few more minutes, then rose, brushed the dirt and blood from her hands and face, and raised a fist, yelling something in French at the house.

Something that very much sounded like a threat. Then she turned and limped away.

My gaze returned to the house. Dark silence had returned.

As tempting as it was to go closer, I resisted, and instead tried to follow Jaqueline and get some idea where this place was.

But tiredness pulsed through me, and an awareness of danger rose. I was draining what little remained of my strength and if I was on this plane when my strength failed, then it was possible I could be stranded here. I closed my astral eyes and imagined my room, my bed, and my sleeping body, then expressed a wish to return.

In an instant, I had, but I didn't wake. I simply sank deeper into sleep and finally got the rest I so desperately needed.

I woke to the realization Aiden hadn't made it home, and panic surged, even though I knew there were a dozen different and very logical reasons why he might not have, including him simply not wanting to disturb me. Logic played second fiddle to fear, however, when there were two angry vampires prowling the reservation.

I reached for my phone and called him. The phone seemed to ring on forever, which only increased my tension.

He did finally answer, though.

"Sorry," he said, sounding tired. "Didn't hear the phone over the noise."

Said noise was evident in the background—sirens, men shouting, the crackle of fire. "God, don't tell me we've been hit with another fireball?"

"No, just a regular old bushfire this time. It's in the heart of the old forest behind the Eureka Reef area."

"Meaning the smoke we smelled when we were up there was the start of it?"

"I don't think so, because we did send a drone aloft and couldn't find anything." He paused, and a voice in the background said something I couldn't quite catch. "And now we've got some fucking tourists sightseeing up on one of the fire roads. I'll have to go and guide them out."

I hesitated, wanting to tell him about what I'd seen on the astral plane, then simply said, "Okay."

"What, no 'be careful out there'?"

I half smiled. "You always are, aren't you?"

He laughed. "See you soon, love."

He hung up. I drew in a deep breath and released it slowly. It didn't help ease the inner fear any, but at least this time, it was due more to the unpredictable nature of a bush-fire rather than a vampire.

I scrolled through my contacts and rang Jaz. It was pointless ringing the station, because the station no longer existed. She answered immediately. "Hey, Liz, it's a bit hectic here right now—is the reason you're ringing pressing?"

"Could be."

"Then give it to me."

I described the house and then said, "Do you know of any place resembling that?"

"Not offhand, but I can get Maggie to ring around the real estate agents to see if they know anything. Why?"

Maggie was the station's receptionist and a ranger in training. "It's the current lair of one of our vamps."

"Well, that's *definitely* a pressing matter. I'll get Mags to call you if she uncovers anything."

"Thanks, Jaz."

"No probs. Gotta go."

She hung up before I could ask where they'd temporarily set up. Not that it really mattered, because Aiden would no doubt tell me later. I tossed the phone onto the bed, then got up and quickly dressed before heading downstairs. The magic buzzing around the reading room told me Belle was in there with a client, so once I'd checked with Penny that everything was under control, I headed back upstairs, made myself something to eat and drink, then settled down to do some more paperwork. When it came to running your own business, it was a never-ending task.

Belle came up a few hours later, carrying two bottles of water and a plate stacked with sandwiches. I hit the save button and closed the laptop. "How'd the readings go?"

"There were tears, and they weren't all the client's." She half shrugged. "Readings involving kids are always the hardest. But I do have some good news."

"So do I. Well, sorta."

She handed me a bottle of water then placed the sandwiches on the coffee table. "Define 'sorta.'"

"I astral traveled last night and discovered Marie's lair. Unfortunately, I have no idea where in the reservation it is."

"Of course not, because your dreams aren't always the most helpful of things, so why would your astral traveling be any different?"

I reached for a sandwich half—which was thickly sliced ham and cheese—and bit into it. "I called Jaz—she's asked Maggie to contact the real estate people and see if they can place it."

"Why Maggie?" she asked, taking one of the sandwiches. "And where's Aiden?"

"He—and just about everyone else—is dealing with a

bushfire—a regular one rather than one caused by Marie—out Eureka Reef way."

"Well, let's hope they get it under control before the wind kicks up again and blasts it toward the town."

"Amen to that." I lightly touched my half-eaten sandwich against hers. "What's your news?"

"My spirit guides finally came through."

I frowned. "On what? Because it's not like you've set them any task of late."

"Oh, how quickly you forget. Remember the telepath who attacked Roger?"

"Don't tell me they've actually gone and found him?"

"Indeed. He is, apparently, staying in the Colonial Motel no more than five minutes away from here."

"Why did it take the guides so long if he's only a few minutes away?"

"Because he's only just driven back into town. They felt his resonance when he telepathically stepped into the mind of the hotel's receptionist and altered her memories, making her believe a couple had registered into his room rather than a solo."

"Why would he do that when no one here knows who he is?"

"Marie does."

"Yeah, but if he was afraid of her, he wouldn't have come back here."

"I guess it depends on *why* he's back and how much he's actually being paid." She finished her sandwich and reached for another. "I'm thinking we need to go talk to him."

"I'm thinking you're right." I paused to lick the excess pickle spread from my fingers then reached for another sandwich. "I wonder if he's been brought back in an attempt to take you out?"

"My guides suggested the very same thing, and then laughed at his gall."

Well, at least we finally agreed on something. "Are we going to confront him directly or hit him from a distance?"

She hesitated. "Probably best to maintain a distance until we've got him snared and are sure it's not a trap."

"Given we're dealing with vampires who use magic to step from one place to another, it's probably safer to just presume every situation from now on could be a trap."

"There has to be a limit to how often they can use their transport spells, though. It's not an easy magic to perform, and Marie, at the very least, has to be running out of blood donors."

"She had two with her last night," I said.

"Two is better than ten."

"Yeah, but it's not like she needs human blood for blood spells, and the roos are almost in plague numbers in the reservation at the moment."

"I still think that, with all the fireballs she threw last night, she has to be riding low on the energy scale. Hopefully, this damn telepath might give us some information so we can capitalize on that."

"Hopefully." I finished the last bit of my sandwich. "Where's Monty?"

"He, Ashworth, and Eli are researching a means of tracing the mage balls back to the point of origin."

"How, given the mage balls and their fires are both out?"

"The ranger station one is, but the one at the house burned into the morning, and Monty was able to snare a lingering bit of flame and keep it activated."

It was worth giving it a go, I guess, although I personally hoped we'd seen the last of those goddamn mage balls.

Belle dug her phone from her pocket and brought up Google Maps. "The motel is here on Barker Street, with an exit into Campbell, and it basically sits between two old churches. Our telepath has the room situated at the back of the lot, right next to this church." She pointed to the red brick building in Campbell Street. "According to my guides, the church sits higher than the hotel, so there are no fences between the two. We just have to scoot through the church grounds and drop down into the service walkway that divides the two properties."

"He'll sense us coming though, won't he?"

Belle smiled. "You forget just how good a telepathic range I have these days. That man will be under my control before he knows what has hit him."

"Excellent." I rose. "Shall we go?"

She hesitated, her expression slightly unfocused as she talked to her spirit guides. "He's there, so yes."

I walked into my bedroom to grab my phone, then followed Belle downstairs and out to the rear parking area. Ashworth had returned the SUV a few hours earlier, as promised, and had even cleaned the thing, which, considering all the bullet holes, wouldn't have been an easy job.

The hotel was only three blocks away, but in the afternoon heat, it was way too far to walk. Belle parked several houses up from the red brick church and then climbed out and raised a hand, shading her eyes as she studied the motel's rooftop.

I walked around the back of the SUV and stopped beside her. "He still there?"

She nodded. "According to my guides, lounging on the bed in his underwear drinking a beer."

"Oh, that's going to be a sight to behold."

"You have no idea. Hang on while I grab him." She narrowed her gaze, and, through our link, I felt the fierce wash of her mental energy as she reached out and snared the other telepath. After a few seconds, she nodded and pushed away from the SUV. "Right, got him. Let's go."

We hurried down the street, cut through the church-yard, and then dropped down into the small service lane. There were three units along this side of the property, and rather handily, all three had back doors. Our target was the last in the line, nearest to the street. I pressed my hand against the door and raised a quick unlock spell. The door also had a chain latch, but that was even easier to undo.

I pushed the door open, waved Belle through, then followed and locked the door behind us. The room was small, consisting of little more than a queen-size bed, a small wardrobe, a bathroom, and one of those old-fashioned meal hatches to the left of the main door. There was a small TV on a swinging arm thingy to the right of that, and on the wall on the other side of the door, an air conditioner.

The gentleman was lying on his side, his head propped up on one hand and a beer clutched in the other. He looked to be in his mid to late thirties and was well-built despite the slight belly he was developing. He was also extremely hairy. With a rug that thick covering his front, back, and legs, it wasn't any surprise he'd stripped off to his boxer shorts. Especially since the old air conditioner, while running, didn't seem to be doing a whole lot.

I walked over to the front window, crossed my arms, and leaned against the frame to keep watch. Belle squatted in front of our captive, plucked the beer from his hand, and placed it on the bedside table.

"If you answer our questions honestly, you will be

253

allowed to leave this reservation without harm. Attempt to lie, shout, break my hold on your mind or in any other way attack me, and I will turn your brain to mush." She smiled sweetly. "And you know I have more than enough power to do that. Understood? You may nod if so."

The man obediently nodded.

"Right," she continued, the force of her telepathic control easing a little, no doubt to allow him to speak. "Why have you returned to the reservation?"

"I was reengaged to neutralize a woman named Isabelle Kent." He eyed her for a second. "That's you, I take it?"

She raised an eyebrow. "You don't know?"

"I was told you were the dark-skinned woman who ran a place called The Psychic Café. She said I shouldn't have any problems, that you were a Sarr witch and therefore underpowered in both magic and psi skills." He grimaced. "They lied, obviously."

"Obviously," Belle intoned dryly. "Who reengaged you?"

"Marie Bouchier."

That Marie had made direct contact was a little surprising. She'd seemed the type to let her underlings handle this sort of stuff—but maybe she was simply running out of them.

"How did she get in contact with you?" Belle continued. "And when were you supposed to 'neutralize' me?"

"How else does anyone contact anyone? Via a phone, of course." It was crossly said, though he seemed to be taking the whole situation rather well, considering. "And it was supposed to happen this afternoon, right after closing time, when you were heading home."

Meaning Marie isn't aware you and Monty are staying

at the café, I said. *Which surprises me—I would have thought she'd have a watcher on the place.*

Maybe you're right—she's simply running out of manpower. To our captive, she added, "You've got her number?"

He reeled it off and then asked, "Who are you, really? Because I'm one of the strongest registered telepaths around, and you snared me like I was a babe."

"The key to your question is *registered.* I'm not. What, exactly, did Marie want you to do once you'd 'neutralized' me?"

"I was to bundle you into my car and take you to the address I was given."

"And that is?"

He gave us map coordinates rather than an actual address.

"And do you know where that is?" Belle asked.

"Up in the Muckleford Nature Reserve, near the Red, White, and Blue Mine, according to Google. I'm supposed to take you there and hand you over."

I couldn't help snorting, and he looked at me. "What?"

"Have you met Marie? Face-to-face, I mean," I asked.

He frowned. "As I said, all our dealings have been via phone, so I've never actually met her. But that's not unusual when it comes to this sort of job. Why?"

"Because," Belle said, "Marie Bouchier is a very old vampire, and you, no doubt, would have provided a nice little snack once you'd handed me over."

His gaze flicked between us for a second, disbelief evident. "If that was her inclination, she could have killed me the first time I was here."

"When you mushed Roger's mind, the war between vamps was only just ramping up," I said. "At this current moment in time, both Marie and her opposite have lost multiple people, including vital feeders, so they're on the prowl for new blood."

"Well, that's fucked." His mouth twisted. "I guess I should thank you ladies for intervening, even if it is decidedly unpleasant to be captured like this."

"You might want to remember that next time you're employed to ensnare someone," I said.

His smile flashed. "When there's gobs of cash in the offing, memory tends to go AWOL."

"And is there?" I couldn't help asking curiously. "Gobs of cash in memory smearing or mind-napping, I mean."

"Nah, them jobs are rare, and I don't often take them anyways. I only did this time because the cash offered was off the charts." He sniffed. "Memory theft is my gig. You know, bank details, corporate secrets, stuff like that."

"Maybe you should stick to that in future," I said. "But I'd advise you to do so a long way from here."

"Oh, you can be sure of that." His gaze returned to Belle. "At least in my own patch, I'm in no danger of being mind-napped, however politely it was done."

"I won't be so polite next time, so make sure there isn't one," Belle said. "What time were you supposed to take me up to the meeting point?"

"At dusk tonight. She said I just needed to keep you knocked out until the exchange is made."

"Was she meeting you? Or was one of her people?" Belle asked.

"I was supposed to meet a gent called Hank." He shrugged. "She said he'd be arriving in a white van, and I was to help transfer you over."

"And that's it? That's all you had to do?"

He nodded. "The rest of the payment would be handed

over—cash, rather than transfer this time—and I would be allowed to leave." He paused. "That wasn't going to happen, was it?"

"Unlikely." Belle's telepathic grip on his mind tightened a fraction. "I would suggest you have no further contact with her. I'd also suggest you get dressed, check out, and leave this reservation within the next hour. Otherwise, the next time we meet, I won't be so pleasant."

He half smiled. "Well, it's not like you've given me a choice in the matter, is it?"

"A gentle compulsion is very different to an overt command, as you well know. Call it a professional courtesy that will not be extended again."

"Understood." He paused. "What of Marie?"

"We're dealing with her."

"As in, she's one dead vampire once you track her down?"

Belle pushed to her feet. "That is definitely the plan."

"Then I will hold off on the refund."

"You'd offer a refund for an incomplete mission?" I asked, surprised.

"Of course." He looked and sounded offended. "Reputation is everything is this business."

"Yeah, well, you and your reputation have an hour to get off this reservation once I release you," Belle said. "Don't waste it."

"As soon as I finish my beer, I'm out of here."

You had to admire the man's nonchalance, if nothing else. I walked over to the back door, waved Belle through, and followed her down the service lane. We were back at the SUV when I felt her release him.

"You think he'll actually leave?" I asked once we were both back in the car.

"While he's probably strong enough to break the compulsion I placed on him, he's not really the type to invite trouble, despite his shady business. So, yes, I do think he'll leave." She started the SUV, then glanced at me. "What's our next step?"

"I think you and I should make that meeting."

"It could be dangerous."

"It could also be our one chance to snare Marie and stop this rot."

"She's not going to be there—Hank will be, whoever he is."

"Yes, but you can sneak into his mind and steal her location information before he actually shows himself."

Belle waited for a few cars to pass, then did a U-turn and headed down the street. "If Hank is a fledgling or even a feeder, she'll feel me in his mind and kill him before I can steal too much information. Or, even worse, she'll flick another goddamn fireball at us. She's got a penchant for doing that, remember."

"I could hardly forget, but I still think it's worth the chance."

"Are we telling Monty and Ashworth? Because I don't think it's wise to do this without backup."

"I agree." If only because very little so far had gone to plan. "They'll need to be far enough away that the vamp can't hear their heartbeats, though."

"Which will be difficult when we're in the middle of a forest and we have no idea which direction they'll be coming from."

"True." I tugged my phone from my pocket and googled the mine he'd mentioned. "Okay, the mine is basically one of those metal tower thingies, but there are a couple of old dams not all that far away. The satellite image has a car parked close to the largest and shows some people in the water, so it's obviously in use as a swimming hole."

"Handy cover, given the heat." A smile twitched her lips. "Though Monty's lily whiteness might just blind Ashworth at the wrong moment."

I laughed. "They don't have to strip off and actually go in."

"But he will, because under all that whiteness, he is a fish. Shall we head over to Ashworth's and update them?"

I nodded and sent him a text to let him know we were on our way.

I'll put the kettle on, he sent back, making me smile.

It only took a few minutes to get over there. Once Belle had parked behind Monty's old station wagon, we made our way through the front gate and up the path. Eli opened the door and ushered us into coolness, and Ashworth had the promised cup of tea waiting on the table.

"Any luck with the tracer spell?" Belle asked, dropping a kiss on Monty's cheek before sitting beside him.

"Yes and no," he replied. "The bit of mage fire I snared flamed out before we could test the spell, but we think we can apply it to active mage fires. Its reliability will, of course, depend on how soon we notice the mage fire."

"Given we've tended not to notice them before they're almost on us, that's not sounding too hopeful."

"No, but it's better than nothing, which is all we would have otherwise," Eli said. "To what do we owe this unexpected honor?"

"We found the telepath that mushed Roger's mind," Belle said, "and had a quiet chat with him."

"Did you now?" A smile twitched Ashworth's lips. "Was it a willing chat or a forced one? From his point of view, I mean."

"It was a pleasantly compliant one, so a bit of both," she replied. "He was given a big cash incentive to come back, kidnap me, and then hand me over to one of Marie's people at a prearranged time and place. Liz and I believe we should keep that meeting."

"We've nothing to lose by trying," Monty said. "Whereabouts is the meeting set up?"

I gave him the coordinates then added, "It's apparently up near a metal thingy over the Red, White, and Blue Mine."

Monty pulled the location up on his phone. "According to my longitude and latitude app, it's actually the intersection of two tracks a few hundred yards away from the poppethead—the metal thingy you mentioned—which means it should be far enough away from the meeting point that they won't hear our heartbeats or sense our presence, but close enough for us to ride to the rescue should the shit hit the fan."

"They would surely do a check of the area before they revealed themselves, though," Ashworth said. "We are not dealing with stupid vampires, unfortunately."

"What other choice is there? We could do an invisibility spell, but they're likely to sense it," Monty said. "Besides, a lone car or a truck isn't going to cause too much alarm, and surely they'll be anxious to get the exchange over with quickly, given they'd know Liz and Aiden would be pulling out all stops to find Belle."

"Speaking of Aiden," I said. "Has anyone heard how the fire is going? Is it under control as yet?"

Eli shook his head. "Not according to the Vic Emergency app."

"Is Castle Rock in any danger?"

"If the wind changes, it might be, but right now it seems centralized in the forest above Eureka Reef."

"That fire happened at a very convenient moment, if you ask me," Monty said. "It's certainly kept the rangers busy."

"There's no indication it was deliberately lit, is there?" I asked sharply.

"No, but there's no indication it wasn't either." He tapped his phone screen. "Dusk is around nine tonight. Our main problem is the fact that these vamps will be expecting a man to bring Belle in, and they're familiar with all of us,"

"I'd normally suggest we grab a ranger," Ashworth said. "But aside from the fact they're all occupied, there's a good chance they know them by sight, too."

"What about Levi?"

I glanced at Monty. "What about him?"

"He has a van, and he'll be able to scent anyone approaching long before we could magically. And, as a bonus, by werewolf standards he's built like a brick shithouse. That could come in handy if things kick off into a fight."

While that was true, the last thing I wanted to do was put someone else in the path of danger, especially when that someone was Jaz's husband. "He's not protected against magic—"

"We can make another band easily enough," Monty cut in. "Hell, I'll even give him that telepathic protection band I have sitting around. Between both of those, he'll be better protected than any of us."

"We could ask," Belle said, glancing at me. "The worst he can do is say no."

I hesitated, then dragged out my phone and made the call. Levi didn't say no. In fact, he was surprisingly enthusiastic. But then, werewolves were never shy about stepping into a fight, and Jaz had no doubt kept him updated on everything that had been going on over the last few days. I just hoped that the shit didn't hit the fan, because if he got hurt, Jaz might never forgive us.

"He said he'll meet us at the Muckleford Community Center at eight fifteen."

"Should give us plenty of time to set everything up," Monty said. "In the meantime, we should get down to the business of constructing the protective charm for him."

We finished our teas and coffees first, then Ashworth pulled out everything we needed to construct the charm for Levi. By the time we'd finished layering in the multiple protective spells, it was close to five.

After arranging for Ashworth and Eli to pick us up at eight—Ashworth's truck was probably the lesser known of all of ours—we headed back to the café. As we climbed out of the SUV, a luminous thread of power drifted toward me—it was from Katie's wellspring rather than the main one.

"I'll be in in a minute," I told Belle, and held out a hand to the thread.

As it wrapped around my wrist, Katie said, *You need to step into our wellspring. Now. Today. The Fenna are saying it is urgent, that the danger is reaching its culmination and you are not ready.*

I frowned. *Did they say why they believed the danger is peaking? Because, aside from the fireballs Marie has thrown our way, there's been no overt sign of the fight ramping up.*

Even if my dreams did seem to be suggesting otherwise.

They say the darkness is growing, that it is staining an ever-wider area.

If that's the case, why haven't they contacted me and

given me the location? We can't deal with what we don't know about.

They say they have not mentioned it because you are not ready. That what you have seen in your dreams is only just the beginning.

They were in my dreams? Well, fuck. *I don't know, Katie—*

We have to take the chance. Whatever these vampires are raising is foul—

Wait—what?

Something is being called. There is blood staining the ground, and it feels foul. I do not know what it is beyond evil, and Gabe is by no means a master when it comes to such things.

Is it just the one evil? Or are there two? Meaning, was it just Marie raising evil, or had Maelle well and truly leapt off the sanity bridge and was now calling something even worse than her punch monster?

She hesitated. *I can only sense the one, but that is not a guarantee there is not another. The Fenna do imply there is more than one.*

I wearily rubbed my eyes. This wasn't what I needed right now, especially given our plans for tonight. *Okay, I'll head up there now.*

Thank you.

Her thread unwound from my wrist and floated away. I glanced around, looking for a thread from the older wellspring, but there was nothing. Maybe they simply didn't want me questioning them any more than necessary, and that thought only had the doubts ramping up.

It's better to take the chance than not came Belle's thought. *In the end, whatever else they're up to, they need you to survive so that your daughter can become one of them.*

If stepping into Katie's spring affects me as badly as stepping into the main wellspring did, I'm not going to be in any fit state to help tonight.

"We've got four witches, a telepath, and a werewolf," she replied, coming back out the door with a small chiller bag and my backpack. "If all of us can't cope with a solitary vamp, then this reservation is doomed."

I accepted the bags and tossed them both onto the front seat. "Given what Katie just said, it might not be just the one vamp."

"If either of them are conjuring the mother of all supernatural nasties, then they're not going to waste them against us."

"I hope you're right."

"Even as you fear I'm not."

Her voice was dry, and I smiled. "Just remember that Maelle seems to be following our every move with unnerving ease, so it's always possible she'll send something nasty up to the meeting point to kill whoever Marie sends."

"Then we will need to be well prepared." She motioned toward the front seat. "Make sure you drink the revitalization and strength potions I made."

"Potions? Plural?"

She smiled. "One for before the hike up Katie's mountain; one for after the immersion."

I groaned. "Seriously? Two in one day is just cruel."

She laughed. "You'll be thanking me if you come out of the wellspring in a less than pristine state. I've added a few special herbs."

I raised my eyebrows. "That's sounds ominous. Maybe even illegal."

She laughed. "If this meeting goes like every other one

you've had with Katie, you'll somehow lose time, so it might be an idea if we simply meet you at Muckleford."

"Hopefully I won't be that late, but ..." I hesitated, wanting to ask them to wait for me but also knowing how important it was that we gained whatever information we could from this Hank.

"We'll be fine," Belle said gently. "If it's a trap, well, we'll deal with it. You'd better get going, before the older wellspring starts getting shitty with you again."

"I've a feeling shitty will be the defining word of our relationship over the next sixteen or so years."

Belle grinned. "Well, they signed you up as caretaker until your daughter is old enough; now they have to suffer the consequences."

I laughed, jumped into the SUV, then reversed out and headed toward the wellspring. The roads were reasonably clear, but smoke filled the air, cutting visibility down. Right now, the wind wasn't strong, and I couldn't help but hope it remained that way. The last thing we needed was the wind changing and Castle Rock coming under threat ... although it was always possible that, if this fire had been deliberately lit by our vamps, that might be their intent. After all, if the town was evacuated, then we'd lose the one place we were generally safe from their attacks. Fireballs aside, of course.

When I reached the parking area at the start of the track up to Katie's wellspring, I gulped down the first of Belle's potions, then washed the foul taste away with a bit of water. After locking the SUV, I grabbed the backpack—mainly so I could throw the second potion, a bottle of water, and my keys into it—then headed up the mountain. Smoke tainted the air, scratching lightly at my throat, and the day was still but not quiet. The waves of noise coming from the cicadas just about drowned out all other sounds, but in this heat, it wasn't like there'd be much moving about anyway. Even the snakes would have found somewhere sunny to bask rather than moving about in the shadows haunting the tree-lined path.

I was about halfway there when the wellspring's luminous threads appeared. Their gentle song surrounded me, creating a harmonious wall that at least went some way to muting the wretched cicada song.

The clearing, while not large, was noticeably cooler than the rest of the forest, despite the fact a good percentage of it was baked in sunshine. It was also strewn with rocks due to the distant landslip that had taken out a good portion of the cliff directly opposite. At the base of the slip was an ankle-deep rock well. The water bubbling up from a seam near the cliff's base lapped over the edge of the basin, then wound down the gentle slope, eventually joining the larger streams farther down the mountain. Unlike many other tiny streams in the area, though, this one had not evaporated in the heat.

But that tiny well was the source of the wild magic, and the air above it shimmered with its force. Its output had increased further since I'd last been here, and was now a gently swirling vortex of rainbow brilliance taller than me and at least five feet wide.

And I had to step into it.

Unease stirred, but I tried to think of the positive—at least this time, I didn't have to step into a goddamn mine and drop who knows how many feet into the earth to reach the heart of the spring.

Katie stood next to the spring, her form solid rather than ghostly, although if you looked hard enough, the wellspring's shimmer was faintly visible through her figure. She was a typical O'Connor in looks—tall and rangy, with short blonde-brown hair and a sharp but pretty face. Gabe stood next to her, his figure wispier, but his scarlet hair glowing in the rainbow wash of light coming from the wellspring.

What I didn't expect to see here were the luminous wisps from the older wellspring. The Fenna were here to watch.

I motioned toward them. "How long have they been here?"

"Little more than an hour" came Katie's response. "Just before I contacted you, in fact."

"And the weight of that spell?"

"Grows heavier."

I frowned. "It's very unusual for a spell to take more than an hour to develop. They must be doing something else."

"It started when the fire started," Gabe said. "We believe they might be feeding it."

"Which would explain why it has been stubbornly hard to put out." I swiped at the trickles of sweat running into my eyes. "Why didn't you mention it when we talked earlier? Monty or Ashworth could have gone out to check and maybe mute its force."

"Because we believe the fire is a distraction—a means of taking the rangers and perhaps even some witches out of the equation," Katie said. "If they intended true harm, they would have swept it toward Castle Rock, but it remains in the hills."

Meaning Monty's suspicions had been right on the money.

"However," Gabe added, "the weight on the earth suggests there is more to that spell than merely feeding a wildfire, because it deadens the earth underneath it."

I frowned. "Why would they want to do that? That makes no sense."

A silvery thread from the old wellspring wound around my wrist and the whispers of the Fenna filled my mind.

Wild magic could not be called from dead earth. They were creating a cage for me, one that I couldn't call the wild magic into.

Which, while scary, also suggested they didn't know about my inner wild magic. Didn't know it was a part of my being rather than something I could simply use and control. Would that matter in this dead zone they were creating? I didn't know—and hoped like hell that we could stop them before it ever became necessary to find out.

"I still don't understand why it's become so urgent that I step into the wellspring," I said. "Even if they successfully prevent me calling on the wild magic through the earth, I've always been able to gather it from the air, and what deadens the earth shouldn't affect that ability, should it?"

Again, the whispers ran through my mind. They believed that what I gathered from the air, even when combined with my own, would not be enough to fight Marie and whatever remained of her coven.

The key words there being "they believed."

But did that mean I dared discount it?

I swiped at another trickle of sweat and glanced at the shimmering pool. Dread surged, but so too did determination. If stepping into this wellspring meant not only my survival but that of everyone I cared about, then really, I had no real choice.

I returned my gaze to Katie, though I aimed my question at the Fenna. "How does my stepping into the wellspring affect Katie? She and Gabe gave their lives to protect this place, and I don't want to do anything to jeopardize that."

The whispers rolled again, this time including Katie and Gabe. My stepping into the wellspring could usurp her control, but this was not something that had been done before and was not a certainty.

"It is a risk we must take," Katie said. "Too much is at stake."

I studied her for a minute and then glanced down at the thread on my wrist. "What if Katie and I step in as one?"

The Fenna's whispering rose in a wave that spoke of uncertainty and doubt. I waited and, after a few seconds, the wave died back to understandable levels. While in theory it should heighten her control as much as it did mine, it was a risk, with an unpredictable outcome.

"For me, or Katie, or your plans?"

The wave rose again. They were displeased with my distrust.

Tough.

I glanced at Katie again. "We do this as one or not at all."

"Merging takes a toll on your body, and you can't afford—"

"Stepping into the wellspring will take an even greater toll, but maybe if I'm sharing body space with you—the spring's guardian—those effects will be lessened."

Katie looked at Gabe for several seconds, and I had a feeling they were conversing. Finally, she nodded. "We can but try."

I stripped off my backpack, tugged off my boots and socks, and, after placing them beside the pack, held out a hand. "Let's do it."

She placed her fingers in mine a heartbeat before her energy swept into my body and two became one. The surrounding light became bright and fierce, the wellspring a kaleidoscope of not just color but sound, and Gabe flesh and blood rather than merely corporeal.

This was the world as Katie saw it—beautiful, colorful, fantastical.

We took in a deep breath, then walked toward the shimmering wall of raw power. It burned across our skin, sharp and yet comforting, a force that both welcomed and warned. There were no voices singing within this powerful river, but the danger it represented to life and limb nevertheless echoed through the raw energy of its song. This was the same sort of force Mom had confronted when she'd been unknowingly pregnant with me. This was the force that had fused to my DNA and forever changed my life, even if I wasn't aware of that fact until years later.

And here I was stepping into this one, in much the same manner as Mom had so long ago, binding my daughter to not one wellspring but two.

I hoped to God she understood why.

We are sealing all our fates, not just hers. Katie's voice echoed through me, as gentle as a summer breeze. *We do this, and the three of us will be forever linked, for as long as you live on this earth. And even after you have passed, I will be here, not just for her, but for all her children and grandchildren.*

You can't be sure of that, Katie.

I can.

The Fenna?

No, I can hear it in the spring's song. This will be our spring, not theirs.

I drew in a deeper breath. *Then let's do this.*

We moved forward, into that stream of energy. It flowed around us, through us, a song as bright as the day and as deep as the earth itself. It streamed through blood and bone, through muscle and nerves, electrifying and empowering, taking the connection that was already there and forging it into something far stronger, far deeper. Something that could not be broken by man, woman, or magic. It filled us with its music and energy, and it made our entire body vibrate to its sound.

This spring, unlike the older one, rejoiced rather than rejected, and there was a part of us that wanted to dance forever within its song. But enough awareness remained to sense the danger in that desire and force us out of the spring.

Two became one.

That one staggered forward several steps, then fell. I landed on my hands and knees, my breath ragged gasps that tore at burning lungs. Everything hurt—even my goddamn hair seemed to be on fire. I closed my eyes against the pain in my brain and concentrated on breathing slow and deep, trying to calm the racing of my heart and the painful ache in my chest.

It seemed to take forever.

But as the pain subsided, awareness increased. The earth was warm under my fingers, and her gentle music swam around me, a soft vibration that was both oddly comforting and one I suspected was now forever inescapable. It was a force that was mine to call, in a way the power of the older spring never would or could be.

Why, I had no idea, and I wasn't quite ready yet to ask that question, if only because I suspected the answer had more to do with the Fenna's wants and needs than my own.

Movement brushed past me, and I opened my eyes. It

was Katie, moving with speed into the trees that surrounded the clearing and briefly disappearing before quickly returning, her expression a mix of wonder and joy. I tried to speak, but the words got stuck in my raw-feeling throat. I crawled over to the backpack, pulled out Belle's second potion, then sat back on my haunches and drank it. Apparently, my body was so desperate for sustenance that I didn't even notice the taste. But, as Belle had promised, I did feel better once I'd finished it. Those herbs, whatever the hell she'd added, were indeed magic.

I tucked the empty bottle away and noticed sunset was beginning to paint the sky with flags of pink and yellow. Once again, time had slipped past way too fast in this place, and the urge to get up and race back to Muckleford rose. But Belle was right—Marie had no reason to expect a trap, and they were more than capable of handling one lone vamp, however capable at witchcraft he might be.

I still couldn't help mentally crossing all things that neither of us were wrong, that this time, for the first time in a long time, things went as expected rather than ass up.

I turned and spotted Katie and Gabe standing next to the wellspring, their hands clasped, and her expression filled with wonder.

"I'm free," she was whispering. "Truly free."

I frowned. "What do you mean, "free"? You've always been free."

Her gaze came to mine, her blue eyes shining. "Not in the sense that I could wander where I wanted at will. My spirit has always been restricted to this clearing; the only means I had of stepping into the greater reservation area was via the wild magic. It was my eyes and ears. But the barrier that bound me here has now gone."

"Because you've now got a deeper connection to the wellspring?" I hesitated then added, with just the slightest bit of trepidation, "Or because stepping into it with me destroyed your connection?"

Her smile was really all the answer I needed. "Our actions here this evening mean I am now truly one with the magic of this place. I can move through the reservation unhindered, and I can use the wild magic to defend, as we always intended."

"Defend, not attack," I said.

She nodded. "The rules do not change—the wild magic cannot be used to kill, nor can it touch that which is killed."

I scrubbed a still shaking hand through my sweaty, tangled hair and glanced at the waiting threads that were the Fenna. "While I'm pleased Katie's restrictions no longer exist, what the hell was the whole point behind me stepping into the wellspring if I remain unable to do anything more than defend? Defending isn't going to stop these vampires."

A luminous thread floated over and once more wound itself around my wrist. Even though Katie and I had bound ourselves to each other and the spring, it obviously had not deepened the connection to the Fenna. At least for me.

This spring is an outlier thanks to the spell performed here on its emergence, the voices said in unison, clearer this time than they ever had been. *It is not part of us. Not until your child is of age and able to make the full reconnection. Until then, you will be able to use it as a Fenna would.*

Which was why they'd been so insistent I come here. By forming a direct connection to this spring—giving me the ability to use its power without the danger of drawing too much from the other and risking the life of both me and my child—I'd given *them* a means of eventually drawing the spring back into their main network. There was a part of me that wanted to be mad about their duplicity, but in truth, how could I be truly angry when Katie was so filled with joy? When my daughter and all those who came after her would have Katie as their guardian, at least while they lived in this reservation.

"That still leaves one major question you haven't answered—what is the point of containing either of the vampires or whatever they might currently be conjuring if I can't kill them within it?"

You cannot be directly connected to the spring's wild magic when the death occurs, came the answer. *But that doesn't mean death cannot occur within its boundaries or that you cannot create your own barrier around theirs.*

"And what of my inner wild magic? Isn't that basically connected to the wilder stuff twenty-four seven?"

Unless you form a direct connection—which you have done subconsciously in the past—no. Like your native magic, it is a separate power.

Which was good to know. I glanced at Katie. "I guess this means you'll need to be my co-pilot when it comes to the wild magic when we're dealing with these vamps."

"And I am more than happy to do so." Her smile flashed, but quickly faded. "What develops may take both of us and more to stop, however."

Which once again brought me back to what I'd seen in those dreams and the clearing I'd entered alone, without the wild magic or the people that had followed me through the forest. Perhaps the reason they hadn't was the deadness the Fenna and Katie had mentioned earlier.

"How do I feel the location of this stain?"

Press your hands and feet into the earth, as you did earlier, the voices said, *then close your eyes, and allow the veins of her energy to flow through your being. You will be able to both feel and see the blight—it will be a shadow within the glowing network of energy.*

I bent and pressed my fingers into the ground. Though it was hard thanks to being baked under countless days of summer heat, it gave way to my touch, allowing my fingers to easily sink knuckle deep. As my toes also slipped into the soil, a deeper connection formed; in my mind's eye, the wellspring's magic was a heartbeat that ran through the ground, a stream of power that flowed from this clearing, a network of bright fingers that merged into a deeper river that spread out through every corner of the reservation and then beyond.

And in that river, I saw the distant blot of darkness. It was a tiny paint splat of black in the rivers of moonlight.

"Katie, where is that?" I whispered.

She placed her hands over mine, her skin warm and real rather than ghostly—a sensation no doubt due to our wellspring-forged bond—and a heartbeat later, her energy slipped into the streams of power beside mine. Which was interesting, because I'd thought Gabe's spell meant she was permanently connected. I was obviously wrong.

"It lies in the forests above Sandon," she replied. "The rivers that flow from both this wellspring and the main one follow the topography—if you concentrate, it should become more like a map than a mere network."

I narrowed my gaze and concentrated, but saw nothing other than the glow of power.

"Maybe with time and a deeper understanding of the reservation's geography it will, but right now, I don't think we've the time to waste. We need to get over there and stop whatever they're currently attempting." I paused as a vibration ran across the bright rivers and echoed through my fingers. Something dark was on the move ... I frowned, staring at the network, trying to gain some sense of what it was.

"There," Katie said, mentally directing my attention to the left. "Whatever it is, it touches the ground lightly for something that feels so dark."

I glanced to the area she meant and caught it—faint splashes of black pulsing across the network of power, dark footprints that faded as quickly as they appeared. "Is that coming from Castle Rock, and moving up this way?"

She hesitated. "It seems to be moving directly west rather than toward us."

Directly west ... My pulse skipped, and fear surged. "Would the Red, White, and Blue Mine be considered directly west of Castle Rock, by any chance?"

"It lies here." She pointed to an area directly ahead of the dark footprints. "This monster cannot be one of Marie's, as she surely wouldn't be in Castle Rock when Maelle's lair lies there. Or has Maelle been lying all along about knowing her maker's location?"

"Oh, she's undoubtedly been lying, but I'm not sure if she's lying about that."

"But you think this darkness is Maelle on the move?"

"No," I said, pushing to my feet. "It's possibly worse."

"What could be worse than a mage vampire?"

"A monster that punches holes through flesh and blood with the ease of a knife through butter." My voice was grim. "And it's heading straight for Belle, Monty, and the others."

"And Aiden?" Katie asked quickly.

"No." I swept up my boots and backpack. "He's still dealing with the fire up past the Eureka Reef."

"That's under control now, is it not?"

"Not the last time I heard."

"Odd," she said. "Because the heat radiating from it suggests it has been confined."

"Maybe it is then, and they're just monitoring it in case the wind changes." I strode out of the clearing and hurried down the path. It was lit by multiple streams of luminous threads—not just those in the air, but also those under the ground. They pulsed under every step, sending warmth echoing through the souls of my feet.

Katie appeared beside me, her pace matching mine, though her feet never truly touched the ground. "Why on earth would Maelle send her monster to attack Belle and Monty? She still needs your help, doesn't she?"

"She's probably sending her monster to attack Marie's messenger, but I fear everyone in the area may become collateral damage in the ensuing battle."

"Maelle's mind might not be what it once was, but surely even she can't be that far gone."

"She came very close to attacking me at the house," I replied. "Without Roger, she seems to be reverting to baser instincts. Even if her control over her monster remains absolute, I can't help but worry that her need to kill Marie's people will flood over to any others there once the bloodshed starts."

"Then I'll go protect them."

I stopped abruptly and glanced at her. "You can do that?"

Her laugh ran across the dying light of the day. "Were we not discussing our merger gifting me the ability to protect the reservation only a few moments ago?"

"Yes, but—" I half shrugged. "I guess I hadn't thought the implications of it through enough."

"Obviously not." She hesitated. "You should perhaps warn Belle I'm on the way. They'll no doubt sense the wild magic, and she will definitely see me, given her strength as a spirit walker, but best to be safe."

"I will. Thanks Katie."

As she nodded and left, I couldn't help but turn and stare back at the clearing. Gabe remained at the very edge of the trees, his hands in his pockets staring down at me. Katie might be free, but his ghost remained bound to the clearing where death had claimed him.

I lifted a hand to acknowledge him, then ran on down the bright path and reached out to Belle. *There's a big problem headed your way, I'm afraid.*

I wouldn't call one lone vamp in a van a big problem, she replied. *Unless, of course, you're sensing something I'm not.*

Got it in one—Maelle has sent her punch monster out to take care of that one lone vamp.

She told you this?

No, the wild magic did.

Well, if that's the fucking case, we need to retreat—

Maybe not. How far away is the vamp? Is he close enough to snare telepathically?

There was a brief pause. *A few more minutes. How far away is Maelle's monster?*

Hang on, I'll check. I stopped and pressed my fingers into the ground again; the network of rivers jumped back into focus, and I swept my gaze across it until I felt the dark footprints. My stomach dropped. *I'm guessing he's about three minutes away at the speed he's moving.*

Three minutes will make it tight. She paused. *What did you mean by "maybe not"?*

I pushed up and ran on, moving so fast down the trail that the trees were little more than a blur. The wild magic was boosting my speed while somehow ensuring I didn't stumble or fall. *Katie is on the way down to protect you.*

Meaning the wild magic she directs?

No. Long story, but Katie's no longer restrained to the wellspring.

Your merging with the wellspring extended to her?

Kind of. I leapt over the small fence dividing the track from the parking area, threw the backpack and my shoes into the back of the SUV, then jumped into the driver's seat and started her up. *Can you tell the others what is happening? I should be there in ten or so minutes.*

By which time, all the fun should have happened. She paused. *Katie's here. Physically, I mean. How the fuck did that happen?*

She's still a spirit—

One who is extraordinarily solid. She stopped again. *The vamp is within reaching distance. I'd better go.*

Be careful.

Always.

I didn't smile. I just concentrated on keeping the SUV on the treacherous dirt road. When I reached the highway, I hit the accelerator and tried to reach Aiden again. The call rang on, then switched to voicemail. Worry stirred, partially fueled by Katie's surprise that the fire wasn't yet under control, and I rang the ranger station's number instead. The station no longer existed, but the call would be switched through to whoever was currently taking them.

Tala answered. "Castle Rock ranger station, how may I help you?"

"Tala, it's Lizzie—is Aiden there?"

"Last I heard, he was heading toward the O'Connor compound to deal with some problem there. Why?"

"Because he's not answering his phone."

"Odd, because he rang here twenty minutes ago to check in."

"Are you able to ping him on the radio and get him to call me?"

"Is there a problem?"

"Our vamps have something big brewing, from the feel of things. Depending on where it is exactly, we might have to arrange a local evac."

"I can do that—"

"I know, but I still need to talk to Aiden."

"I'll ping him, but he may not answer immediately, as he should be at the compound by now and may be out of the truck."

"Thanks, Tala. I'll be back in contact when we know more about what's happening."

I hung up and returned my full attention to the road and getting to the mine as quickly as possible. I was belting down a dirt road, only a kilometer from the mine site according to Google Maps, when Belle reached out again.

You can ease up on the speed and the worry. We're all fine.

What happened?

I can hear the SUV, so you're nearly close enough to see for yourself.

Well, that sounds ominous.

And it would have ended badly if not for Katie.

Well, fuck.

Her laughter rolled through me. *That was definitely said a few times over the last few minutes, and not just by me.*

I slid around the last corner and then slowed down. Before me lay carnage. Trees were down all over the place, the wooden railing fence that surrounded the mine tower was smashed in several places, and there were deep trenches dug into the side road on the left.

There was also a body in one of the remaining trees in the section to my left. A body that was so damn large, the tree was bowing under its weight. A body that had one arm longer than the other and a fist the size of a stockpot.

Our punch monster. Or rather, Maelle's punch monster.

She wasn't going to be pleased. Not at *all*.

Belle, Monty, and Levi were all standing next to a truck parked to one side of the intersection directly ahead, the latter looking somewhat bemused. In the middle of the road in front of them was what looked like a pile of black tree limbs. What I couldn't immediately see was the vamp they were supposed to be meeting, or either Ashworth or Eli—though the thought had barely risen when the two appeared out of the tree remnants to my left, dragging another bit of black wood toward the pile.

I stopped the SUV and climbed out. That's when the smell of death hit; it was so damn strong that I briefly gagged and had to switch over to breathing through my mouth. It did help, though the scent coated my tongue with a foul taste.

I grabbed my phone from the backpack, then walked toward them, the warm streams of wild magic running across my toes telling me that Katie was no longer in the area. I couldn't help but hope she was heading toward the compound, looking for her brother.

The closer I got to the pile of sticks, the more evident it became that it actually wasn't wood, but rather some form of creature. Or rather, *creatures*. I skirted around the pile to get out of the wind's path and stopped close to Belle.

Levi greeted me with a nod. "Hell of a show you invited me to."

"Glad you enjoyed yourself."

He grinned. "I wouldn't call it fun, per se, but it was interesting to finally witness some of the weird action my wife has been spouting about."

I smiled and motioned toward the pile of wood. "And what the hell are these?"

"Stick golems," Monty said cheerfully. "And nasty little creatures they are too. They got transported in when Belle read the vamp's mind and Marie subsequently melted him."

"I've heard of heard of stone and mud golems, but never stick."

He pointed toward the tree holding Maelle's now dead monster. "These sticks did that, so don't you be dissing them."

"Anything raised by Marie is nothing I'm going to diss." I glanced at Belle. "Did you manage to get anything from the vamp before Marie melted him?"

She shook her head. "His van is around the bend ahead, but I'm thinking there's not going to be much left of him to pull any clues from."

"What about the van itself?" Levi asked. "The rangers should be able to at least pull some location data from the GPS."

"Trouble being, the rangers are all caught up in that fire event," Monty said.

Levi frowned. "No, they're not. Jaz called just before we met and said the thing was under control. Duke and Ric are remaining up there to monitor the roads and stop sightseers, but the rest of the team has either returned to base or are out on patrol."

Monty glanced at me. "Then you should contact Aiden and get—"

"Aiden's up at the compound and not answering his phone at the moment."

He groaned. "God, what has his witch of a mother gotten up to now?"

"Hey," Ashworth said, as he and Eli threw the stick golem on top of the others. "Don't be insulting us witches by such a comparison."

Monty laughed and motioned to the odd-looking pile of wood. "You want to do the honors, old man, or shall I?"

"This old man will box your ears if you don't start respecting your elders." The sharpness in Ashworth's voice was countered by the smile creasing his eyes. "And the fire is all yours, given we did most of the hard work killing these beasties."

Monty snorted but quickly crafted a fire spell and flung it onto the pile. The golems went up with a whoosh, and a thick column of black smoke rose skyward.

I frowned. "Hadn't we better ring the fire brigade and rangers and let them know—"

"Already done," Monty said. "They've asked us to hang around until the fire is out."

"Which won't take long, given how quickly the fire is consuming the golems," Eli commented.

My phone rang sharply, the ringtone telling me it was an unknown number. I was tempted to ignore it, but trepidation and instinct were stirring. I tugged the phone free, put the call on loudspeaker, and then warily hit the answer button. "Liz Grace speaking."

"Elizabeth, how pleasant it is to hear your dulcet tones."

My stomach dropped. Marie. It was Marie.

"Ah, fuck," Monty said softly. "This can't be good."

"What do you want, Marie?" It came out flat and cold, which was surprising given the thick knot of fear that had settled in the middle of my chest.

"I want you to bring Maelle to me tonight. I will accept no more excuses or delays."

"And if I don't?"

Though I asked the question, deep in my heart I already knew the answer.

"If you don't," she drawled, "your wolf dies."

CHAPTER TWELVE

"What guarantee do I have that he's not already dead?" I said, somehow keeping my voice even.

"I would give you my word, but we both know how little faith you now put in that. Ranger, your dear partner wishes to speak to you."

There was a pause, then, in a voice that shook with pain, he quickly croaked, "Staked, silver rods, long and hooked, located behind—"

The rest was cut off by the sharp sound of flesh hitting flesh, followed by a low, frustrated growl that was also abruptly cut off. Whether by magic or something else, I had no idea. I clenched my free fist against the wild magic that burned across it, sending bright sparks spinning into the deepening shadows.

"If you do not appear at my desired time and meeting place, I will slowly remove pieces of your man until you do."

"Is she kidding?" Levi asked softly. Incredulously.

"Sadly, no." Belle's reply was somewhat absent. Her attention was on me, ready to step in and help in any way I needed.

I didn't need help. I needed revenge. Needed these two vampires dead and gone.

There'd been enough pussyfooting around them. I had the power now to contain them both, and I sure as fuck was going to use it.

And, if necessary, I *would* kill them. Both of them, no matter what it took.

I couldn't be connected to the wild magic when I did it, but ending their lives with my own damn hand would be a fucking bonus.

There is no "I" in this revenge strategy, Belle said in the background of my thoughts. *There is only "we."*

"Where do you want to meet?" I growled.

"I will contact you at twelve-fifteen to give you the GPS location." Amusement drifted through her voice. "Wouldn't want to give you the time to plan a surprise attack now, would I?"

"I guess not," I said. "Talk to you soon."

"You will. Oh, and before I forget—I will be setting a spell around the meeting point. If you do not have Maelle with you, you will not get in. And I will take your wolf apart, as promised, while you watch."

"We'll be there."

And with that, I hit the end button. It took every ounce of control I had—and a little extra help from Belle—not to throw the goddamn thing at the nearest tree and scream in utter fury.

"I know it's the whole point, but how the hell are we going to plan a proper response when we won't have any idea where we need to go until after midnight?" Monty asked.

"We can still prepare," Ashworth said. "And make any necessary adjustments once we have the location."

"Except we don't need to wait," I said. "I think I know where they are—or at least, Katie does."

"What?" Monty said. "How?"

"Over the course of the last few hours, a 'dead zone' has developed in the forests above Sandon, preventing the wild magic from accessing the area. That has to be where she's holding Aiden, given she's aware of my control over the wild magic."

"You can't enter a dead zone. Not alone," Eli said sharply.

I glanced at him. "I can and will. The dead zone won't apply to my inner wild magic, and she's not aware of its existence."

"You can't be sure of that, Liz," Ashworth growled. "And these two vamps will try to control and use your power."

"I know, but they'll fail."

"Pride comes before a fall, lass."

"It's not pride. It's determination. I will *not* let these bastards destroy my happiness. Besides, you four will be situated outside Marie's barrier, hitting it with everything you can to distract and hopefully weaken her."

"I'm not liking it," Monty said. "But I'm thinking we really don't have any other choice."

"Other than hanging around letting her call the shots yet again, no, we don't." I bent and pressed my fingers into the ground to form a deeper connection as I reached for Katie. The luminous rivers once again danced through me like a wildfire, making my whole body vibrate and burn.

There was a sharp intake of breath and a soft "Fuck me." Monty.

What's wrong? What's happened? Katie asked. *There is a deep fear and anger in you.*

Aiden is in trouble. I need you to give me the exact location of the dead spot and then head over there to scout. But be careful—Marie is aware of my connection to the wild magic and might just get spooked if too much of it appears.

I'll keep back and just send in a few threads. She gave me directions. *How soon will you be there?*

Within the hour.

I detached and pushed to my feet.

"That," Ashworth said gravely, "is yet another new development."

"You were glowing, Liz," Monty added. "The wild magic—it was all over you."

"I'm linked to Katie's wellspring," I said. "It isn't as strong as the main one—"

"If what we just witnessed is anything to go by, that's probably just as well," Eli said. "For several seconds, you weren't flesh so much as a network of power."

"Power we'll need every bit of," I said. "Katie's given me the location of the dead patch and is heading over there to investigate. She'll let me know what she finds."

"And Maelle?" Monty asked. "How the fuck are we going to drag her out of her stronghold?"

"We don't. We convince her that her best option is working with us rather than against us."

"Yeah," he said wryly, "because she's shown every inclination to date to willingly play along with our plans."

"I think she will this time."

"And if she doesn't?"

"Then I'll snare her with wild magic and drag her out."

"Giving her time to raise nasty spells."

I smiled. "I didn't say she'd be conscious when I dragged."

"And remember, Maelle, like Marie," Belle murmured,

"has seriously underestimated not only Lizzie but also the combined might that is all of us."

"And with that worthy bit of motivation ringing in our ears, we should get moving," Ashworth said. "We'll need to detour past home to grab extra supplies and weapons."

"Including every bottle of holy water we have between us," Monty said. "Even if we don't use it on any conjured monsters, it will be the only thing that can counter the deadness."

"You three do that, then. Belle and I will go for Maelle." I glanced at Levi. "I'm afraid you can't come along on this one."

"I gathered that," he said, voice dry. "I'll stay here and keep an eye on the fire—I take it regular water will put it out if it flares up suddenly?"

"Yes, it will, and that would be brilliant."

"Just remember," Belle added. "If that charm around your neck starts to burn, jump into your van and get the hell out of the area."

He smiled. "After the weirdness I've just witnessed, I'm not about to hang around if another monster makes an appearance."

"Good man," Monty said, then pushed away from Levi's van. "Shall we get this shit show on the road?"

I glanced at my watch. "How long will you need to gather everything?"

"Probably not as long as you'll need to convince Maelle to accompany you," Eli said, amused.

"Then shall we meet at the post office in Newstead in forty-five minutes? The dead zone is roughly ten minutes away from there."

Ashworth nodded, and the three of them headed over to his truck, which was parked close to the mine's tower. Belle and I walked over to the SUV. I tossed her the keys. "You drive. I'd better ring Karleen and let her know what's happening."

It was, in truth, the last thing I wanted to do, but if the situation were reversed—if it was my son or daughter's life on the line—I would want to know, no matter how much I disliked the would-be rescuer.

Belle nodded without comment and reversed around, following the men out of the forest as I dragged out the phone and made the call.

"What is it you want?" she said without preamble.

"A situation has developed—"

"What sort of situation?" The edge in her voice suggested she already suspected what it was. Karleen was many things, but she wasn't stupid.

"Maelle's counterpart has kidnapped Aiden—"

"What do you need? I can call out all three packs—"

"*That* is the last thing we need, and the surest way to get him killed."

"I cannot simply—"

"Karleen," I cut in again, "you have to trust me. You have to believe I will do everything in my power to save him, no matter what it takes. But neither you nor any other pack member can go out there after him. The woman behind the kidnapping is one of the most powerful mages I've ever seen, and that's speaking as someone whose parents are the strongest witches in Canberra. She could magically squash you, and everyone you send, like bugs."

"Then what is there to stop her doing that to you?"

"The wild magic. She wants to taste it, and me."

"So, you're bait? I do not think Aiden would approve—"

"Oh, he definitely would not, but we have no other option. They currently hold all the cards."

"But you have a plan."

It was a statement, not a question. "Yes, indeed."

There was a long moment of silence, then she said softly, "I cannot lose him, too. Please, bring my son home."

"You can be sure I will do whatever it takes, Karleen."

There was another long pause. "I will wait to hear, then."

"One of us will call when we can."

"Thank you."

She hung up. I sucked in a relieved breath. "Well, that went better than I thought it would."

"Let's just hope everything else does," Belle said grimly.

There was nothing I could say to that, other than a soft "Amen."

Our plans were set, our path determined.

Now we just had to hope we all survived it.

It didn't take us long to return to Castle Rock. I drove over to Maelle's and once again parked out the front. Though the interlaced web of protection spells still ran around the building, there were no guards out the front. What was new was the dark weave of emotions that emanated from the heart of the club. It was so damn thick that it actually darkened the glow of the streetlights in the nearby vicinity.

"Oh dear," Belle said as we both climbed out of the SUV. "That cloud suggests Maelle is not in a good frame of mind."

"No." I studied the cloud for a second. Fury was the dominant emotion, of course, along with the deep desire for revenge, but there were also threads of grief and loss, and even a touch of guilt. "If she isn't in a sensible frame of mind, can you snare her telepathically?"

Belle hesitated. "Most likely, but I'd prefer not to if her mind is as fractured as that cloud suggests. Any attempt might well risk utter destruction—and Marie won't be happy if we turn up with what amounts to a vegetable."

"Right now, I don't really give a fuck about Marie's happiness." Not when she was holding mine prisoner. "Let's go."

We headed across the road, but before we reached the pavement, the club's doors opened and Maelle appeared. Instead of her usual riding habit, she was dressed in black boots and jodhpurs, a waistcoat adorned with blood-red buttons and stitching, and had tied her hair up in a bun that was wrapped in black ribbons. Her pupils were pinpoints of black in a sea of white, and the sheer weight of black and bloody fury radiating from her was so damn strong it was almost overwhelming.

I stopped, unease briefly fracturing my determination.

"Marie sends you, I take it?" she said, her voice cool and calm, at odds with the emotional turmoil that surrounded her.

"She has Aiden hostage, Maelle. I have no choice."

"There are always choices, but I understand yours would not be mine in a matter such as this." She smiled her scary smile. "Let us go, then."

Surprise hit like a punch to the gut, and I couldn't help the gasp that escaped. She raised an eyebrow lazily, amusement lending a brief moment of humanity to her porcelain features. "I will not be dragged to any confrontation like a piece of parceled meat, and any battle we have here only weakens us three and works to Marie's advantage."

"Does that mean the oath you took when you were turned no longer prevents you from attacking her?"

"That remains in play," she said. "But she has taken Roger from me, killed my monster, and had a hand in releasing my demon. The bonds of that oath are now wafer thin and, in truth, I no longer care. Even if that oath destroys me, I will see her dead first."

I glanced at Belle. *Is she spinning a tale to catch us off guard?*

No. She means what she says. She paused and briefly—cautiously—reached out mentally. *Her mind is clear and focused, even if her emotions are out of control.*

I returned my gaze to Maelle. "Our meeting point is in a dead zone for wild magic—one Marie has created. I also suspect the magic that rings it will be designed to hamper you as much as me."

Maelle's answering smile was back to being as scary as fuck. "That is a certainty, but what stops your magic and hampers mine will also hamper hers, as I am made in her image."

I hesitated, then moved to one side and motioned to the SUV. "Let's go, then."

She stepped clear of her club, then turned and locked the door. It was then I noticed the bracelets on her wrists. It was the first time I'd seen her wearing jewelry of any kind, and it seemed fitting that—given they were her creatures to call—these bracelets were obsidian snakes that curled up her arms. With the club secured, she walked across the road and climbed into the back of the SUV.

I glanced at Belle. "I don't like the thought of her sitting behind me."

A smile twitched her lips. "No, though I doubt she'll attempt to taste you until she's dealt with Marie. But I'll sit

293

beside her, just in case. If she so much as twitches the wrong way, I'll freeze her."

I nodded, walked over, and climbed in. The back of my neck crawled with awareness, and tiny sparks of magic danced across my fingers. I did my best to ignore both, started the SUV, then did a U-turn and headed out of Castle Rock.

Belle's phone pinged about ten minutes later. After a second, she said, *They've just left Monty's, so they're not far behind us.*

Good. The less time we have to wait in the car with Maelle, the better.

She might not be saying or doing anything, but the closer we got to our target, the deeper and darker her emotional state became. Which only made me suspect she did indeed know exactly where her maker was.

So why, if she was now so determined to break her oath and confront Marie, hadn't she done it earlier, when Marie had been distracted by summoning and sending those stick golems? Why wait for us to chauffeur her there?

Backup, Belle said. *She may be confident that her skills are greater than that of her maker, but she's taking no chances. If she can't kill Marie, she wants to make damn sure someone else will.*

Which we certainly would. Hell, I wasn't even sure we could leave Maelle alive. Not now. I continued on at speed, and we quickly reached Newstead. The post office was a cream-colored weatherboard building with a rusting tin roof, and looked more like an old house than a place of business. I parked opposite, turning off the headlights but keeping the engine on so that we could still run the air con.

Maelle immediately said, "Why do we stop? This is not the meeting location."

A statement that confirmed my suspicion that she did indeed know where Marie was. "We're waiting for the other three witches. They can deal with any other traps or nasties Marie might have waiting."

"Which she undoubtedly will. She is not one to take any chances."

Silence fell again. Maelle remained a dark blot of furious turmoil that neither moved nor even seemed to breathe.

Just over ten minutes later, a car swept around the corner, pinning us with its headlights. A heartbeat later, Belle said, "That's Monty. He said to lead the way."

I started the SUV and drove off again. We sped through Newstead, then turned left onto the Creswyn-Newstead Road. About halfway down, we turned left again, this time onto a dirt track that wound up toward the darker gloom of a forest. I followed the track until we ran out of road and then stopped and climbed out.

The minute my feet touched the ground, Katie appeared. *A house lies through that path to your left. It looks abandoned, and no one is there at the moment, but it shows signs of being occupied until very recently.*

I'd bet everything I owned that the house was the same one that I'd seen in my last astral journey, the one from which Jaqueline had been ejected. *And the dead zone?*

Two hundred or so meters behind it. Darkness stirs through the trees, though.

Spirits or demons?

She hesitated. *They feel the same to me, so I cannot be sure.*

Huh. I turned as everyone else climbed out of the vehicles. "Apparently there're creatures a-roaming, so be ready for an attack before we get to the meeting point."

"She will not attack the two of us before we reach her dead zone." Maelle's voice was calm and assured, everything the turbulent net around her was not. "She *will* attack once we are within."

"Don't take this the wrong way, Maelle, but I don't think we can take your word on this matter."

She glanced at Monty, her gaze glacial and amused. "That is only wise, young witchling. Let us proceed."

Belle held out my backpack. *Monty's put a half dozen stakes in there. Thought they might come in useful in case your magic is totally leashed in that clearing.*

I hope he's left a couple for everyone else. We still have no idea how many vamps Marie has left.

Oh, trust me, she said, mental tones wry. *The man ordered enough to stake an entire vampire army.*

I couldn't help but chuckle. *Let's hope that's not what we're walking into.*

Though, in many ways, a vampire army might actually be easier to defeat than the monsters Marie would undoubtedly send our way.

I swung my pack around my shoulders and headed down the path Katie had pointed out. The night closed in, thick and shadowed, and the silence was oppressive. Nothing stirred in the area—no night creatures and no insects. It was as if the evil that waited ahead had scared them all away.

About five minutes in, we found the house. It was exactly as I'd seen in my astral vision, right down to the broken windows that looked like eyes staring desolately into the darkness.

"There is no one inside," Maelle said. "No one who lives or who walks the edge of life, anyway."

I glanced at her. "Meaning something else awaits?"

Her smile flashed, though it held little humor. "I would advise you not go inside. I would also advise those who remain outside the dead zone watch their backs."

"We always do when dealing with evil," Monty murmured, looking Maelle's way.

She raised that eyebrow again, but otherwise didn't respond.

"We should also spread out a little more," Ashworth added. "We're a bit like skittles at the moment—easily taken out by one well-placed ball."

A well-placed ball would probably be the least of our problems. No one said it, but it was pretty obviously what most of us were thinking. I moved on cautiously, leading the way down the side of the house. Its broken "eyes" seemed to follow us, and my back itched as we moved into the trees behind it. The others fanned out, walking to my right and left, the wild magic floating along beside them.

It was my dream come to life, though the shadow walking by my side was Maelle rather than Aiden or Belle.

The closer we drew to Marie, the more the dead area of ground stood out. It was a widening gap in the music that surrounded me, a blot on the landscape I wasn't sure could be healed.

And yet, in the middle of that deadness, fires flickered. It wasn't magic. It was silver.

The staked body in that last dream ... It had been Aiden, not Roger.

Anger surged, but so too did hope.

Silver might be very deadly to werewolves, but it was also very good at countering dark magic. Where those silver stakes plunged into the earth, wild magic stirred.

Marie had made a mistake.

Now I just had to hope I could make full use of it.

The mage fire I'd seen in my dreams began to flicker through the darkness up ahead. I stopped, dug my toes deeper into the soil, and reached for Katie. *Can you raise that barrier now?*

Luminous threads of moonlight immediately crawled around the flickering mage fire, creating a barrier around it without ever touching it.

Marie would know we were coming, if she didn't already.

That thought had barely crossed my mind when the shit hit the fan.

Creatures roiled out of the trees all around us, creatures that were little more than shadows with bloody red eyes and long, vicious claws. I swore and cast a repel spell past Belle. It hit the creature that had leapt toward her and sent it tumbling back into a tree. Its diaphanous body splattered like paint across the trunk. It didn't remain that way—globs of black began to roll back toward each other as the creature reformed.

"Liz, keep on going," Ashworth shouted, his magic searing the night. "We'll take care of these beasties."

Belle? I said silently. *You coming or staying?*

Monty and I are both coming. She paused to cast another shadow into a tree. *Someone needs to have your back, because I doubt these things will be the last of them.*

The four of us moved on but had barely gone a dozen steps when something thin, white, and armed with a wickedly gleaming axe lurched out of the trees and came at us.

"Keep on keeping on," Monty said. "I'll deal with whatever the fuck this is and catch up when I can."

And then there were three, I couldn't help but think.

Maelle, I noticed, was smiling. Either she approved of

her maker's tactics, or she was simply anticipating the final battle. Maybe even both.

The purple glow of the mage fire now peeled back the darkness, and its caress burned the air, sharp and unpleasant, a stark contrast to Katie's net.

More movement caught my eye, this time from the trees to the right. Human-based rather than demon or spirit. Five of them at first, with more movement in the trees suggesting there were others. They were thin and disheveled, their wild eyes showing little intelligence and their teeth long and pointed. Vamps. New turned, totally untutored, and without restriction. They were snarling as they ran at us, their hands slashing at the air, eager to rent and tear. I flung a cage spell, capturing two and pinning them to ground. Belle pinned one magically and the other two telepathically, brutally sweeping into their minds and destroying their motor functions. As they crumbled to the ground, she said, "Go. Monty and I will take care of the remainder."

I glanced past her, saw Monty running toward us, then nodded and strode on.

"Should we expect any more of her creatures to hit us?" I growled, glancing at Maelle.

She smiled her horrid smile. "One should always expect more, but not necessarily creatures that belong to the opposition."

I glanced at her sharply. "Meaning?"

"Nothing more than what I said." She waved a hand toward the flickering, foul mage fire that burned through the trees. "We should hurry. My victim and your lover await."

I increased my speed and did my best to ignore the continuing sounds of fighting behind us and the multiple flashes of spells being created and countered. There was at least one dark mage or a witch back there somewhere now, but their magic wasn't overwhelming anyone, and probably wasn't meant to. Distraction was the intent here, not death.

Not yet, anyway.

The closer we got to the mage fire, the more my skin itched and the deeper my dread became. I didn't want to go into that clearing, and given the choice, would have cheerfully pushed Maelle inside and let the two of them fight it out until only one—or even none—stood. But Aiden lay staked within it, and he would pay with his life if I made so much as one wrong move.

Katie lifted the curtain of wild magic to allow Maelle through. *Be careful in there.*

I nodded. It was all I could do because, a heartbeat later, I was stepping through the mage fire. It was thick and gelatinous, filled with tiny fingers of flame that danced across my skin with sharp little claws that dug and tore at my skin. My inner wild magic flared to life, creating a barrier of magic just under my flesh, preventing anything more than superficial cuts.

We came out the other side of the barrier into silence. Utter silence. All sounds of fighting, and all feel of magic, had been completely cut off. The rivers of wildness no longer ran under my feet; the ground here was as dead as the air felt. Worse still, my connection to Belle was no longer active, though I suspected the cause was the pulsing wall of wild magic surrounding this place more than any of Marie's spells. I glanced down at my hand and tried to construct a repelling spell. Nothing. My native magic had been curtailed; thank God she hadn't known about my inner wild magic.

I stopped just beyond the wall of flame, just as I had in the dream. Blood trickled down my bare arms and across my chest, but I paid it no heed. Marie stood on the other side of the clearing, and in the center between us lay Aiden. He was naked, and he was staked by a thin rod of silver through his left shoulder and right thigh. The red lines of silver poisoning were already creeping out from the wounds, and sweat dotted his forehead and body. I couldn't see any signs that Marie had dined on him, though I couldn't see the far side of his neck yet, either.

Every instinct within wanted to run over, drop to my knees, and rip the silver from his skin. But that was what Marie wanted, what she anticipated, so it was the very last thing I could do. At least for the moment.

My gaze rose to hers. I'm not sure what she saw in my eyes, but uncertainty flickered through hers.

I think, in that moment, she finally realized she might have underestimated me. Then her natural confidence and self-belief returned, and she smiled. "Thank you for being so predictable, Elizabeth, though I am surprised you managed to convince Maelle to reveal my location. She knows that doing so is a breach of contract."

"So was killing Roger and taking my daughter as a lover," Maelle said evenly. "Though I did not breach the contract by revealing your location, it is, as far as I am concerned, void."

"The contract cannot be voided unless I directly attack you, as you are well aware."

"I believe you to be wrong, but shall we put it to the test?" Maelle replied. "It is the only way to see who might be right, after all."

"The usual rules?"

"That sounds ideal."

"Before you get into any of that," I said, not quite able to believe how polite these two were being. "How about you release Aiden? I've played my part and brought Maelle here."

Marie laughed, the sound falling like death around me. "Child, I never promised to release him. He is, in fact, hostage for your good behavior. Once I deal with my wayward fledgling, you and I shall discuss the matter further and come to some arrangement."

"Arrangement" being code for blood donor, I suspected. I glanced at Aiden again. His eyes were open, and though they were little more than blue slits of pain, I felt the fury in him. Fury aimed at himself for putting me in this position.

"Fine," I said. "Do what you have to do, but leave Aiden and me out of it."

"Ah, the innocence of youth. Were we ever that naive?" Marie didn't wait for Maelle's answer—not that she provided one—her gaze instead coming back to mine. "You will not be able to free your wolf, because he has been well anchored. But on the off chance that you do manage the impossible, you will not be able to leave this clearing. Not until I release my shield."

I didn't say anything. The moment I'd stepped through that barrier it had become damnably obvious that the only way I was going to leave was by her death or mine.

"Shall we begin?" Maelle said.

"I believe we should. But first, my dear Maelle, you must prove yourself a worthy opponent, now that you are without your demons to draw power from."

And with that, Marie waved her hand, and dozens of different critters appeared out of nowhere and ran straight at us. Maelle laughed and raised her arms; the bracelets on her wrists came to life, slithering free and dropping to the ground, their forms growing, thickening, and lengthening, as they went right and left to attack the nearest creatures.

Then Maelle launched into the fray.

I swung my pack around, freed the silver knife, and ran for Aiden. It was tempting, so damn tempting to reach for the wild magic that burned through my body, but the last thing I needed was to unleash my one good weapon too soon—and certainly not before Aiden was fully protected.

Something brown and fuzzy leapt at my face and I slashed sideways with the blade, severing legs and eye stalks. The rest of its body hit mine, and teeth tore into my T-shirt, ripping through the material but not into skin. I tore it free, tossed it into the air, and stabbed it as it fell back toward me. It squealed and went limp, and I flicked it free from the blade and ran on. Another critter, this one a long streak of black with skeletal wings, swooped toward me, wickedly sharp black talons held out in front of its body. I dropped to one knee and raised the knife, slicing its leathery underbelly open as it went past. Blood and gore and God knows what else fell like rain all around me, stinging where it hit bare flesh. I cursed, but scrambled upright and continued on, reaching Aiden just as another one of those spidery things leapt at me. I slashed wildly at the thing, splitting its fat body in two. As the two sections fell either side of Aiden, I dropped my pack beside him, grabbed the holy water and blessed salt, and quickly circled him, creating a temporary barrier around the two of us. It might be basic, it might not hold back any sort of magic, let alone the type Maelle and Marie could raise, but it was enough to stop the critters and give me time to help Aiden.

But to do that, I had to leave the silver in his body a little bit longer.

I dropped to my knees, reached for another bottle of holy water, and carefully poured it onto the wound in his thigh. He hissed and clenched his hands.

"I'm sorry, I'm so sorry," I whispered, "but I can't remove the silver rods just yet. I need their deep connection to the ground, but the holy water should at least stop the silver infection from getting any worse."

Or at least, I hoped it would.

His mouth moved, but no sound came out, and there was deeper pain in his eyes and tears trickling from the corners. But his hand found my knee and squeezed lightly. Acceptance. Trust. I blinked back my own tears, opened another bottle of holy water, and poured it over the wound in his shoulder.

Movement caught my eye, and I glanced up sharply. Several hairy brown spiders were skittering around the edge of my circle, looking for a way in. I needed to hurry, because I had no idea just how long that circle would hold or even if it would stop something airborne. That scenario had never been mentioned in any of the books I'd ever read.

Once I'd doused the wounds, I splayed my hands around the two sharply pointed, blood-streaked rods, being careful not to touch the silver myself, and then reached for my inner wild magic. But I didn't use it to throw a net around the two of us. Instead, I arrowed it along each one of the stakes, following them through Aiden's body and into the ground. The rods, as he'd said earlier, were several feet in length and had a cross-like end that anchored into the soil—no doubt to ensure they could not be easily ripped free.

But it also meant she'd had the stakes already embedded and just dropped him onto them.

Fucking bitch ... I swallowed the anger. In many respects, Marie's actions had actually helped us, because those ends were anchored below the dead zone, right in the heart of the luminous rivers, providing not only a connection point but also a means of guidance through the deadness.

Katie? You there?

Her energy swam through the rivers, then around me. *Ready and waiting.*

Then follow me back through these rods and protect Aiden.

I quickly withdrew my inner wild magic, and she chased me up the silver shafts, an almost volcanic force that erupted from the two wounds in Aiden's body and quickly formed a fierce, bright dome around the two of us.

Nothing was getting through that dome or Katie. Of that, I was certain.

I touched a hand to Aiden's face, and he opened his eyes; the blue depths were filled with fury and pain. "I'm going to lift you free of the stakes. It'll hurt."

He half laughed, then croaked, "Not as much as being slowly pushed onto them, I assure you."

Fury bit through me again, but once again I shoved it aside and reached for the wild magic that still flowed into the clearing via the bridges of silver, bolstering Katie's dome even further. I caught several strands and swept them around and under Aiden. Then, with a glance of warning his way, I ripped his body free from the silver. He screamed, a sound that tore at my soul and my heart, then went limp in my grip. I swore, placed him gently on the ground, then scrambled across to him, my heart racing and panic filling my veins. I pressed two shaking fingers against his neck, my breath caught somewhere in my throat.

I found his pulse. It was too faint and too rapid, but nevertheless there.

Relief surged, and I briefly dropped my head, once again fighting the tears that stung my eyes. It wasn't over yet. Couldn't be over while the two vampires remained alive.

I retrieved the silver knife and then drew three stakes from my backpack, shoving two through the belt hooks at the back of my jeans and gripping the other. Then I rose and glanced at Katie, who nodded at my unspoken question.

I severed the connection between me, her, and the wild magic, then stepped through the protective dome.

Into utter chaos.

There were bits and pieces of critters everywhere, and plenty more moving on the ground and through the air, the main concentration currently over the two women. One of Maelle's snakes encircled them, spitting venom that instantly melted any creature that came too close while it swatted others away with its whiplike tail. I couldn't see the other snake, but there were chunks of shiny black stone scattered about the clearing that had a rather scaly appearance.

I stalked toward them, knife in one hand, stake in the other, my knuckles white with the force of my grip. A creature whirled away from the tempest ahead and dove toward me. I slashed with the knife, killing it. More left the tempest, coming at me from several different angles. I briefly switched the stake to my left hand and called to my inner wild magic, lassoing the lot of them before drawing them closer in a more controlled manner so I could dispatch them with the knife. After tossing their lifeless bodies on the ground, I stepped over them and continued. The snake eyed me, hissing, but threw no acid my way. A warning, nothing more.

The two women continued to fight, battering each other with clenched fists one moment, slashing at flesh and limbs with nails as long and as sharp as any knife the next. Both were bleeding heavily, and Maelle's movements were hampered by what looked to be the skeletal wing of one of the bone creatures driven deep into her thigh.

I had no idea who would win if the fight ran to its natural conclusion, and didn't really care. I just needed it to end quickly, and I needed Marie dead, because that was the only way her barrier would drop and I could get Aiden to the hospital.

I stopped several yards behind Marie. Maelle's snake continued to roll around the two of them, and Marie's critters continued to attack it. I wrapped wild magic around the stake, then stepped forward and raised the knife. As I'd hoped, she sensed the movement, but she sent her remaining creatures at me rather than attacking me herself. I slashed wildly with the knife, striking several but missing more. Maelle's snake reared into the air, venom spraying from its teeth. Marie screamed as her critters fell around her, then spun and dove at me, her nails sharp talons aimed at my throat.

That was the moment I flicked the stake at her. It cut through the air so fast it was little more than a blur, but Marie nevertheless sensed it. She threw herself to one side, hit the ground, then rolled away as Maelle's snake attacked. As my stake flew harmlessly over her head and plunged into the ground, her hand flicked up, and silver glittered briefly before lodging in the snake's left eye. It reared up again, hissing in fury, shaking its head as its body convulsed, shimmered, and began to dissipate.

Maelle screamed, the sound so high-pitched it hurt my ears. Marie laughed and raised a hand, and all her remaining creatures flew at Maelle, completely covering her. Then she rose and strode toward that writhing, screaming, clawing mass, a smile of anticipation etching her thin lips.

She'd forgotten I was here.

I quickly slipped another stake free from my belt straps, wrapped it in wild magic, and once again flung it as hard as I could.

This time, I didn't miss.

The stake flew through the now vaporous snake and arrowed on. A heartbeat before it plunged into Marie's chest and buried deep in her heart, I released the wild magic.

Just to be safe.

Marie gasped, her eyes wide, her expression shocked. Her gaze came to mine, and she raised a hand, though I had no idea what she intended to do or say, because Maelle stepped free from the black mass, raised her bloody claws, and slashed her maker's throat open. Marie made a gurgling sound and fell back, her head rolling to one side of her body, connected only by a few remaining strands of muscle.

As flickers of fire began to erupt from where the stake had plunged into her body, I sucked in a breath but didn't relax. One monster might have fallen, but another remained. I had no idea what the state of Maelle's mind would be now that she'd finally killed her nemesis, and no intention of allowing her out of this clearing until I knew she presented no danger to anyone else.

Katie, I said, *release the dome around the clearing. I need to speak to Belle.*

She immediately did so, and as my telepathic link to Belle once again came online, I said, *You okay?*

A few cuts and bruises, but otherwise, we're all good. You?

Same. Could you call an ambulance? Aiden's alive, but in a bad way.

And Marie?

Dead—staked by me and decapitated by Maelle.

Excellent. She hesitated and concern flickered through our link. *Jaqueline's here.*

What? Why?

I don't know. She paused again. *Her mind is a mess. All I'm basically getting is fury. You want me to stop her?*

I hesitated. *No, not unless she threatens any of you.*

That could be dangerous.

She can't hurt me or Aiden, not with the amount of wild magic now in this clearing. I paused, eyeing the mage fire that still burned, even if with far less ferocity. *I'm not entirely sure she can get into the clearing or hurt Maelle, given how slowly Marie's barrier seems to be falling.*

Just stay wary. Don't trust either of them.

I won't. I returned my attention to Maelle. She stood over Marie's body, her fingers clenching and unclenching, her sharp nails digging into her palms and drawing blood. She didn't seem to care.

"She was my everything," she said softly, after a while. "And then she destroyed everything."

She wasn't the only one who did that, I wanted to say, but kept the words locked within. Though her voice remained normal and she no longer radiated the driving, desperate need for revenge, darker emotions still skated around her.

Jaqueline's just come out of the trees and is walking toward the left edge of the clearing, Belle warned.

I glanced up. So did Maelle. "A familiar heartbeat runs through the air."

"One that belongs to a heart you gave birth to and then

309

betrayed in so many ways." Jaqueline stopped right on the edge of the trees, her body in shadow but her face lit by the dying purple embers of the mage fire. It made her look as if she were wearing some form of grotesque mask.

"I never betrayed you. I gave you what you asked, protected you as much as I could, and saved you from the death that found Marie."

"You saved me from nothing and took all that I ever wanted, all that I ever loved," Jaqueline retorted. "But no more. I gift you, dearest Mother, what you refused to gift me. And I wish you long centuries of torment in whatever hell claims what remains of your soul."

With that, she raised her arm and pulled the trigger of the gun she was holding.

Maelle didn't react. Perhaps didn't even have time to do so before the bullet hit her forehead, smashed through her brain, and then exited through the back of her head, splattering brain matter through the air.

She fell, almost in slow motion, to the ground.

Perhaps in defeating Marie she'd drained herself so completely of magic she was unable to raise a protective barrier against the bullet, or perhaps a mix of disbelief and surprise had slowed her reactions for too many vital seconds. Either way, she was dead, as surely and completely as her maker.

My gaze returned to the woman in the shadows. For several minutes, she didn't move, didn't react, the gun pointed unswervingly at the unmoving body of her mother.

Then, slowly, her gaze came to mine, and in her eyes I saw death.

But not mine.

She pressed the end of the barrel under her chin and pulled the trigger. She was dead before she hit the ground.

I sucked in a deep, quivering breath, and then walked somewhat unsteadily back across the clearing. Katie pulled the dome protecting Aiden down, creating a waterfall of luminous threads that splashed all around me as I knelt beside Aiden.

He shifted shape and is no longer close to the edge, Katie said, *but the silver wounds will still need attention.*

Belle's called the ambulance. I pressed a hand lightly against his cheek, and his eyes opened. Relief stirred through blue depths still washed with pain.

"Is it over?" he croaked.

I nodded. "All vampires are dead, and the only true casualty on our side is you."

"Well, better me than you, given I still heal a little faster." He caught my hand in his, brought it to his lips, and kissed it. "But sadly, I'm thinking my plans for a Christmas Eve wedding might have to be changed."

I laughed. "You just wanted to save some money and buy a two-in-one gift."

"No, I just need to make you all mine, and that was the earliest date the celebrant gave us."

I laughed again, gently pressed my hands to either side of his face, and then kissed him. Slowly, gently, deeply.

The darkness had finally left the reservation, we'd all survived, and he and I could now start planning the rest of our lives together.

And the sooner, the better. A Christmas Eve wedding might be off the cards, but New Year's Eve was definitely on.

EPILOGUE

I married my wolf on a warm summer evening six days after Christmas. Ashworth and Eli had created magic in their garden, somehow managing to keep the roses at their best despite the withering heat. Fairy lights twinkled like stars through the greenery, lining the path through the garden and ringing the half-circle seating area at the bottom.

Aiden waited in the middle of that circle, wearing suit pants and a deep blue shirt that matched the color of his eyes and the bridesmaids' dresses. I only had two—Belle and Jaz. Aiden's two brothers—Michael and Dillon—were the groomsmen.

We didn't have many guests. Belle's parents and siblings were all here, of course—they were my other family, closer to me than my real family, and I simply couldn't imagine them *not* being here. Mom was here, too, looking happy and relaxed, sitting next to Eli, the two of them chatting like old friends. Aiden's entire family was here as well, even his mother. She'd recently thanked me for saving Aiden and had apologized for her attempts to turn the pack against our marriage, but had avoided any reference to actions beyond that. I guess I couldn't expect miracles, and it was a step in the right direction. She and I would never be friends, but at least I no longer had to worry about her causing future problems for me with the pack.

Katie was also here, her whole body radiating with happiness, luminous threads of wild magic dancing around her, signaling the connection between her and Gabe. He might not be able to leave their clearing, but she'd found a way for him to witness the wedding.

"Well, are we ready to go?" Ashworth asked. "Or are we planning to be fashionably late and make the lad sweat a bit longer?"

I glanced at him, laughing. He'd insisted on wearing a dress suit, shirt, and tie because it would be unseemly to give his adopted granddaughter away in anything else, apparently, and though he had to be hot, he seemed unfazed by the heat.

"If we make him wait too much longer," Belle said, "he's likely to race up here, sweep her off her feet, and carry her down to the celebrant."

"Because that man was not made for waiting." Jaz paused, amusement touching her lips. "Though I guess it depends on the situation, doesn't it?"

"Indeed, it does." I took a deep breath to settle the silly nerves fluttering in my stomach and then nodded. "Let's get this show on the road."

Dillon, who was now as tall as both Aiden and Michael, despite only being fourteen, offered his arm to Jaz, and the two of them walked out onto the patio and down the steps. He still limped, but finally seemed to be at peace with his disability.

Belle did a final check of my dress—a simple sheath style with a plunging neckline, made of a material that shimmered like the rainbow threads dancing through the garden—then caught my cheeks and dropped a featherlight kiss on my lips.

"You look stunning," she whispered. "I'm so happy for you."

I gave her a fierce mental hug rather than a real one, knowing she'd scold me for mussing the dress or my makeup. "It'll be your turn next."

She laughed. "Not for a few years yet. I'm planning for your daughter to be my flower girl."

I grinned. "Have you told Monty about this long engagement you're planning?"

"Not yet. But he wants to get a house and new car first, anyway, so I can't see him complaining."

She stepped back, slipped her arm through Michael's, and the two of them headed out. Leaving me and Ashworth.

I smiled, took his hands in mine, and squeezed them lightly. "Thank you for everything you've done for us. Thank you for being here for us. Thank you for becoming the grandfather and father I never really had. I know you are going to be the absolutely best great grandfather our daughter could ever have."

"Ah, lass," he said, blinking rapidly. "You're going to make a grown man cry."

"Before you do, let's get out there."

I released one hand and turned to face the garden. He cleared his throat and then, as one, we stepped out onto the patio and followed the twinkling line of fairy lights down to the bottom of the garden. Aiden's gaze followed me every step of the way, warm and loving.

When we reached the end of the seats, Ashworth kissed my cheek and then sat down beside Mom. I walked the remaining few steps toward Aiden alone and stopped in front of him.

"You look glorious," he murmured.

I smiled. "So do you."

He caught my hands in his and then glanced at the celebrant, who immediately began the ceremony. It was a simple thing—a promise to cherish each other always, to honor and sustain each other, in sickness and in health, in poverty and in wealth, and to be true in all things until death alone parted us. We placed the rings on each other's fingers, the celebrant declared us married, and as the cheers began, we kissed.

Then Aiden whispered, his breath warm against my lips, "You are my heart and my soul, my reason for living, as necessary to me as the air that I breathe. I love you, Elizabeth Grace, and I cannot wait to spend the rest of my life with you and our many, *many* children and grandchildren."

I half laughed, blinking back my tears of happiness, and then kissed him again, long and slow.

This wolf—this stubborn, sometimes frustrating, big-hearted, beautiful wolf—was mine, now and forever.

Who'd have thought, all those years ago, that the frightened teenager who'd left Canberra as a powerless failure would not only come into her own, magic wise, but also find the family she'd never really had and the love of a man who she absolutely adored, and who in turn adored her?

Fate, it seemed, played a long game and held her cards as close to her chest as the wolf in front of me. But in the end, both had come through.

Spectacularly.

"Shall we go celebrate?" he asked softly.

"We should."

He twined his fingers through mine, and as one, we headed into the throng of well-wishers.

Taking the first steps toward our long and happy life together.

ALSO BY KERI ARTHUR

Drakkon Kin Trilogy
Of Steel & Scale (Nov 2024)
Of Scale & Blood (TBA, 2025)
Of Blood & Fire (TBA, 2025)

Relic Hunters Series
Crown of Shadows (Feb 2022)
Sword of Darkness (Oct 2022)
Ring of Ruin (June 2023)
Shield of Fire (March 2024)
Horn of Winter (Nov 2024)

Lizzie Grace Series
Blood Kissed (May 2017)
Hell's Bell (Feb 2018)
Hunter Hunted (Aug 2018)
Demon's Dance (Feb 2019)
Wicked Wings (Oct 2019)
Deadly Vows (Jun 2020)
Magic Misled (Feb 2021)
Broken Bonds (Oct 2021)
Sorrows Song (June 2022)
Wraith's Revenge (Feb 2023)
Killer's Kiss (Oct 2023)

Shadow's End (July 2024)

The Witch King's Crown Trilogy
Blackbird Rising (Feb 2020)
Blackbird Broken (Oct 2020)
Blackbird Crowned (June 2021)

Kingdoms of Earth & Air
Unlit (May 2018)
Cursed (Nov 2018)
Burn (June 2019)

The Outcast series
City of Light (Jan 2016)
Winter Halo (Nov 2016)
The Black Tide (Dec 2017)

Souls of Fire series
Fireborn (July 2014)
Wicked Embers (July 2015)
Flameout (July 2016)
Ashes Reborn (Sept 2017)

Dark Angels series
Darkness Unbound (Sept 27th 2011)
Darkness Rising (Oct 26th 2011)
Darkness Devours (July 5th 2012)
Darkness Hunts (Nov 6th 2012)
Darkness Unmasked (June 4 2013)

Darkness Splintered (Nov 2013)

Darkness Falls (Dec 2014)

<u>Riley Jenson Guardian Series</u>

Full Moon Rising (Dec 2006)

Kissing Sin (Jan 2007)

Tempting Evil (Feb 2007)

Dangerous Games (March 2007)

Embraced by Darkness (July 2007)

The Darkest Kiss (April 2008)

Deadly Desire (March 2009)

Bound to Shadows (Oct 2009)

Moon Sworn (May 2010)

<u>Myth and Magic series</u>

Destiny Kills (Oct 2008)

Mercy Burns (March 2011)

<u>Nikki & Micheal series</u>

Dancing with the Devil (March 2001 / Aug 2013)

Hearts in Darkness Dec (2001/ Sept 2013)

Chasing the Shadows Nov (2002/Oct 2013)

Kiss the Night Goodbye (March 2004/Nov 2013)

<u>Damask Circle series</u>

Circle of Fire (Aug 2010 / Feb 2014)

Circle of Death (July 2002/March 2014)

Circle of Desire (July 2003/April 2014)

ABOUT THE AUTHOR

Keri Arthur, the author of the New York Times bestselling ***Riley Jenson Guardian series***, has written sixty novels–35 of them with traditional publishers Random House/Penguin/Piatkus—and is now fully self-published. She's won seven Australian Romance Readers Awards for Favourite Sci-Fi, Fantasy, or Futuristic Romance & the Romance Writers of Australia RBY Award for Speculative Fiction. Her Lizzie Grace series won ARRA's Fav Continuing Romance Series in 2022 and she has in the past won The Romantic Times Career Achievement Award for Urban Fantasy. When she's not at her computer writing the next book, she can be found somewhere in the Australian countryside taking photos.

for more information:
www.keriarthur.com
keriarthurauthor@gmail.com
Buy Direct from Keri & Save:
www.payhip.com/KeriArthur

facebook.com/AuthorKeriArthur
x.com/kezarthur
instagram.com/kezarthur

9 781923 169067